To Haran Banjo and Squall Leonhart:
This dream started with you.

ACKNOWLEDGMENTS

To my editorial team, Robert S. Malan and Sharon Bekker.
Thank you for your tireless and exceptional work.

CONTENTS

RE-ENTRY

Julius McCoy woke up with a jolt. It took him a few seconds to remember where he was. As the burbling of voices outside his cabin and the familiar drone of the engines carried to his ears, he relaxed and lay back again, rubbing his eyes wearily.

'Attention students,' bellowed a voice over the intercom system. 'We will be entering Zed orbit in ten minutes. Collect your belongings and report to deck B.'

Julius couldn't believe they had arrived already. He had left Alpha Fornacis just three hours earlier and yet here he was, 46 light years later, back in his own solar system. 'That's hyperjump for you,' he mumbled, groggily.

He dragged himself out of his bunk and moved to the small metal sink by the window. There he washed his face with cold water and ran his wet hands through his dark hair. *'I could do with a haircut,'* he thought to himself – the jagged strands were looking more unruly than usual. It wasn't his fault though. At Summer Camp, he had been constantly occupied with spaceship catalysts and how to use them during Combat. It had been pretty difficult at times but, then again, it *was* an advanced course designed for Mizki Seniors. And it was only because Julius had shown how capable he was in Flight fighting that he had been given special permission to join the older students. His friend, Skye, had also been allowed to go with him, for similar reasons. There was no question that they had both proven their skills in the past year.

He dried his face and looked out of the window. The stars, yellow dots in the pitch black sky, streamed by him, glowing eerily. He had been kept busy that summer, but no matter how tired he had felt when he went to bed, his last thoughts had always strayed back to Queen Salgoria and the events of the previous April.

He remembered clearly their fight with the Arneshian hologram army, led by Salgoria's henchman, Red Cap; how he, Skye, Faith and Morgana had escaped from the hangar; the desperate flight to the Arneshian outpost, where the remote control for their army had been positioned, and the draw he had performed to destroy it. It amazed him still that he had even survived that. As much as he had done though, he knew what he owed to his three friends for their part in that battle.

'McCoy, are you decent?' called Skye from outside the cabin.

'Coming,' shouted Julius over his shoulder.

He grabbed his backpack and moved towards the door, which slid open silently. Skye was leaning against the opposite wall, his blonde curls partly hiding his light grey eyes.

'Are we there yet?' asked Julius, who had set off in the direction of deck B.

'Almost,' said Skye, hurrying to catch up with him. 'The Seniors are all assembled. I thought you might be asleep, as usual.'

'I was, actually. Mind you, I don't think I managed more than an hour or two, but it's better than nothing.'

'Why do you sleep so much? There'll be plenty time for that when you're dead.'

'That's a cheery thought. Thanks.'

'Besides, there are other things to do here,' said Skye with a sly grin.

'What are you on about?'

'Ife Alika,' he said quietly.

'What's that?'

'Not what – *who*.'

Julius stopped and looked at him. 'Is that what you've been doing all those hours in the hangar – chatting the pilots up?'

'Not quite. You can't chat up a Senior just like that. It could be quite embarrassing ... and possibly dangerous. You have to play to your strengths. I'm young, you see; inexperienced but willing to learn and, of course, interested in *everything* she has to say. That way she thinks I'm cute and likes talking to me. She feels ... understood, and in control. Believe me McCoy, that's how you do it,' he finished, like a professor who had just explained some highly advanced scientific fact to an ignorant pupil.

Julius opened his mouth to say something, but he knew there was no point, so instead just shook his head and continued walking. Skye didn't seem at all bothered by that, and proceeded to list Ife's many fine qualities, then abruptly stopped again as soon as they reached the deck where the Seniors were. Skye, who had just spotted Ife, nudged Julius in the ribs and pointed her out to him. Julius had to admit that she really was very pretty indeed. The only useful information he had gathered from Skye's admiring words was that she came from Nigeria and was among the best of the 5 Mizki Senior pilots. She was surrounded by a group of giggling girls just then, and when she saw Skye, she gestured for him to join them.

'Come with me,' said Skye to Julius under his breath, and wandered over to them.

Julius stayed where he was, feeling partly amused but also quite nervous. He had never been much good at socialising with strangers, especially older girls, so instead of joining his friend, he retreated to one of the hatches by the opposite wall. Ever since the draw incident, he had the feeling most people were unsure what to say to him; so generally they avoided talking to him altogether. That suited Julius just fine, and he had spent his time concentrating on ship catalysts instead.

The only Senior who had been chatting to him at all was Bernard Docherty, a 6MS student. Up until the previous November, Docherty had been the only student from Tijara School to make it into the top ten of the all-time Solo rankings: a simulated single player competition that tested an individual's mind-skills to the very limit, by way of Combat scenarios, Flight games, or a mixture of the two. In fact, he was currently the reigning champion for the whole of Zed. Just making it into the rankings was an achievement, given how difficult the Solo games were. To his surprise, Julius had managed to shoot straight into the charts in ninth, the youngest ever from Tijara. He shuddered, thinking about that game and his battle with the weird, morphing villagers. Certainly, it had caused quite a stir among the other students when they had viewed replays of it afterwards.

The group games were much more enjoyable for him though – something to do with the fact that no one was allowed to use their mind-skills in them and they had to work together in teams. His thoughts turned to his own team, the Skirts, so formed and named almost by accident on their first visit to Satras's famous Hologram

4

Palace. A smile crept onto his lips as he remembered how he and Skye, along with Faith and Morgana, had gained quite a reputation for their gaming skills.

The ship juddered slightly as it entered orbit and Julius peered out of the porthole next to him. The Zed Lunar Perimeter was just coming into view, sitting proudly on the surface of the Moon. He stared beyond it for a minute, to where Earth shone blue, green and white in the distance and he wondered for a moment how his parents and his little brother Michael were getting on.

As the ship continued its descent towards Zed's dock, Skye joined him by the hatch. 'Today is our first Mooniversary, you know?' he said, pointing out the window.

'Yup,' said Julius. 'Exactly one year ago we were just arriving, and we didn't even know each other then. Do you think we'll get our new uniforms tonight?'

'Hope so, buddy boy,' said Skye, throwing an arm over Julius's shoulders. 'We're 2 Mizki Juniors as of today.'

'Bet your life we are,' said Julius with a grin. 'Listen, remind me to write to my folks later, OK? They'll be worried sick wondering if I've survived the summer. Have you written home at all?'

'Yeah,' answered Skye, stepping to the side and turning to prop his back against the wall. 'You can send messages between all of Zed's space stations. It's only the relay to Earth that doesn't work from so far away. Besides, you can be sure my Mum would've had a search party out if I *didn't* get in touch.'

'Imagine what *that* would have done for your star-rep with the ladies,' said Julius, with a wink.

Skye shivered at the thought, 'Don't even joke about it.'

*

By the time they docked, it was almost seven o'clock. The Zed shield's artificial illumination had grown dark, so mimicking the twilight sky of the last day of August on Earth. Julius and Skye hurried off the ship and boarded the Intra-Rail train which, after a brief stop at Satras, delivered them to the outskirts of their school. Julius stretched and drew in a breath of Zed's warm air. After two months on a cold space station, the heat felt like absolute bliss to him. Tijara looked as inviting as always, a spherical sandstone structure with the appearance of a tropical island, covered as it was in palm trees and gentle waterfalls. They walked over to the security entrance, where their retinas were scanned by Tijara's front-gate guards, the Leven twins, who were never seen anywhere without each other, much to the puzzlement of all the students.

Once through, Julius and Skye headed straight for the boys' dorm and boarded the lift.

'Remember to press -5. We're one level up this year,' said Julius to Skye. He was getting quite excited at the idea of seeing his new bedroom and uniform.

The dorms had six underground levels in all. 1MJs slept on -6, as Julius had the previous year. As a person progressed through each new school year, so they were moved higher up the levels, getting ever closer to the ground floor.

The lift came to a stop at their floor and opened onto one end of a long corridor, which had four closed doors on each wall. All school-level groups were limited to thirty students each, with an equal number of boys and girls, so there was never any need for more than eight rooms per year. The same rule applied for the girls' dorm.

They exited the lift and stopped in front of the third door on the right. 'Here we are, darling,' said Skye. 'Just like last year.'

'Allow me, dear,' said Julius, looking into the retinal scanner that acted as security lock for the room.

The bedroom had the same layout as their previous one, with a control panel for electronically raising or lowering partitions and furniture. Neatly folded on each of their tables were their new Tijaran uniforms. Julius grabbed one of the blue jumpers and looked for the label on the left sleeve. Written in silver, the letters spelled out "Julius McCoy-2MJ-Tijara".

'This is just!' he said excitedly.

'Hey, there's a message from Faith,' said Skye, who was checking his personal holoscreen. 'He's with Morgana in the garden. They'll meet us for tea around eight.'

'Great. I've got time to wash up then. I want to wear my new clothes.'

After a refreshing shower, as he waited for Skye to get ready, Julius sent a quick message home. A few minutes later, feeling crisp and refreshed, the boys made their way up in the lift and emerged onto the school's circular promenade. When they arrived in the mess hall, they saw that most of the tables had been taken up by the latest batch of 1MJ recruits, who had just spent their very first day on the Moon. Judging by their expressions, they had been having a great time of it so far.

'Wait till they get their timetables tomorrow morning,' said Julius to Skye, with a wry smile.

Just then, Morgana and Faith waved to them from the back of a long queue for the food. Morgana was so happy to see Julius again that she was positively beaming, her lovely almond-shaped, green eyes shining brightly. They had met many years ago when her family had moved from Japan to Scotland, her father's homeland, and had always looked out for of each other as they grew up together. When Julius was close enough, she threw her arms around his neck; Morgana was the only girl in the whole world who would actually be allowed to do that, given how naturally reserved Julius was.

As she turned to greet Skye, who was visibly pleased at being considered hug-worthy as well, Faith hovered towards them, sporting his now famous conical, metallic skirt. It was amazing to Julius thinking about how, when he had met Faith the year before, he had been restricted to a wheelchair. Not that a wheelchair could *actually* limit someone as technologically gifted as Faith who, even at that young age, had already managed to alter the chair so it could hover and fly about. The 'skirt', as everyone called it, was an invention of Pit-Stop Pete's, the owner of a docking base in the lunar orbit, where Faith had just spent his Summer Camp. Julius knew that it had made a great difference in his life and, even if Faith didn't ever talk or make a fuss about his disability, it was clear how happy he was just to be able to stand up like the rest of them.

'How's it going, boys?' asked Morgana.

'Had a great time in Fornax,' answered Julius, truthfully. 'But it was hard work. We spent every waking hour with a catalyst in our hands, shooting anything that moved.'

'That sounds fun,' said Morgana. 'I did a fair amount of flying myself this past month. The apprentice camp is *really* advanced. I don't know why they gave me permission to join them so early. At least I didn't crash any of the Cougars though. And Kaori was there too, which was brilliant of course.'

'How *is* your sister?' asked Julius, edging slowly forward in the queue.

'She's good, thanks. She says hi.'

'What about you, Faith?' asked Skye.

'I spent the best part of the summer zooming in and out of Pete's dock on a sky-jet, salvaging debris from the battle with the Arneshians.'

'A what?' asked Julius.

'A sky-jet. It's a jet-propelled personal aircraft, or to put it simply, a space-scooter. Pete has hundreds of them. They're actually really fun to drive.'

'I got a shot at it too, when I was there in June,' added Morgana. 'There were so many Cougar parts floating about, it was getting dangerous for everyone. So, as part of our Summer Camp, Pete made all of us go retrieve them.'

'Sounds like you actually did something useful *and* had fun,' said Julius.

'To be sure. The luck of us Irish is never-ending,' said Faith, with a theatrical wink.

Finally they reached the counter, where the resident chef, Felice Buongustaio, was dishing out *tagliatelle al ragù*, a dish of fresh pasta dressed in tomato and mince sauce.

'Can I have a double portion please, Felice?' pleaded Skye, almost on his knees, much to the amusement of the first year students.

'*Va bene, va bene*! Of course,' cried the chef in a thick Italian accent. 'But only because you remind-a me of my son and you've spent three months on-a that piece of floating junk in-a outer space. What have they been feeding you, eh? You look-a too skinny. You're a boy in full growth. You need-a to eat. Eat, I say!' he finished with a flourish of his hands.

'You're very right and I'm so glad to be back, Felice. It's like going home to my dad when I see you,' said Skye, pursing his lips as if he was about to cry for all the emotion he was feeling.

It was all too much for Felice, who couldn't resist being called a father, and proceeded to dish out a portion of pasta sufficient enough to feed a small platoon. Skye walked away with a large smile and a humongous plate of food, leaving the others standing there quite stunned.

'I'm gonna call him the *Black Hole*, from now on,' said Julius.

'Where does he put it?' asked Morgana.

'Who knows,' said Faith. 'If I ate that much I wouldn't fit in me skirt. Mind you, I think I must have grown a bit over the summer, 'cause it feels tighter around the waist.'

'Tell me about it,' said Morgana. 'I feel like all my clothes are getting smaller in the oddest places.'

Julius and Faith froze, looked at her, and then quickly glanced away.

'What?' asked Morgana. 'What's the matter?'

It was only when the boys had turned a dark shade of red around the ears that she understood. 'Honestly, guys,' she said, pragmatically. 'It's called puberty, and it's going to happen a lot from now on, to *all* of us. You better get used to it.'

Julius and Faith mumbled an apology, but it was clear from their faces that the embarrassment wouldn't fade away so quickly. Come to think of it, Julius *had* started to notice a few changes to his own body over the past few months and, looking at some of his classmates he had become aware of more than one boy developing a slight moustache shadow.

Once dinner was finished, they all moved to Tijara's private garden, where they lay down on the grass under their favourite oak tree. The other 2MJs were also milling about and Julius took the chance to chat with most of his classmates, discussing the new gaming season in Satras and exchanging stories about the various Summer Camps. Everyone seemed to have had a great break. None of them talked much about the fight with the Arneshians anymore. Julius supposed that was understandable, given that ultimately they were completely unaware of the real reason for that attack on Zed. How could they, when they knew nothing of Salgoria's secret experiments, or how he was the *White Child* she had been trying so desperately to kidnap?

Tijara's Grand Master, Carlos Freja, had revealed as much to him following the attack. Salgoria had discovered about the existence of a White Child, someone with the exact blend of DNA that she needed. Julius had just joined the Zed Academy at that point, to train in the White and Grey Arts: the White to develop his mind-control abilities; the Grey to enhance the logical side of his brain. Arneshians, by their nature, were highly skilled only in the Grey Arts. The White Arts, however, were a gift that only a small portion of the Organic population possessed, and Julius was that rarest of things: an exact blend of both Arts.

If they had succeeded in grabbing hold of him, and mixing his DNA with an Arneshian's, Salgoria would have been able to create a being powerful enough to finally help her overthrow Earth's leadership. Morgana was the only other person Julius had shared this information with and he was sure she had kept this to herself, as he had asked her to. She didn't even discuss it with him, unless he brought it up. Still, Julius knew it was playing on her mind. He could tell she was worried by the grey wisps of smoke rising from her head when she looked at him silently. He had come to rely on the colourful wisps he saw above people; they helped show him their true and deepest feelings.

Still, there wasn't really a lot he could do about the situation. If Salgoria decided to come back for him, as Freja thought was likely, he could only hope to be ready for her.

*

At seven o'clock the next morning, Julius's alarm marked the beginning of a new year in Tijara. To his surprise, he awoke rather more easily than usual, and for the first time he was dressed and out the door before Skye. As he walked along to the mess hall, he met Morgana in the corridor.

'You're up early,' she said.

'I thought I might start the year properly this time,' he replied. 'Besides I want some extra time to digest the timetable, you know, in case it's nasty.'

As they reached the mess hall entrance, Julius saw a table with two trays lying on it, one for each junior year. He picked up two copies from the second tray, placed them in his back pocket and headed to the food counter. Once they had finished eating, Julius pulled them out onto the table.

'Here,' he said handing one to Morgana. 'Break it to me gently.'

Morgana glanced over hers. 'Sorry. We have two extra hours of lessons and we *still* need to keep a diary for each subject.'

Julius sighed and scanned his own copy. 'Spaceology, Draw, Telekinesis, Meditation, Martial Arts and Pilot Training,' he read aloud. 'Plus two new subjects: Shield and Telepathy. What's Shield?'

'Did I just walk in during an episode of *"There's No Such Thing As A Silly Question"*?' asked a familiar voice from behind him.

'Morning smarty-metallic-pants,' said Julius, shifting along the bench to let Faith in.

'Morning, lovelies,' he said. 'To tell the truth, I was actually wondering the same thing.'

'It's probably a defence course, or something. As for Telepathy ... it sounds straightforward enough,' added Morgana with a shrug of her shoulders.

'We've not got either of them till Monday though,' said Julius.

'What's the story for today then?' asked Faith over his cereal bowl.

'Let's see. Wednesday ... double Spaceology, double Draw and, after lunch, double Telekinesis,' said Julius. 'Not too bad.'

'Ooh, I almost forgot,' said Morgana suddenly. 'You'll never guess what happened to Billy Somers.'

As the name was mentioned, the boys stopped eating abruptly and plonked their forks down on their plates. Somers was a token of everything a Mizki student shouldn't be. Considering how much grief he had given them when they had met him at the Zed Test Center back on Earth, it was a surprise to them that he had even got in. And sure enough, once enrolled, he had continued his obnoxious behaviour towards everyone he met, not least of all Faith. Fortunately they had not heard much from him in a good while.

'What's he done now?' asked Faith, pretending not to care.

'Remember Marion Lloyd, the girl who passed the test with us?' continued Morgana in a conspiratorial tone. 'I met her yesterday in the dock, and she told me Somers left Zed last year!'

'He what?' said Julius. 'Why would he do that?'

'That's the thing. No one knows,' she answered. 'It happened a few weeks after that first game we had against him last year. Marion just said one day he was called out of class and that was the last anyone saw of him.'

'He probably got kicked out for being a prat,' said Faith, 'and was too ashamed to show his ugly face around Zed again.'

'It's still weird though,' said Julius. 'Not that I miss him. Thankfully, bullies like him are few and far between, and they stick out like sore thumbs. But Faith's right, I'm sure: he probably got booted.'

Certainly, it seemed obvious that Somers had not been missed by anyone at the school, and Julius was sure he wouldn't lose any sleep over it either. He returned his attention to his new timetable, while the mess hall slowly filled up.

When Skye finally joined them, it was time to head to their first lesson. Professor Lucy Brown was waiting for them outside her class, in the Grey Arts sector. She was an excitable, aging English lady in a blue Tijaran uniform, with long white air gathered in a plait. Julius, followed by Faith and Skye, took a seat as far towards the back as he possibly could, knowing that his eyes might close involuntarily at some point during the lesson, while Morgana moved quickly towards the front, since this was a favourite subject among aspiring pilots like her.

'Welcome back, 2MJs,' she said, bowing to the students.

They all bowed back respectfully and then sat down.

'This year we will be concentrating on the constellations, all 88 of them, as defined by the International Astronomical Union back in 1930, long before the Chemical War of 2550. Now, can anyone tell me who the astronomer was who listed the *first* 48 constellations?'

A hand shot up timidly, that of Barth Smit, Faith's professionally clumsy Dutch roommate. They all looked at him in surprise, since Barth had yet to excel in any particular subject.

'It was Ptolemy the Greek,' he said in a squeaky voice. 'He listed them in *The Almagest*, in 150 AD.'

Everyone in the classroom stared incredulously at him, clearly impressed.

'Well, Mr Smit, that was quite the answer. I take it you like the topic, then?'

But Barth was too embarrassed to speak and simply nodded his head rapidly.

'In that case you might want to keep your eyes on a career as a navigator,' she said, smiling kindly at him and resuming the lesson. 'During the course of the year, you shall learn the system of names, letters and numbers used to recognise the celestial objects present within each constellation, and the fastest routes between us and them.'

Julius let his head fall heavily to the desk. With all due respect to Professor Brown, he would rather have been eaten by mutant grannies in a Solo game than learn to do a job that a computer was going to do for him anyway. Faith and Skye seemed to be of that opinion too, since they promptly began a match of Mindless. This was a game that Julius had invented the year before, during a lesson about the moons of Jupiter. It required two players, who had to mind-push a small ball of paper towards the other's nostrils, and score as many of these goals as possible. Obviously, retrieving the ball was the harshest part of the game, which included a lot of sneezing from both players, and the occasional nosebleed.

The two hours eventually passed and the 2MJs walked over to the White Arts sector for their Draw lesson. There, they bowed to

Professor Cathy Turner, who was standing fidgeting by the door, wearing her white lab coat. Julius, Faith, Skye and Morgana moved automatically towards their usual counter, where a set of leafy pot plants awaited them.

'She seems more wired than usual. Are we sure she's not on drugs?' whispered Skye to the others.

'I think her nose is getting longer,' added Faith.

'Hey! You two,' said Morgana, 'Cut it out. She's a nice lady.'

'And she's coming this way,' added Julius under his breath.

Professor Turner was indeed moving closer to their station, where she stopped in front of Julius.

'Mr McCoy,' she said quietly. 'I need to inform you that over the summer you have been officially registered with the Curia and the Grand Masters of the three schools, for the inorganic draw you performed last April.'

'Oh ... thanks,' said Julius. He knew this was going to happen, but he still felt a little embarrassed.

'I would have liked seeing that very much indeed. Ever since the day you made my digital watch stop, I figured there was something different about your draw ability. I've read all the papers published by Doctor Walliser on your draw. It was fascinating. Most of all though, I'm glad that you are alive, McCoy. It was a tremendous risk you took back there.'

Julius nodded. 'Thanks, Professor. I'm glad to be here too.'

The teacher smiled at him and then turned towards the rest of the class. '2MJs, it's a pleasure to have you all back. You have completed your first year of Draw training with excellent results. Now that we all know *how* to perform a draw, we are going to practise the fine art of controlling *the amount* of energy we need to obtain from a target.' She paced between the counters and pointed at the various pot plants in front of each student as she walked. 'These specimens are more delicate than your average cactus plant, so we shall work on them for a while. Let's start by drawing just enough energy to wither only the tip of each leaf.'

For the rest of the lesson, they worked in silence, while Professor Turner moved around the class replacing any dead plants with new ones. It seemed that everyone was finding it hard to control their draw. Even Julius wasn't able to limit his to smaller quantities – it was always the entire leaf. By lunch, no one had managed to fulfil the criteria.

'Not to worry, Mizkis,' said Professor Turner as they left the classroom. 'You'll manage. Just keep trying.'

'You've gotta love her optimism,' said Faith, once in the corridor. 'She managed to smile even after bringing me the fourteenth plant.'

They all agreed and used up their lunch time trying to guess where she kept her seemingly infinite stash of shrubbery. The last two hours of the day were spent with Professor Paul King, the Telekinesis teacher. He had decided to celebrate the beginning of the year in his typical *unusual* style.

'Today, we shall move a meteorite!' he cried ecstatically, his face growing deeply red – in stark contrast to the blue of his uniform. 'I want to see the powers seeping from your skin, permeating the air. Focus! Concentrate!'

Julius and his classmates could only stand there, transfixed by Professor King's drive and ambition, but most of all by the mammoth-sized rock before them.

'How the heck are we supposed to do that?' whispered Morgana.

'I think I know why he's always so red: he gets internal bleeding every time he tries to move something bigger than him,' said Skye.

'If I try to move that thing, it'll be me brains seeping through me nostrils and permeating the floor,' added Faith.

'I'll probably pee myself,' finished Julius miserably, trying not to think about the numerous glasses of orange juice he had drunk at lunch.

The recommended approach, according to the Professor, was for the whole class to try it all together, which they did for the next two hours. The meteorite moved roughly five centimetres, while the students strained themselves so much that in the end the majority had to go to the infirmary to get headache shots.

Five minutes from the end of the lesson, an anonymous student even succeeded in getting an enthusiastic holler from Professor King, for farting loudly under the strain. 'Air biscuit!' he cried jovially. 'We have ourselves an official air biscuit!'

That did it – Julius and his classmates collapsed on the floor in hysterics, which prompted the Professor to call it a day. He strolled off nonchalantly and left them there, like a bunch of gasping fish, struggling to regain their composure. By the time that evening arrived, news of the "air biscuit" had made its way throughout the entire school. Some of the 6MS pupils had even promised a cash reward to the proud owner of said biscuit but, no matter how many Fyvers had been promised, nobody came forward to claim the prize.

*

That Thursday morning, the 2MJ students started the day with Professor Len Lao-Tzu, who helped them ease back into their meditation routine, seeing as they were quite rusty from the long summer break. His classroom had the peaceful atmosphere of a temple, and indeed looked like one too. He was kneeling in front of them, clad in a loose white tunic and trousers. In his usual serene manner, he calmly announced that they were all expected to lower their trance threshold from one minute to thirty seconds. That really worried Julius, seeing as the previous year he had been required to attend remedial lessons just to get his time down to *one* minute, never mind *half a minute*. He sincerely hoped he didn't have to endure private tutoring again. It wasn't even so much that his VI tutor had ended up helping the Arneshians invade Zed, but more because he had been forced to wake up at 05:00 every morning for a month to do those extra lessons. That was just *not on*, in his book.

As serene and quiet as that morning was, that afternoon in the martial arts dojo was far more energetic. Professor Lee Chan, the only other one of the teachers who didn't wear the official Tijaran uniform, welcomed them back to their Mindkata lessons in high spirits, running them through a training session designed specifically for a seasoned athlete, with the promise of many more wonderful surprises to come, starting the following Monday. By the end of training, Julius was too exhausted to think about surprises and went to bed straight after dinner, aching all over.

*

As was the case the previous year, Fridays were wholly devoted to Pilot training, everyone's favourite subject. Professor Farid Clavel met them in Tijara's underground holographic sector, where the Sim-Cougars were kept. Naturally, Morgana was waiting outside the classroom by eight thirty, eager as always to fly. When Julius didn't see her at breakfast, he grabbed two brioches and a latte and went to meet her.

'Thanks! How did you know I was here?' she asked, biting into her pastry.

'Not difficult, really,' he said, sitting down on the floor next to her. 'It's Friday, and a full Clavel day. Where else *would* you be?'

'It's just in case he gets here early, so I can go in and do some warm-up. You know me,' she said.

'Yes, I sure do,' said Julius with an exaggerated sigh.

As if in answer to her prayers, Professor Clavel did indeed arrive a few minutes early, dressed as ever in his pristine uniform.

'Miss Ruthier,' he said holding out his hand and helping her up. 'Why am I not surprised? And Mr McCoy, it's a pleasure to see you again.'

Julius liked Clavel. He had a warm smile and always managed to make him feel comfortable. 'Likewise, Professor,' he said with a quick bow.

Clavel invited them inside, listening with genuine curiosity to Morgana's tales of her Summer Camp.

'Sounds like you had a good summer, Miss Ruthier. I hope you won't find my lessons too easy now,' he said.

'Not at all!' she answered vehemently. 'I really enjoy you ... I mean ... your lessons!'

'Excellent,' said Clavel, clearly pleased by her enthusiasm.

Julius noticed a thick pink stream of smoke shooting upwards from her head; he recognised it as Morgana's "embarrassing moments" wisp, his cue to remove her from the scene before she could dig herself an even bigger hole.

20

'I can't believe I said that,' she whispered to Julius as he led her away by the elbow.

'Well, you did. Now, let's go look at the pretty Cougars, yes?'

Mercifully for Morgana, the rest of the class joined them soon after and, by the time the lesson had started, there was not a pink wisp to be seen. Clavel had decided to use their first training session of the new year to revise all the flying techniques they had previously learned. Not all of the students had had the opportunity to fly during their Summer Camps, and he needed them all to be comfortable with their Sim-Cougars. By the end of the day, the 2MJs had left the holographic sector with renewed confidence. Julius was in particularly high spirits. Tijara was beginning to feel increasingly like home to him. Plus, next year, his brother Michael would be able to join the Zed Academy, hopefully even the same school as him too. Thinking about it made Julius eager to speak to his family again, so he hurried back to his room and spent the next two hours talking to them on his computer.

That night, he slept peacefully. Yes, it was really good to be back.

AUGMENTATIONS

That Monday morning, the 2MJs gathered in a classroom on level -5 of the Grey Arts sector. Everyone was visibly excited, as they would soon be meeting a new teacher. Julius, Morgana, Faith and Skye were chatting in a corner when the door suddenly opened. The students fell silent at once and bowed towards the entrance.

'Good morning, Mizkis. I am Professor Calandra Morales and this is your first Shield lesson. Welcome.'

Julius didn't need help in identifying her accent as Spanish and could quickly tell that Professor Morales had a vibrant demeanour. She had long, dark wavy hair that covered her shoulders and a pair of large, smiling brown eyes.

'This course will teach you how to protect yourself, and others, against different types of external attacks. We will have lessons in this room in the morning, when you will be studying the theory of the various Shield techniques. Then, after lunch, we will continue our training in the dojo. There you will learn to use your own shields while using your Mindkatas in a more flexible way. After January we will also use most of the mornings for practice. Sounds fun, no?'

Julius certainly thought so. On Mondays he did prefer more active subjects, as there was less risk of him falling asleep.

'Now, here's the best part,' said Professor Morales stepping into the centre of the room. To all of their surprise, she removed her blue jumper, boots and socks, remaining bare footed in her Combat trousers and t-shirt. She bent her left arm and brought it up in front of her chest, parallel to the floor. 'Watch,' she said.

Suddenly a shimmering magnetic field sprung out of her forearm, creating a shield that protected her from head to toe. The class let out a gasp.

'How did you do *that*?' said Lopaka Liway, completely forgetting protocol.

Professor Morales smiled and continued her demonstration. With the same ease, she produced another shield from her right forearm and proceeded to walk among the students, moving her arms in a smooth flow around her torso. It was obvious from this demonstration that it would require a high level of agility to use the shields properly. To stun the Mizkis even more, she produced two further shields from the tops of her feet. Then, just as quickly as they had appeared, they all vanished. The students erupted into applause, while several of them were shouting for more.

'*Muchas gracias.* Thank you,' she replied, bowing. 'The shield is powered by my own mind-skills, but it *isn't* created from out of nothing. Today, we are going to Dr Walliser and each one of you will be fitted with a special microchip in both forearms. Those chips are for your shields.'

Julius, like the rest of the class, was too surprised to say anything. They were still in a dazed silence as Professor Morales put her shoes back on and led them out of the class, to the infirmary.

'How come Kaori never told me about the shields?' asked Morgana. She didn't seem best pleased.

'Maybe she didn't want to spoil the surprise for you,' answered Faith.

'And how come I've never seen Calandra before?' said Skye, following her every move with his eyes. 'She's *muy caliente*.'

'Don't you start with her too, you hear?' whispered Julius. 'And don't call her Calandra. She's our teacher, man!'

'I need to learn some more Spanish,' continued Skye, oblivious of what Julius had just said. 'Hey, Valdez! Come here a second.'

Manuel Valdez, a short, dark-haired boy, walked back towards Skye.

'Valdez, you speak Spanish, right?'

'I'm Mexican, chico,' replied Manuel, raising an eyebrow at him. 'What do you need?'

'Give me something clever to tell *her*,' he said, pointing at Professor Morales.

'*Ay caramba, amigo*! You wanna play with fire, huh?' said Manuel with a grin. 'Come with me.' He dragged Skye away from the others and began chatting quietly to him.

'What's got into him?' said Morgana, amused.

'His hormones, that's what,' said Julius, half exasperated. 'He's spent the summer chasing this girl called Ife, which is risky enough 'cause she's a Senior. But the teacher ... he could get expelled!'

'He's a nutter,' said Morgana.

'At least *he* has a chance,' replied Faith. He looked at Julius and Morgana and pointed at his skirt. 'A lot more chance than I'll ever have.'

Julius was taken aback, as this was the first time he could remember Faith making any sort of negative comment about his situation.

'Faith, that's not true,' said Morgana, putting her arm around his shoulders. 'Who cares if you can't walk, right? That's not what makes someone special. Besides, how many people do you know who can hover?'

Julius saw Faith's smile grow a little wider. Only Morgana could have made someone feel better so easily, and he had seen her doing that ever since the first day they had met.

When they reached the infirmary, Dr Walliser was standing in the foyer with the nursing team. 'Good morning,' he said to the students. 'Today is a special day for the 2MJs, because you will not only receive your shield-chips, but also for the first time ever, all Zed students will be fitted with a PIP-chip.'

The Mizkis seemed understandably confused, so Dr Walliser extended his left hand in front of him, touched the centre of the left palm with his right index finger and activated a small, circular holoscreen which popped into life above his hand.

'This Personal Information Planner, or PIP, contains all the information that you would normally access from any of the Tijaran terminals. Among other things, it has your timetable, an alarm clock and a map of Zed, and it will link you to any other student in the Lunar Perimeter. Plus, you can type notes on it, by simply touching the screen, which will take a bit of getting used to because it feels like you're touching fresh air.'

'Paint me pink and call me an android,' said Faith, shaking his head. 'Last year I ended up metal-plated and fitted with sensors all through me legs. This year they're implanting more chips in me arms and hands. By the time I graduate, there'll be nothing left of me!'

That made everyone within earshot giggle.

'Well I'm glad you're all so comfortable with the thought,' said Faith, half seriously.

'There are a couple of things still to tell, Mizkis,' said Professor Morales. 'The good news is that there's a nice shop in Satras called Going Spare, which sells upgrades for all your chips. You might want a different colour for your shield's magnetic field, yes? Or some extra functions for your planner, like spare memory in case you want to store books, movies or music.'

'There you go, guys,' said Skye. 'That shop will be the go-to place for all our birthday presents this year.'

'Agreed; absolutely; bet your butt,' answered Julius, Morgana and Faith, almost in unison.

'The bad news,' said Morales, 'is that, in order to allow your shield implants to properly bond with your muscles, you will not be able to use them or play any games in Satras until November.'

A chorus of disappointed grunts echoed through the infirmary at that news.

'However,' continued the Professor, 'for this very same reason, all your Monday afternoon classes will be cancelled until November, to give your body a chance to rest.'

'Now that's what I call good news,' said Faith.

Dr Walliser began to call the students one by one, in alphabetical order. When it was his turn, Julius went into a room with a nurse by the name of Federica Primula.

'Lift your sleeves, please,' she said, typing his name into the terminal. 'Place both arms inside this tube, palms down.'

Julius did as instructed. The tubes were transparent, so he watched curiously as two green lasers marked a spot in the middle of each of his forearms. Next, a pair of small metal boxes was lowered automatically over both marks. As they touched his skin, he felt a sudden sharp pain, similar to an injection.

26

'Ouch!' he said, jerking his arms back.

'Don't worry. It'll pass,' she said, disinfecting the two red marks on his skin. 'See? You can barely notice them. Now, where do you want your PIP-chip?'

'I'm right handed,' he answered.

'In your left hand then. Palm up.'

Julius gritted his teeth and inserted his hand into the tube once again. The pain was sharper this time than before, but it was also thankfully brief. Once the nurse had disinfected the skin on his palm, he left the room.

By the time the remaining 2MJs had been fitted with chips, it was already midday. Professor Morales told them to make good use of the free time and practise using their PIP-chips. The Mizkis were more than happy to oblige, and for the rest of that afternoon there was not one boy or girl from their class who didn't have his or her nose buried in their PIP. That evening in the garden, when Julius finally lifted his eyes to look around, he felt like he was in the middle of a firefly convention, as all that was visible was a myriad of yellow circular holoscreens, glowing dimly among the trees.

*

When Julius woke up on Tuesday morning, his forearms still felt quite bruised and sore, thanks to the shield implants. As he walked over to the shower, he couldn't help but muse over how the invention of body augmentations had helped humans to enhance themselves with everyday tasks, but *also* how it was surely moving them a step closer to the creation of a different species altogether. Julius, who loved Earth history, had studied extensively on this topic from a young age. He remembered that, ever since the twentieth century, humans had been talking about cyborgs, fictional beings that were part robot, part human. The subject had been widely discussed in popular literature and entertainment, while tentatively experimenting with the technology in existence at the time. Slowly but surely, advances in bio-mechanics had started a revolution that had eventually led to the use of chip-implants to fulfil many different tasks, like sending and receiving data and curing various previously incurable diseases. And now he too was being sent down the path of augmentation – he didn't mind too much though, as long as the "real" Julius still owned the majority of his body.

When he had finished getting ready and arrived in the mess hall for breakfast, Faith waved at him from a table in the corner, where the rest of the gang was also sitting. Julius grabbed some porridge from the counter, covered it in honey and ginger puree, and headed over to join them.

'Morning, folks,' he said, sitting down.

He got general nods in reply from Morgana, Faith and Skye, who were all busy swallowing or chewing.

'So, does anyone have any idea who the Telepathy teacher is?' asked Julius.

'Kaori didn't tell me much,' said Morgana. 'All I know is that he's called Oleron Beloi and he's from Russia. And he doesn't actually *speak*.'

'What do you mean?' said Faith.

'I'm not sure if he can't or just won't, but he never utters a word. Apparently he's also the best Telepathist the world has ever known.'

28

'This White Art should be right up your alley, Julius,' said Faith, through a mouth full of toast.

'Yes,' added Morgana. 'You do mind-talking all the time.'

Julius nodded. 'Guess so. But so do you guys.'

'Sure,' said Faith. 'Maybe not as well as you, but we do. What *you* do that I can't, though, is that scary *entering-my-mind-to-see-what-I-see* thing.'

Julius grinned. 'I've only done it once, with your permission. Last year on the train to Tijara, when you couldn't describe the school salute to us, remember?'

'Oh, I remember all right. I felt so violated!'

'*2MJs. Please report to holographic sector, Level -5,*' said a male voice, inside Julius's head.

'What the ...' cried Julius, jumping up in surprise.

'What's happening?' said Morgana, looking worried.

Julius looked around. 'Did you hear that voice?' he asked them.

Morgana and Skye nodded.

'I think it was the teacher,' said Faith.

Julius noticed that all the 2MJs looked just as traumatised as him.

'I take it we need to go to class then ... ten minutes early too,' said Skye gathering up his things. 'Come on, guys. Best we obey the voice.'

'I hope he didn't hear my reaction,' said Lopaka Liway, walking past them. 'I wasn't kind, or polite.'

With that, they hurried from the mess hall and headed left along the promenade. Gabriel List, the senior technician, was at his desk at the entrance of the sector, welcoming the students. When he saw Julius, he smiled.

'Mr McCoy,' he called. 'How are you? Did you have a good summer?'

'Yes, thanks Mr List. And you?'

'I was kept very busy repairing our Holopals because of ... well, you know. Any more problems with Meditation?'

'No. The first lesson went fine. I think I'll be all right.'

'Good. On you go now. Professor Beloi doesn't like to be kept waiting.'

Julius went back to the others and together they caught the elevator down. When they reached Level -5 there was only one door open, so they headed inside.

'Whoa,' Julius gasped, looking around him with wide eyes.

Morgana, Faith and Skye stared, awestruck at the sights in front of them.

They were standing on a stone ledge no more than a few feet wide, overlooking a massive labyrinth of mirrors. The ledge ran off to either side of them, and followed the edges of the square room. As the rest of the Mizkis arrived for class, Julius and several others were running excitedly here and there along it, exploring the labyrinth with their eyes. The light was reflecting off the mirrors in all directions, creating shiny shapes against the walls.

'*Good morning, Mizkis*,' said the same voice in Julius's mind.

He looked around, searching for the source of it. Without the sound, it was impossible to tell where it was coming from.

'Over there!' cried Lopaka, pointing at a small circular platform, which was hovering above the labyrinth.

The students faced towards it and bowed. The platform moved closer to where they were gathered, along the ledge, and Professor Beloi bowed in return to the students. He was a tall man, with broad shoulders and a short, thick neck. His eyes and hair were dark brown, and he had a quite remarkable handlebar moustache.

'*Since, no doubt, you will be wondering why I do not speak, let me explain it to you now. I have always believed that actions are better than words when it comes to learning. Therefore, forty years ago, I decided to stop talking altogether. Telepathy was to become my sole means of communication, and, if I was to master it to perfection, I was going to have to practise it constantly.*'

Julius was stupefied. He couldn't imagine spending even one hour without talking, never mind forty years. No wonder this guy was the best in the world.

'*You are all capable of receiving messages from experienced teachers like myself, but less so at transmitting to, or communicating with, other less accomplished people. This year, we shall practise transmission, and the many valuable uses of this White Art. I understand that it might be frustrating at times, but necessity is the very best reason for learning.*'

Julius watched, enthralled, as Beloi moved closer to the ledge.

'*I want you to pair up now. One person from each couple will join me on my platform and I will place them in random parts of the labyrinth, while the rest of you up here will guide them toward the centre of it, using only your minds to communicate the directions to them. As you can see, the ledge follows the room around, so make good use of it.*'

Julius was sure all the others would probably try to pair up with him, given his skills, but in fact the four of them just stood there facing each other.

'This is ridiculous,' said Morgana, shaking her head. 'We can't all pair off with Julius. Skye, you want to join me?'

'Madam,' he replied, with a little bow.

Julius looked at Faith. 'What's it going to be?'

'I've got a bit of a sore head, actually,' said Faith with a sly grin. 'I'll go in and you guide me out, methinks.'

'OK,' said the Professor, in their heads again. *The fifteen who are going into the labyrinth, come with me.'*

So Faith, Morgana and another thirteen students hopped onto Professor Beloi's platform, and were dropped off at different points along the labyrinth's perimeter.

'Remember, guides, you cannot talk and you cannot use your hands either. To the person in the labyrinth, I would suggest a little meditation for a few minutes, to clear your mind. It'll make things easier.'

While Faith meditated, Julius took the opportunity to study the labyrinth's layout. It seemed simple enough and, by the time Faith was ready, Julius had almost memorised the path to the centre.

'OK, fly-boy,' said Julius to Faith. *'Can you hear me?'*

'Loud ... clear ... you?' Faith's voice in his head sounded a little disjointed and faraway.

'Sort of. Try to concentrate harder on each individual word. Visualise them in your mind.'

'I'll try. That better?'

'Yes, much. You ready?'

'Is me skirt metal? Sure am.'

Julius smiled. *'Keep facing that direction. Start walking and take the first left.'*

Faith began to move, and spent the next twenty minutes following Julius's directions. Occasionally, Julius would ask him to focus more, especially when he took the opposite path to the one advised, or got so disorientated that he would walk straight into a mirror. But he was still the only student in the labyrinth making any progress at all.

'Almost there. Take the next left, then the second on the right and Spock's your uncle.'

32

'*Ain't you handy to have around?*' said Faith, emerging in the centre of the labyrinth. '*I'll just sit here then, and wait.*'

Julius smiled contentedly. He had wanted to make a good impression on the teacher and was sure he had done just that. As he looked at the other students, he had to hold back his grin. Barth Smit, notorious menace, was bouncing from mirror to mirror and was sporting a swollen forehead as a result. Siena Migliori and Astra Evangelou were both trapped in the same corner – in the absence of any clear directions, they were trying to feel their way out. Morgana, meanwhile, was advancing slowly but steadily along the maze, while some others were still sitting at their starting positions, like Jiao Yu, her new roommate. The temptation to give them a hand was strong, but Julius thought better of it.

When all the stragglers – some with the teacher's help – had finally been rounded up in the centre of the labyrinth, Professor Beloi gave them a fifteen minute break, and then made them swap roles. It was Faith's turn to guide Julius through the maze, and he did so rather well. It wasn't quite as quick as when he had been doing the guiding but, despite that, he was the first to the end point.

'*I still think it's 'cause you're good at receiving,*' said Faith, while they were waiting for the others to finish.

'*Maybe, but you know how to use telepathy, Faith, or you wouldn't be here on Zed. You can do just as well as me.*' Faith made no reply so Julius let the topic drop.

By the end of their first lesson, everyone had tried both roles, with different degrees of success. Professor Beloi had not made any individual evaluations, probably a good thing given that some of the students hadn't actually made it to the centre, but he promised them more of the same for the next few lessons.

33

For the next three weeks, Julius and the Mizkis got busy adapting to their second year subjects, both the old and new ones. So far, there were no troubling topics for him – in fact, he was doing rather well. It made him think that perhaps Freja had done a good thing by telling him that he was a White Child; he felt as if that knowledge had given him a little more confidence when it came to learning new things. Morgana had noticed this too, and had mentioned it to Julius on a few occasions. But then again, Morgana had *always* believed in him and his abilities, so maybe she didn't really count. What was beyond question, though, was that Julius was very happy with his start of term and hoped to keep it that way for the rest of the year.

September quickly came and went, and October brought glimpses of Satras and of a new gaming season. They were only to be allowed back on the third weekend of the month, which for Faith meant no birthday presents for another two weeks. Despite that, Julius, Morgana and Skye made sure he got a nice chocolate and carrot gateau for his birthday dinner – courtesy of Felice Buongustaio – with fourteen candles to blow out.

'Thanks, guys,' he said that night, passing slices of cake around the table.

Julius, Morgana and Skye had transferred fifteen Fyvers into Faith's account, as a present.

'Any idea what you're going to buy?' asked Morgana, licking her fingers.

'Actually, between upgrades for the PIP-chip and the shields, I have no idea. I guess I'll just have to wait and see what they're selling in Going Spare.'

'What about your skirt?' asked Julius, 'Can you still get gadgets for it?'

'I think so, but I forgot to mention it. Pit-Stop Pete wants to see me for a skirt-service.'

'That sounds fun,' said Skye, ramming an entire slice of cake into his mouth.

'Very,' said Faith, 'if I was a Ferrari. By the way Skye, you can't eat the candles.'

Skye stopped chewing, produced a blue wax ball from his mouth and put it down on his plate, while the others observed him with silent, comical looks on their faces.

'You really are a human trash compactor – you know that, right?' said Julius, amused.

*

On Saturday the 16th of October, Julius met the others at Tijara's main gate at eight o'clock sharp. It meant getting up as early as a normal school day but, given the number of people that would soon be clogging up the Intra-Rail System, it was well worth it. A handful of 1MJ students were also waiting for the train, chaperoned by a couple of Mizki Seniors.

'I wish someone had warned *us* last year to make sure we got here before the masses,' said Morgana.

'I almost got me new skirt torn off of me, the crowds were so bad!' added Faith, reminiscing.

'That might happen again, and worse, if you don't move away from the tracks by the way,' said Julius, dragging him back away from the edge of the platform.

When the train arrived, they boarded it without any difficulties and, following two brief stops for the early birds from the Tuala and Sield schools, they reached their destination. After a whole summer away, walking through the gates of Satras and standing on the terrace overlooking the emerald lake felt like a sweet homecoming to them.

'I so missed this place,' sighed Morgana.

Julius looked past the lake and the hundreds of shops flooded in neon lights, to a tall tower protruding from the Moon's jagged rocks and stretching all the way to the ceiling – the Hologram Palace, home of the Skirts.

'I know we can't play yet,' he said to the others, 'but let's go sit in the arena later on. I wanna check the score boards and see what's been going on.'

'Afraid someone's beaten your Solo score?' said a voice behind him.

Julius whirled around in surprise, and saw Bernard Docherty standing there.

'Hi Julius, how's things?'

'Bernard. Have you met my friends?'

'*Everyone* knows the Skirts,' he said jovially.

Julius noticed the pinkish wisps emanating from the tops of his friends' heads. It seemed a compliment from Docherty was enough to get them blushing.

'So, what's up, McCoy?'

'Just shopping. They've implanted our shields, so we can't play until November.'

'I remember that day, all right. It'll be worse when you get the chips in your feet, trust me. Well, maybe we'll meet in there this year,' he said pointing at the Palace. 'Enjoy your day.'

They watched as he boarded one of the platform lifts into Satras with two other Mizki Seniors, and waited for the next one so they could go too.

'He's a nice guy,' said Morgana, observing him from afar. 'I mean, he's made Zed history with his Solo record so he could easily have been a real stuck-up number because of that. But, in fact, he's quite the opposite.'

Julius nodded in agreement. He remembered the first time he had seen him, in the garden of Tijara. He had been surrounded by girls and boys, all positively spellbound by him. Now it made sense. He was a gracious winner, in true Tijaran style, and he hoped that one day he could follow suit.

As they stepped off the elevator, a unanimous vote called for an opulent breakfast at Global Brioche, the only place in Satras where you could find all of the different foods used for breakfasts around the world. A few minutes later, armed with custard-filled doughnuts in one hand and lattes in the other, the Skirts discussed the plan of attack for the day. Once they had managed to prise Skye from the pastry display, they headed straight for Going Spare, which they were very keen to explore. As he stepped inside the shop, Julius was immediately struck by the number of gadgets and gizmos spread over the seemingly hundreds of shelves.

'I could waste the whole day in here,' he said to no one in particular.

There was no answer from the others. Like a flock of oversized magpies, they were completely mesmerised by the shiny objects. Knowing that he needed to do other things that morning, he decided it would be best to ask for help, and walked towards one of the shop assistants. He asked to see the colour choices for the shields and was led towards a display.

'Choose the one you like,' said the man, 'and then put your arms inside these tubes, with the chips under the light. I'll do the rest.'

His favourite colour was sapphire blue, so he told the assistant and placed his arms in the tubes. The man selected the required tones for the colour and when the light shone over the scars on Julius's forearms, he pressed a button and a needle shot down into the chips. Julius flinched, expecting to feel the usual sharp pain, but it didn't arrive.

'Is that it?' he asked, quickly massaging each of the tiny scars.

'Yes. When you use the shields for the first time, you'll see. It's beautiful. Anything else I can help you with?'

'I would like more memory for the PIP, a different colour for my holoscreen – red this time – and an Earth Link so I can video-call home, please.'

'Coming right up,' said the man.

In ten minutes, he had fulfilled all of Julius's requests, for the price of thirty Fyvers. Each week the students could earn up to ten Fyvers to spend in Satras, depending on how well they had performed in class and, since Julius had done really well and couldn't spend any of his money on games, he had enough for the upgrades and a long overdue haircut.

'Guys, I'm going to head over to the *Barber of Seville*,' he said to the others.

'Wait for me,' said Faith from where he was standing, by the till. 'I need a trim too.'

'I'm meeting Kaori for more shopping and lunch,' said Morgana, who was still browsing over the merchandise. 'How about we meet at one in the Palace arena?'

'Fine by me,' said Skye, 'This morning I'm sort of busy ... with ... just busy.'

'Who are you meeting?' asked Julius with a knowing grin.

'No one,' said Skye, vaguely.

Julius and Faith quickly moved over and cornered him.

'Go on! Tell us,' said Faith.

'Wait!' said Julius. 'Don't tell me – it's Ife, right?'

'Maybe. Well, OK. Ife is far too old for me, so I decided to bring it down a level or two.'

'Yes but *who* then?' persisted Faith.

'You don't know her. She's from Sield School: Pippa Coleman, 3 Mizki Apprentice.'

'And when did you meet her?' asked Julius in surprise. 'You haven't really left Tijara that much.'

'I'm good at social networking,' said Skye, proudly. 'That's one good use of the PIP-chip.'

'You're quite something, you know that?' said Faith, amused. 'Will we see you at one?'

'Of course. Friends before girls, right?'

'Don't let Morgana hear you saying that, ever, if you know what's good for you,' said Julius, 'OK then, we'll see you later.'

They waved to Morgana and left the shop and then burst into laughter. It took a while before they were able to stop again.

'What is he like?' said Faith. 'And how many crushes is this now?'

'The third since August, including the teacher. But never fear, we have another seven months until the end of the school year.'

'Anything could happen between now and then,' added Faith, grinning.

When they entered the barber shop, a short, dark haired man came quickly to welcome them in and ushered them into two of his high leather chairs.

'Good morning, gentlemen,' he said with an obsequious bow and the vocal flourish of a tenor. 'My name is Figaro Rossini, factotum and owner of this fine establishment. Now, from the obvious absence of facial hair, I assume that you are here for a haircut, no?'

'To be sure,' said Faith. 'See if you can untangle this brown carpet parked over me head please. Not too short though.'

'Right away, sir,' said Figaro, tipping Faith's head back and beginning to wash his hair in a basin of water that was attached to the back of the chair.

Julius relaxed in his own seat, which Figaro had reclined to make him more comfortable.

'Sir,' asked Faith, 'I don't mean to be out of place, but am I right in saying that your name is related to the name of this shop?'

'Why, yes! Figaro *was* the barber of Seville, in the opera by the Italian composer Rossini, my ancestor. Hence my name. My family built this shop in the days when Marcus Tijara and Clodagh Arnesh were first founding the Zed Lunar Perimeter. But I am very surprised that you know of this opera.'

'I'm Irish, see, but me mum's family is Italian. They used to play loads of opera in the house.'

'Well, good for you! It's truly a balm for the spirit.' As he said this, he turned on the stereo and selected the opera in question.

Julius waited patiently for his turn, enjoying the music and the smell of aftershave permeating the leather of his chair. Figaro meanwhile had removed the basin of water and was vigorously drying Faith's hair. The sound of the barber working as he snipped away rapidly at his friend's locks was almost hypnotic.

When Figaro finished with Faith, he moved over to Julius, attached a clean basin of water and washed his hair, then tilted the chair upright once again. 'What shall it be for you, young master?'

'I like my hair longish, but the jagged strands are getting out of control. They need to be less Amazon Forest and more botanical garden type of vegetation.'

'I'm sorry, but I have no idea what you're talking about.'

'Just tidy it up, please,' said Julius.

When they left Figaro, Julius and Faith looked a lot neater than when they had entered.

'Let's just grab some food and go to the Hologram Palace. There'll be plenty of entertainment there, till the others arrive,' said Faith.

'Sure, and it's free. I don't want to finish all of my money today.'

So they stopped by one of the many stalls along the Emerald Lake and bought sandwiches and a litre of freshly squeezed carrot juice to share. When they reached the Palace, dozens of 1MJ boys and girls were populating the courtyard, some looking rather lost and scared.

'Surely *we* weren't like that, last year?' said Julius, sitting down on one of the large steps of the arena.

'Of course not,' answered Faith, unconvincingly. 'Besides, I was too busy dealing with Somers – he did have a way of gettin' me goat up.'

'You always managed to put him in his place though, Faith.'

'But it's a shame I lost me temper with him – he wasn't really worth it. I should have known better.'

'No one could blame you for that. He insulted you at every opportunity. Heck, I would have done the same thing.'

'I'm fine with me disability, Julius. Well, at least I'm comfortably resigned to it. I've gotten used to the stares, the pity and sometimes even being treated like I'm second class, or a freak,' said Faith. 'Certain things you can't change, and the more I get upset or frustrated about it, the more time I waste, when I could be using that time to find ways of getting around me problems. You would have thought that, with all the technological discoveries we have, somebody would had invented a cure for folks like me, but no.'

Julius stared at his feet for a moment, reflecting on Faith's words. For a start, he was surprised at how much Faith had just told him. This year Julius had already been taken by surprise with the remark about his lack of chances with girls, and now this. Julius thought he sensed a hint of frustration in his friend's voice but, try as he might, he couldn't actually see any form of coloured wisp above Faith's head, a sign that he was probably suppressing his emotions pretty well. Still, he was glad that he had opened up to him. It meant he was trusted at least.

'Ah, don't be too harsh on yourself, mate,' he said, eventually. 'You're a really funny guy so even the worst of your wisecracks makes people like Somers look like the idiots they are. See, that's one way of getting around the problem. Besides, everyone needs to let off steam sometimes. We're only human, after all! Well OK, maybe not you – you're pretty much a cyborg already.'

Faith laughed heartily and punched Julius on the shoulder. 'Don't worry. You'll get there too one day.'

'At the rate they're going with these augmentations, it'll be earlier than we think.'

They finished their food in silence while staring at the scoreboards in the arena. Julius was curious to know exactly why Faith was unable to walk, but he knew better than to ask, or to probe around in his head with the aid of mind-skills. Faith would tell him when he was good and ready, so Julius would simply wait until then.

At one o'clock, Morgana and Skye joined them on the steps.

According to the charts, the Skirts still held the record for flying games among the first year students.

'Guys, what do you say we start this year with a fight?' said Morgana, looking at the scoreboards for the team fighting contests. 'There aren't any particularly impressive records up there, and I bet you no one will be able to beat our Flight score for a long time.'

'I like that idea,' said Faith.

'Why don't we play the first one against the computer?' said Julius, 'To see what it's like.'

'Sound,' said Skye. 'Are we still only competing against teams from our own year?'

'I'd prefer that, if it's all right with you guys,' said Morgana. 'At least for now.'

Julius and the others nodded in agreement. They spent the afternoon wandering around the arena, checking out newcomers and meeting up with students from the other schools. Julius and Faith even managed to drag Skye away from the crowd to enquire about his date, but he was rather mysterious about it and would not share any particulars, with the excuse that it wasn't the gentlemanly thing to do. Julius told Skye it was very thoughtful of him to not kiss-and-tell and so they stopped pestering him. It was just before eight o'clock when they returned to Tijara for dinner. Given that his wrist wasn't hurting too much anymore and that he was dying to use some of his gadgets for the PIP, Julius spent the evening chatting with his family on his new Earth Link from the comfort of the Juniors' common room.

THE FIRST ORACLE

The first week of November felt a century long to Julius, so eager was he for the weekend to arrive. This was in no short part down to the knowledge that on Saturday the 2MJ students would finally be allowed back into the Hologram Palace, now that their shield implants had been given a chance to fully merge with their muscular tissue.

'Merged or not, I'm going to the Palace tomorrow,' said Julius during the Friday evening meal.

'I'll follow you even if me arms fall off,' added Faith, eagerly.

This enthusiasm was shared by all of their classmates, and there was plenty of game-talk that night, as the students decided who to team up with and who to challenge. So it was no great surprise that the Tijaran train stop was packed to the hilt by 08:00 the following morning. Still half asleep, the Skirts had managed to beat all the queues, thanks to sneaking out of school one hour before the others. So while their classmates struggled like so many sardines to cram themselves onto the Intra-Rail System, Julius and his friends were enjoying a small breakfast in the quiet of the arena.

Julius drained the last drops of his latte and stood up. 'Are we ready, Skirts?'

The others nodded. Skye collected everyone's cups and threw them in a nearby nullify-bin, where the rubbish was instantly dematerialised.

When they reached the information kiosk, old Mrs Mayflower greeted Julius with her usual cheeky smile.

'Good morning, madam,' said Julius. 'We would like to sign up for a Combat game please.'

'Now, that's a first for the Skirts. It's good to see you back,' she said smiling at the others. 'We've missed you here at the Palace.'

'We've missed it too, Mrs Mayflower. Like you wouldn't believe,' said Morgana.

'But of course. Well, you're back now. Here's your ticket. Miss Logan will tell you what to do. Good luck!'

They said goodbye to her and passed through the entrance for the group games. The previous year, they had always followed the underground corridor to the right, where the Flight sector technician, Mr Smith, would be waiting to set them up with their holosuits; today however, they took the left path which was marked "Combat". At the end of the corridor, they found a room with two doors and a desk between them. A young blonde woman was sitting on top of it, reading something on her PIP. When she saw them, she closed her hand and got off the desk. Julius handed her their ticket.

'Morning all. I'm Miss Logan. First time in Combat, huh?' she asked, with an encouraging smile. 'Well, no need to fear – it's the same routine as for Flight. Get in, get changed, wait to get called, get holosphered and of course, do your best. You can't use your mind-skills in here, as you know, 'cause this isn't Solo. The big difference is that you don't have a Sim-Cougar to attack your enemies, so you'll be given a Sim-Gauntlet instead. You heard of them before?'

'Well, we've heard of *the* Gauntlet,' answered Morgana. 'Last year, Professor Chan explained that it's a device you wear on the back of your hand, which works like the catalyst on a Cougar, so your mind-skills get channelled through it and you can aim it at a target. But we haven't done any training with it yet.'

'You'll start today then. The energies you use in Combat games aren't your own anyway. They are already pre-programmed into the Sim-Gauntlet. You'll see them coming out in a blue beam. All you need to do is aim and tighten your fist to shoot. Remember, these types of sessions have a set time limit. You have thirty minutes to create as much havoc as possible. You ready then?'

They nodded excitedly and hurried to the respective dressing rooms. Inside, Faith headed straight for the back room, where he could change with a bit more privacy. Julius and Skye quickly changed out of their uniforms and into the holosuits, then waited by the door to be called. As they sat there, Julius examined the Sim-Gauntlet on his right hand. It was made from a hard plastic material, which covered the back of his hand and gathered up into a thin central ridge starting at his wrist and coming to a stop just above the third knuckle. There was a tiny hole set into this end, which was clearly where the beams shot out.

A few minutes after Faith had finished up and joined them, the loudspeaker called for the Skirts to enter the arena through the green portal. As soon as they had done so, they instantly recognised the familiar vast room, with its dozens of long rows of holospheres stretching across the arena. Julius was pretty sure this was every bit as large as the Flight game sector.

'I didn't think it would be possible to have *two* such massive areas,' he gasped.

46

'Between these holospheres and the Flight ones we could have every single Zed student gaming at once,' said Faith, in awe. 'How rapid would that be?'

Once Morgana had joined them, a floor technician showed them to their holospheres. Julius climbed nimbly onto the hovering, metal ring-frame of his sphere, as he had done many times before. Grabbing the handles to either side of him, he placed his feet onto the two small platforms below him and rested his head back against the support. When they were all ready, the technician activated the controls and the lights went dim. Julius felt a familiar tightening sensation around his hands, waist and feet, as the pale blue magnetic field enveloping him began to tremble. Seconds later, the dusk of the room gave way to a growing ball of light and he shut his eyes against its brightness. His body became weightless and he felt himself being lowered gently down onto hard ground. He opened his eyes and quickly jumped back, as he found himself staring over the edge of a precipice.

Behind him, he heard Faith shouting excitedly. 'Me legs! Me legs! I can see me legs! Guys, I can walk!'

Julius turned around and watched, mouth open, as Faith improvised a merry Irish jig. There was a thick green wisp emanating from his head, which Julius immediately recognised as a telltale sign that Faith was genuinely overjoyed.

'This simulator is well cool,' said Skye, who was standing just to the left of Faith and grinning brightly as he watched the dance. 'Just don't go knocking us off this platform OK, you crazy kid.'

As he said that, Julius and Morgana had a proper look around them, and realised that they were indeed standing on a grassy platform, roughly the size of a king-sized bed, which was flying across a clear blue sky.

'I wonder where we're heading,' said Julius. He didn't fully trust the peaceful atmosphere around them. This was a Combat game after all, so it struck him as a good idea for them to stay sharp.

As if they had read his thoughts, Morgana and Skye began to scout the horizon, and Julius did likewise. It took Faith a little longer to recompose himself, but none of them were about to complain about that, seeing as he was so understandably excited about his very own functioning legs. It was Morgana who first spotted something.

'Over there,' she said, pointing with her finger at a spot just below and ahead of them.

The others edged over beside her and looked down.

'Is that a tower?' asked Julius.

'It looks like it,' answered Skye. 'There are people all around its base. What are they doing?'

'It's a siege!' said Faith. 'See there – they're putting ladders against the tower, so they can climb it.'

'But why?' said Morgana, 'There's nowhere to go from its top.'

'I think,' said Julius, worriedly, 'the more important question is, why are *we* heading towards them?'

Suddenly, as if prompted by the words, the platform veered left and started its descent towards the peak of the tower.

'Oh boy,' said Faith, 'Um, guys ... I think they've seen us.'

Julius glanced anxiously at the mob below, who were waving pitchforks and slingshots over their heads and glaring angrily back at him. Without warning, the platform stopped abruptly above the tower and began, slowly but steadily, tilting to the left.

'Shoot!' cried Julius, stepping to the right side of the platform in an effort to counteract the tilt.

'Woah,' exclaimed Morgana, who was losing the battle to stay on her feet. Just in time, Julius grabbed her hand and pulled her back.

'Sit down everyone!' shouted Skye.

'Quick. The roof of the tower – we're going to have to slide down onto it,' said Julius. 'There's no other way.'

'I can't believe I'm saying this, but ...' said Faith scrambling backwards, 'I miss me skiiiirt ...' And with that, he slid off onto the top of the tower.

The others tumbled down right behind him and landed face first on the hard stone floor.

'I hope we get bonus points for this,' groaned Julius, checking his nose to see if it was still intact.

'What was that ab ... ouch!' exclaimed Morgana, massaging the right side of her face with her hand. 'I don't believe it. They just threw a beehive at me!'

'I hope it's empt ... ouch!' cried Skye, shielding his face with his left hand and picking up the projectile with the other. 'It's a blinking pine cone!'

'Death to the ogres!' the crowd shouted as one from the base of the tower.

'Kill the monsters!' added another lone voice, just for good measure.

'Steady on now, you pesky peasants,' called Faith, who was obviously feeling rather put out by all of this and marched over to the edge of the tower. 'I'll have you know that me friends here have a mean aim, especially under pressure. Isn't that right, guys?'

'Too right,' said Julius. 'Come on Skirts, this is *our* game. Pick a side and give 'em grief!'

The rallying call worked wonders and, less than ten seconds

49

later, the air was filled with blue beams of energy firing off in every direction. Every time they hit someone, the target would instantly disappear. Despite their heavy losses however, the attacking horde continued their assault, throwing every manner of weird projectile. At one point, Julius could have sworn that he saw a chicken whizz past his head, closely followed by what appeared to be a loaf of bread.

'Hey!' cried Morgana in between shots. 'They've put a ladder up.'

Julius ran over to her side and took aim at a man who was scrambling up towards them. He squeezed his fist tightly and a blue jet shot out, hitting the man square on his nose. The puzzled expression on his face was the last thing Julius saw before the peasant disappeared into thin air. It took several more minutes of intense firing but at last they managed to eliminate all of the attackers.

'That was hard work and no mistake,' said Skye, panting.

'And you haven't seen anything yet,' said Julius ominously, pointing north. 'It looks like their friends are coming to the party.'

'We've gotta get out of here,' said Morgana. 'Look, there's a forest over there. We *could* try to lose them in it.'

'Works for me,' said Julius. 'Come on. This side. It was nice of them to leave a ladder for us.'

Julius waited for his friends to climb down and then rushed after them. Together, they sprinted for the forest, accompanied by Faith's hollers as he savoured the joy of running with his own legs.

'Keep going!' called Julius, hurrying them on. 'They're catching up.'

As they hurtled through the forest they kept turning and firing at random, hoping to get lucky and hit some of the chasing pack. Some of the shots actually did find their target but, as many as they hit, there were still more who stayed hot on their tails.

'There's an opening to the right,' cried Skye, swerving in that direction.

Julius veered off to follow him, then half stopped and glanced back towards Morgana and Faith, who had stopped briefly to fire off a volley of shots at their pursuers.

'This way. Come on!' he shouted to them. Then, seeing that they were following, he took off after Skye again.

Up ahead, the trees were parting off to either side while the ground sloped steadily downwards. A flurry of pine cones and other random missiles whisked past his head. He wasn't really paying proper attention to where he was going so, when Skye suddenly stopped, Julius simply rammed into the back of him.

'What's the matter with you?' cried Julius in surprise.

That's when he noticed that they had stopped just in time to avoid going over the edge of a cliff. Far below them was a lake that was fed by a large waterfall to their left.

'That was too clo ...' began Skye.

He never managed to finish his sentence though, as just then, Faith and Morgana belted out of the trees and crashed into Julius and Skye, sending the two of them flying through the air and over the cliff.

'AAAAHHHH!' cried Julius, arms flailing.

As he fell, he braced as best as he could for impact and just hoped he wouldn't land on top of Skye. Seconds later he splashed into the lake. The water, which was freezing cold, swirled all around his head and ears. Struggling to orientate himself, he searched desperately for the surface. Finally, he spotted a ray of sunshine filtering down through the water and he kicked upwards, towards it. He emerged in time to see Morgana and Faith jumping off the cliff together just as a line of the pine cone wielding peasants screeched to a halt at its edge. To his left, Skye was swimming for the shore and calling to them as he went. Julius treaded water for a moment, waiting to check that the other two resurfaced safely. He was also slightly worried about Faith and how he would cope with the novelty of swimming. Fortunately they were both fine though and, as soon as they caught sight of Julius, they began to swim in his direction.

'I'm so glad I wore trousers today,' said Morgana, as they reached the shore and heaved themselves out of the water.

'I'm so not,' said Faith, seriously.

Julius chuckled, and then pointed towards the cliff, where a small group of the peasants had just leapt into the lake. 'They're coming. We need to keep going.'

Before them, the forest continued all along the left shore so they hurried inside it, with Julius leading the way. He could tell that the crowd wasn't far behind, because their stomping feet were shaking the ground beneath him. He knew that they needed to somehow either lose them or else find a place to stand their ground and fight.

Just then, he sensed something to his right, and a mental picture appeared in his mind of a cave and a long tunnel. He veered off in that direction and shouted back to his friends: 'Come on, there's a cave here! Let's go – we can hide inside it.'

Behind him, the others skidded to a halt and dived after him. There was a large weeping willow in front of them, its leaves hanging over like a curtain of green. They swatted them aside and scrambled up an embankment that had a rock wall at its head, with the mouth of a cave yawning open there. They hurried inside and pressed their backs against the wall, trying hard to control their heavy breathing. A moment later, the angry hubbub of the mob echoed through the cave, then slowly died off and disappeared. Julius drew a sigh of relief.

The air about them was cool and damp, which wasn't ideal given how wet they all were. As his eyes adjusted to the darkness around him, Julius realised that this wasn't just a small cave they had ducked into – it was a vast cavern, which stretched off into what appeared to be a long tunnel.

'How did you spot this place?' said Morgana to Julius. 'None of us saw it, especially with that tree in the way.'

He shrugged. 'I didn't – it appeared in my mind.'

She looked quizzically at him. 'Hmm, OK. Well, what do we do now?'

Faith peered outside, and quickly pulled his head back inside. 'Some of 'em are still out there,' he whispered. 'Looks like they're searching for us.'

'Well, we can't go that way then,' said Skye, wringing some water out of his shirt.

Julius stood up and took a few tentative steps in the direction of the tunnel. There was a faint glow coming from the far end, possibly from another opening.

'I think there may be a way out up that way,' he said.

Morgana looked distrustfully at the tunnel. 'That's all very good, but we need a torch or something. It's pitch black in there.'

'Problem solved,' said Faith. He was tapping a small button on his Sim-Gauntlet, which was causing a small blue light to blink on and off. 'Try yours.'

They each quickly found the lights on their own Gauntlets and flicked them on.

'You guys check it out,' said Skye. 'I'll wait here and keep watch.'

Julius hesitated, not wanting to leave his friend behind, but also realising it would be better to have at least some kind of warning if their hiding place was discovered. 'OK,' he said after a minute, 'but the first sight of trouble, you come after us you hear?'

'With bells on,' Skye answered, with a reassuring grin, then added, 'Go on, I'll be fine,' after seeing Morgana's and Faith's doubtful expressions.

They nodded and turned to Julius, who was staring purposefully into the darkness. He felt Morgana grab hold of the back of his t-shirt, while Faith in turn drew closer to them. Cautiously, they set off through the cavern, making sure to be careful where they placed their feet on the uneven ground. As they moved further along the tunnel, the faint light from the outside world behind them gradually faded away, leaving them with only their pale lights to illuminate their surroundings and the outcrops of red rock all around. As they went, they became aware of faint squeaking noises above them.

'Bats,' gasped Morgana, looking up at the ceiling, 'My hair hates bats.'

'Do you get them often?' asked Faith, with a chuckle.

'If we keep our voices down, they won't bother us,' whispered Julius.

Eventually the path split into two tunnels, one heading downwards – its entrance half blocked by a couple of collapsed wooden beams – and the other bending right and upwards.

'I don't want to go any deeper into this thing,' said Faith.

'I hear you. Let's try the right tunnel,' said Julius, heading in that direction.

He took only a few steps around the bend and then froze where he was.

'What's wrong?' asked Faith.

'Get back,' hissed Julius. 'Now!'

In the darkness ahead, two large yellow dots were advancing towards them, swaying slightly from one side to the other as they approached.

'What *is* it?' whispered Morgana, anxiety creeping into her voice.

'And what's that stench?' added Faith, slowly backtracking.

There was no way for Julius to tell, but he could hear clicking noises on the ground, like nails or claws, tapping against the rocky surface. Gradually, he raised his right arm in front of him, and prepared to shoot.

'Aim between the eyes,' he said.

Faith and Morgana, who were also slowly retreating, nodded and raised their Sim-Gauntlets in front of them. As they reached the point where the path had split, there was the sound of footsteps hurrying towards them from the direction of the cave entrance.

'They've found us!' cried Skye.

At that moment, several things happened at once: a huge black bear emerged from the tunnel, raised itself up on its hind legs and roared threateningly at the intruders. Meanwhile the bats, who had been peacefully lining the cave ceiling, burst into a chaotic flutter of wings and shrieks, further obscuring the already dim light. Julius squeezed his fist and fired at the bear, aided by Morgana who, to her eternal credit, was somehow managing to ignore the bats. Faith and Skye turned towards the angry mob, their backs touching Julius and Morgana's. A small part in the back of Julius's mind took note of how they had taken that instinctively protective formation, without any prior decision, and the thought of how efficient they were together filled him with a sense of exhilaration. He continued firing at the bear with renewed zeal and, when he saw that the animal was almost finished, turned and said to Morgana, 'Help the others.'

Morgana's arm swung promptly to the left, in the direction of the mob.

'Julius,' cried Skye. 'When you're done playing with that oversized cub, aim for the rocks above the door. We need to stop them from coming in.'

Julius hardly thought "cub" was a suitable description for the hairy beast in front of him, but this definitely wasn't the time to argue about it. He squeezed hard one last time and watched the bear crash to the ground, then whirled around to face the advancing mob. They were still pressing forward but, between the cloud of bats and the sterling efforts of the Skirts, they weren't managing to make any serious inroads yet. Julius looked up at an outcrop of rocks just above the entrance, aimed at them and squeezed his fist. The blue beam shot through the air and exploded against the wall of the cave. Chunks of rocks tumbled onto the crowd, while a growing rumble filled the air. A sudden tearing sound ripped through the cavern, and they all stared up, not daring to breathe, as the entire section of stones above the entrance teetered, then came crashing down, plunging them into darkness.

'Are you guys all right?' cried Julius.

'Shoot first. Ask questions later,' shouted Skye, knowing that some of the mob may have been trapped inside too.

Julius pointed his light at the pile of rubble. There were a few survivors, some still brandishing their bizarre missiles, but Morgana, Faith and Skye quickly eliminated the last of them.

'That was intense,' said Julius, pulling a strand of hair behind his ear.

'I think we're going to get loads of points for this one,' said Skye.

'By the way, how long have we got left?' asked Faith. 'The thirty minutes should be up by now, surely.'

'If my PIP is correct, the simulation should end in the next two minutes,' answered Morgana.

Julius walked back and popped his head into the tunnel that the bear had emerged from. It was a dead end. He returned to the collapsed wall and tried to shift some of the rocks, but none of them would budge. The others had plonked themselves down in exhaustion opposite the split in the path, so he joined them.

'Hmm ...' said Faith, sounding worried. 'Time's up, but we're still here.'

'Maybe they're having some sort of delay. A glitch perhaps,' added Skye.

'Well, I hope it's not something we've done, shooting the place up like that,' said Faith.

They sat waiting for a few more minutes, discussing their performance and how they could improve it for the next game. Suddenly Julius, who had been leaning back on his hands, sat bolt upright; he felt something, a presence of some sort, but he couldn't quite put his finger on exactly what it was. He stood up and glanced around the cave, half expecting to see some crazy new game character come charging out of the shadows. The others looked at him.

'What's up, McCoy?' asked Skye.

'Not sure,' answered Julius. 'Could have sworn I felt something.'

The others immediately jumped to their feet and began to look in all directions.

'There!' said Julius, pointing at the left tunnel. 'There's something through there, I'm sure of it.'

'Guys,' said Morgana, 'haven't we had enough for one day?'

Julius shook his head. 'I say we check it out. There's nowhere else to go and besides, when they extract us from the game, it won't matter where we are.'

'Better than sitting here, I suppose,' agreed Faith.

'The Skirts never run from a challenge, right?' said Skye, not waiting for a reply and moving towards the tunnel entrance. 'Stand back!' he called. With two quick bursts of energy from his Sim-Gauntlet, he pulverised the wooden beams blocking the way.

Julius moved next to him, stretching his right hand forward to illuminate the downward path. Morgana stepped behind Skye, followed by Faith and they set off. The path stretched on and they walked in silence along it for what seemed like an eternity.

'I can hear water dripping,' said Morgana eventually.

'There's also a weird glow ahead,' added Faith.

'Hey, come on!' shouted Julius excitedly. 'There's some kind of chamber along there.'

They had reached the end of the path. At the bottom of a slope in front of them lay a small pool of water, surrounded by a number of tunnel entrances. Water was falling from the jutting rocks into the pool in gentle trickles, creating echoes all around the cave. Right in the centre of this tiny lake was a flat rock, half covered in algae.

'It's kinda pretty, in a strange way,' said Morgana.

'Yeah, but what is it?' Julius asked, and headed down the slope while the others stood and examined the chamber. He stooped over and looked closely at the rock, then stepped back quickly – there was a click, followed by a whirring sound, and a mechanical device, which looked like a scanner of some sort, popped out of the rock. Sure enough, it emitted a flat beam of turquoise light, which spread out in a straight line at his feet, then slowly rose up his body and continued upwards until it reached the top of his head. He stood, transfixed. Then, just as quickly as it had appeared, it was gone.

'What in the name of ...' began Skye. He was cut short as a blinding flash of light filled the cave, forcing them all to flinch and shield their eyes with their hands. When they opened them again they saw, to their amazement, that there was a luminous woman standing on the rock in front of them.

'Um, are we *sure* time is up?' said Morgana.

'Yeah, but maybe this is a bonus level or something,' offered Skye.

'It's a hologram – I'm pretty certain of that – but who is she?' asked Julius, stepping closer.

'Careful there,' called Faith.

As Julius got closer, the woman looked at him and smiled. She appeared to be in her mid-thirties, with long blonde hair outlining her beautiful, delicate face. She wore a flowing, silver tunic with large sleeves.

'I've been waiting for you,' she said.

Julius jumped back in surprise, while the others readied their Sim-Gauntlets.

'Do not be afraid,' she said with a gentle smile. 'I kept telling myself you would come back to me, and here you are.'

'Who are you?' asked Julius. The woman didn't answer, but kept staring in front of her, the same warm smile fixed on her face.

'I don't think we can actually interact with it,' said Faith. 'This could just be a standard holo-message relay station, which, in this case, looks like a lady.'

'Meaning?' asked Skye.

'Well, like I said before, it's just a bonus event that we've found inside the game. We've activated it, but it isn't specifically for us.'

'OK, but what's the point? What do we do with it?'

'Hush,' said Morgana, as the holo-lady began to speak again.

'I am the first Oracle and I will set you on the right path. My time is short, so hear my words. We shall meet again in fifty-five days from now, in the last five minutes of the day.'

Morgana began to type away speedily on her PIP as the lady spoke.

'Go to Lake Smaragdus, where it all began,' continued the Oracle. 'At the feet of the lovers you shall see me, if you can. You will heed my words three more times. Remember, only the bravest can reach the end. Farewell, my bringer of life.'

With those words, the Oracle flickered and vanished.

'Flashy! We got ourselves a little treasure hunt,' said Skye.

Julius was just about to reply when he suddenly felt himself being sucked backwards, and the next moment he was gone.

*

'Apologies, guys,' the technician said, as he helped Faith out of his holosphere. 'The system went mental for a while and we couldn't get you back. I hope you didn't mind waiting too much.'

'No problem,' answered Julius. 'The game has some nice surprises if you have time to find them.'

'I suppose so,' he said, furrowing his brow quizzically. 'Anyway, you'll need to move along. Sorry, but I've got several other kids to retrieve now that the system is back online.'

They thanked him and headed for the dressing rooms. Half an hour later, they sat on the steps of the arena, eagerly waiting for their score to come up as an ever growing number of students queued up for the games.

'I'm so glad we got here early this morning,' said Morgana, watching Mrs Mayflower looking increasingly stressed as the crowd around her kiosk multiplied.

'See Yuri, what did I tell you? I knew they would be here already.'

'Hi Gustavo; Yuri. Always a pleasure,' said Julius, looking over at the two boys as they appeared from the crowd.

Like Skye, Yuri Slovich and Gustavo Perez came from the Zed space stations, and had become a sort of double act, in that they were inseparable. They acted as if they were brothers, but physically they couldn't have been more different from each other: Yuri had a definite eastern European paleness to him, with light eyes and hair, while Gustavo was simply the opposite, with darker skin and hair.

'Why aren't you queuing? Have you played already?' asked Yuri in surprise.

'Got here at the crack of dawn, actually,' answered Faith.

'I didn't think it would be *this* busy,' said Gustavo.

'Well, it is Saturday, plus you know every 2MJ in Zed has been chomping at the bit for a game,' said Julius.

Yuri chuckled and nodded. 'So, what are the Skirts up to this year then?'

'We've decided to start off with Combat actually, but only with teams from our own year,' explained Morgana.

'And how did it go?'

'Well, it was just us early birds this time. We're still waiting for the score,' said Skye. 'There was a problem with the simulator this morning and we got stuck in it, well past our game time.'

'No kidding?' asked Yuri.

'Yep. I was a little worried at first,' said Morgana. 'But then, as we were waiting, we found a bonus level inside the game.'

'Really? I've never heard of anything like that before. Maybe it's a new thing.'

'Perhaps,' answered Skye. 'Hey, look. The score is coming up.'

Julius turned towards the central screen, where that morning's scores were being compiled. The chart started with the first-year results. For Flight, the Skirts were still leading the table, unbeaten since the previous school term. They cheered as soon as they saw it. When the second-year chart appeared, their cheering grew even louder – they had made it to number one in the Combat game category, edging out a team called The Zedinators.

'How good are we?' said Faith, giving low-fives to each of his team mates.

'This is just!' cried Julius, who was beaming happily.

'You are no fun,' said Yuri, shaking his head. 'But I gotta hand it to you, you did well. Congrats.'

'Thanks, you guys,' said Morgana.

'Well, Yuri,' said Gustavo, putting a hand against his friend's back and leading him off towards Mrs Mayflower's kiosk. 'I think it's about time we assembled a team so we can kick their little skirted butts.'

'You wish,' shouted Skye, with a cheeky grin.

'See you guys later,' called Julius.

'So,' said Faith, once they had left. 'What do we do about that bonus thingy?'

'The lady said she'll be back in 55 days,' said Julius. 'That's Morgana's birthday.'

Morgana, who was scanning the scoreboard, turned her head and looked at Julius. '31ˢᵗ of December?'

'Yes. At five to midnight.'

'It'll be right in the middle of the New Year's ball,' said Morgana. 'It might be tricky to get away.'

'Never mind that – we need to figure out where we're going, first of all,' answered Skye. 'But not now, please. I'm starving and it's getting far too busy in here. Let's go to Global Brioche.'

'You'll turn into a global brioche if you're not careful,' quipped Faith.

'Funny guy, hey,' said Skye, throwing an arm around his neck and pulling him along in the direction of the shops. 'I'll pull your skirt over your head if you don't watch it.'

Julius and Morgana grinned at each other and followed them. It was tricky going, trying to find a path through the packs of students, but Julius hardly noticed it, so lost was he in happy thoughts of their Combat result and the news that would surely soon be spreading throughout Satras – the Skirts were back.

VANISHING ACTS

November had started in the best of ways, as far as Julius was concerned. He was still performing well in all of his subjects, the Palace was currently holding not one, but two records for the Skirts, and his Solo score remained unbeaten from the previous year. On top of this, the Space Channel had not reported any sightings of Arneshian fleets. It was as if their defeat in the summer had been enough to send them home with their tails between their legs. Julius didn't really believe that he had seen the last of them, however, but he was pretty sure that they wouldn't try another open attack again any time soon. With these thoughts in his head, he headed to Chan's dojo for his Mindkata session, looking forward to trying to use his shield for the first time. There, Professor Morales was waiting for the students. Professor Chan stood to one side, leaving his colleague to lead the lesson.

'Good afternoon, Mizkis,' she said, bowing. 'Please kneel.'

Julius noticed how quickly everyone obeyed, eager as they all were to finally try out their shields.

'We have spent the last two months learning the theory behind basic Shield techniques,' continued Morales. 'From today, until the holiday, you will learn to use and control your shields as you walk, run and perform basic kata movements. In January, if Professor Chan believes that you are ready, then we can begin experimenting with defence and attack.'

An excited murmur spread through the dojo.

'I'm going to ask you to fan out in a long row. Make sure you have enough space on either side to safely activate your shields.'

Julius positioned himself between Faith and Barth. Although, being all too aware of Barth's propensity for disasters, he put a bit of extra distance between him and the young Dutchman as a precaution. He noted how Lopaka had done the same thing on Barth's other side.

'Now, do as I do, please,' Morales said, bending her arms parallel in front of her, fist against fist and then waiting for the students to do the same. 'Each shield chip is activated by your mind-skills. The actual resistance of the shields is already calibrated into your chips, so you can all withstand the same level of attacks. As you move through the Mizki ranks, your shields will be improved and made more resistant. Take a deep breath now, and *will* your shields into life.'

Julius concentrated on the chips beneath his skin, and soon felt a light jolt of current running up his forearms. Suddenly, a pair of sapphire-blue magnetic fields sprung into being, creating two long, oval walls, from above his head right down to his feet.

'Amazing,' gasped Julius.

The dojo had turned into a multicoloured forest. It appeared that all of his classmates had paid a visit to Going Spare, because every single shield had been personalised with a different tint. Morgana had chosen a delicate shade of lilac. Faith had gone for a lively green, while Skye had turned his shield silver.

'Very good, Mizkis,' called Morales. 'Now, try walking around the dojo for a bit, without bumping into each other.'

Julius began to move slowly, being very careful to avoid the other students.

'You can stop focusing on the shield, by the way,' added Morales. 'It'll stay active for as long as you want.'

'Or until you faint, or die, or get hurt,' added Professor Chan from the corner.

'Yes, thank you, Professor,' said Morales, eyeing him sideways.

'I thought they should know,' he replied, shrugging his shoulders innocently.

Julius relaxed his mind, concentrating more on his own movement than on the shields, and indeed they did stay up. Occasionally there was a zapping sound – the kind of crackling noise a fly made when it hit an electrified zapper – whenever two students allowed their shields to touch. Following these contacts, the shields would normally disappear, given that the students tended to get a fright and instinctively turn them off whenever this happened. Variations on "Sorry", or "Get out of my way – I can't control this thing" could be heard throughout the dojo during that first lesson.

'Very good, Mizkis – you're doing well,' encouraged Morales.

'Carry on as you are,' called Professor Chan to the class. 'Professor Morales and I are going to start moving around the room. Your job is to try to avoid us.'

And, with that, they began to dart here and there among the students, forcing them into swift changes in direction. Julius noticed that Faith was managing to turn more fluidly than anyone else, aided by his ability to hover. With his smooth movements and the green

66

shields surrounding him, it was like watching him waltz with an emerald ghost.

'Stop-stop-stop!' cried Morgana, suddenly.

Julius and the other students turned to see what was happening, and were treated to a curious picture. Several strands of Morgana's hair were being yanked upwards by Barth's shield, who had somehow managed to entangle them inside the magnetic field.

'Oops, I'm sorry. Wait, let me help!' pleaded Barth, trying to pull his arms away and free her.

Obviously that was only making things worse, as Julius could tell by the single tear running down Morgana's cheek.

'Mr Smit, stop moving!' ordered Professor Morales, hurrying over to them.

Barth froze like a statue but continued apologising as he stood there. Julius almost had more sympathy for him than Morgana; the look of anxious worry on his face was that great.

'Now Mr Smit, listen to me carefully,' continued Morales. 'Whenever such a situation occurs, one has to stop, focus on their shield and simply switch it off. This is what I want you to do, on the count of three – one, two, three!'

Barth closed his eyes and took a deep breath ... but nothing happened. Julius stood watching, mesmerised by the scene. He knew how much Morgana loved her hair. She tended to it daily, so that its "Japanese shine", as she called it, would remain untarnished.

'OK,' said Morales, trying to remain calm. 'That didn't work, and unfortunately I can't retract your shields for you, so we'll just have to take you to see Dr Walliser. Try to walk side by side. Yes, that's good.'

Morgana let out a yelp of pain as the Professor led them slowly out of the dojo. Barth immediately hurried out another stream of apologies.

'If anything happens to my hair, you'll be sorry for sure,' warned Morgana, through gritted teeth.

The students waited for the three of them to leave the room, and then collapsed into fits of laughter.

'I can see remedial classes coming his way,' sighed Professor Chan, shaking his head.

It took all of his authority to get the class under control again. It was needed, as it was soon clear that giggling and trying to control a magnetic field at the same time wasn't a particularly good idea. The lesson was punctuated by several more clumsy collisions, but fortunately there were no further tangled hair incidents. At 16:00 hours, they were dismissed from class. Julius, Faith and Skye headed off to find Morgana. Ten minutes later she emerged from the infirmary, looking quite menacing, grasping a bunch of black hair in her fist.

'Don't speak to me!' she growled, storming along the concourse toward the garden.

Julius and Skye exchanged a quick glance, each stifling an amused grin, but they knew better than to pass any kind of comment. Apparently, Faith didn't.

'Don't worry,' he said reassuringly, gliding after her. 'It's just a tiny patch of hair. Who's going to notice such a silly little thing?'

Without turning or breaking stride, Morgana elbowed him hard in the ribs, sending him sprawling into a large pot plant.

'What did I say?' he asked.

'The wrong thing,' answered Skye, helping him out of the shrubbery.

*

It took Morgana the best part of November before she was able to work anywhere near Barth again. Whenever she saw him, her hand would nervously shoot up to her head, where the clutch of hair had been cut off. Julius agreed with Faith that it was barely noticeable, but he kept very quiet about it. As Faith had discovered, girls were quite funny, and unpredictable, when it came to their flowing locks.

But, if Morgana was a bit distracted during Professor Morales's classes, Skye was the complete opposite. Every time he was in a Shield lesson, he turned into an overexcited bundle of happiness, an apparent expert in Shield techniques and lover of all things Spanish. Never mind that every Monday morning Julius woke up to an insane smell of perfume, vile enough to kill a llama, that Manuel Valdez had told him was just the right essence for anyone wanting to attract a Mediterranean women.

'If I ever turn into a moron over some girl, I give you full authorisation to throw me out of an airlock,' uttered Julius to Faith, at the end of yet another Shield class.

'I'll make a note of that,' answered Faith.

'Hey guys,' said Morgana, emerging from the dojo and joining them.

'Hey,' answered Julius, who was not entirely sure whether her mood had improved at all, and was subtly trying to gauge if it was safe to speak to her again. 'Wanna come with us to the garden?'

He obviously wasn't subtle enough, though, as Morgana quickly noticed the hesitant tone in his voice. 'Don't worry, I'm OK now. I had lunch with Barth earlier and told him to forget about it – I wouldn't do anything nasty to him.'

'That was mighty nice of you,' said Faith.

'Maybe,' she said, with a shrug of her shoulders. 'You know, he may be a complete klutz but he just can't help it I guess. Sorry about elbowing you, by the way.'

'No probs. I always wanted to know what was behind that plant anyway,' Faith said, and winked at her.

'So, did you hear the news?' asked Julius, happily moving the conversation along now that all seemed fine.

'I sure did,' answered Morgana. 'We're getting our November reviews done this coming Friday.'

'Yep,' said Faith. 'We've got Mrs Cruci again.'

'I haven't met her yet,' said Julius. 'Last year, I got Master Cress. But not this time, hopefully. I'm pretty sure they won't give me any extra classes. I've been a good boy.'

'Same here,' said Faith.

'I'm fine too. So's Skye – apart from that perfume he's been wearing,' added Morgana, creasing her nose up. 'I'm worried for Barth though. That's another reason why I spoke to him today.'

'Why, is he nervous about some of the subjects?' asked Julius.

'When we were in the infirmary he was really upset – I mean, so was I – but he was really unhappy. He just kept saying that he'd really done it this time and he would be sent packing for sure.'

'Can they do that?' asked Faith, aghast.

'I don't know. It seems they just give you extra lessons if you're not up to scratch, as Julius knows, but ...'

'Yeah, you can never tell,' said Julius. 'He's got the mind-skills though, or he wouldn't be here in the first place. Maybe they'll advise him to go for a desk job. He's a complete menace when it comes to the physical stuff, but he *is* also a smart kid.'

'Well, we'll just have to see. Anyway, if you get a chance, he could do with some cheering up,' said Morgana.

'I'll talk to him,' said Faith. 'He's my roommate, after all. I'll do it before the meeting with Mrs Cruci.'

'Thanks, Faith,' said Morgana, and smiled.

Julius soon realised that Barth wasn't the only one who could benefit from a chat before the reviews. All 2MJ students were required to state their preferences for which subjects they wanted to follow during their next two Apprentice years. Although the actual choice wouldn't be made until the following September, they needed to have a vague idea ready, in order for Mrs Cruci to give them the relevant details. So it was no surprise that, every night of that third week in November, they would meet in the common room to eagerly exchange ideas and information on career choices. Morgana, unsurprisingly, had already decided that she wanted to be a fleet pilot. Faith wanted to become an engineer and Skye was torn between the idea of joining the fleet as a catalyst specialist and a career in politics (Morgana and Faith believed this had everything to do with the fact that these were both considered to be quite sexy career paths by many of the girls in Tijara). Julius, for very different reasons, liked the idea of becoming a catalyst specialist too. It was not only that he was particularly good at it, but also because the idea of joining the fleet to become a strategist, diplomat, or even better, a captain, was a very alluring one. He hoped he wasn't aiming too high though. Freja had intimated to him that a White Child had more chance than others of reaching the highest ranks, but that was no guarantee that he actually *would* make it.

So, when Friday finally arrived, Julius nervously went off to meet with Mrs Cruci. She was a kind, pleasant woman, and quickly put him at ease.

Julius explained his plans to her and watched as his file appeared on the slick screen built into her desktop. Mrs Cruci opened the folder with a tap of her finger and proceeded to type his information into a document simply entitled "Julius McCoy – 2MJ". After she was finished she moved it to one side with a gentle flick and looked up at Julius.

'It may be worthwhile to consider spending the summer serving on a Zed vessel, so you can get a better idea of what it's like doing the kind of work you're looking at,' she said,

'Thanks, I'll definitely think about that,' he answered.

'Well, that's us for now then,' she said with a smile. 'Grand Master Freja is very pleased with your progress, so keep it up and good luck with whatever you decide to do.'

Julius thanked her and stood up to go. He was a little surprised about the personal message from Freja. Then again, he thought as he walked to the door, maybe it wasn't such a shock. He *was* the Grand Master of Tijara, so it was surely only natural that he maintained an interest in how the students were getting on. After all, his deputy, Master Cress, even kept track of how much Julius weighed at any one time and how many hours he slept each night.

He left the office and wandered off back to his dorm, feeling very pleased with how well his review had gone. With that out of the way, his mind drifted to another matter that he had pushed to the back of his thoughts for the past week. Lest he forget, there was a treasure hunt to be solved.

*

The following Wednesday afternoon, the Skirts found themselves sitting at Mario's, drinking milkshakes and searching on their PIPs for information about Smaragdus.

'I have looked at every single name of every blinking sea on the blinking Moon, and found precisely zilch,' cried Morgana in exasperation, throwing herself against the back of her chair.

'What were you hoping to find – the Double Chocolate Ice Cream Sea?' asked Faith, stirring the last remnants of his strawberry shake with a straw.

'Mmm, chocolate,' sighed Skye, greedily slurping down his Nutty Blitz and then scrunching his face as the resulting brain-freeze hit him.

Morgana sighed and said, 'Well, Smaragdus *is* Latin and on the Moon all of the craters have Latin names, so it was worth a shot.'

'Yes, but they're also called *"seas"*, and the lady in the cave said *"lake",'* replied Julius.

'Anyway, what does Smaragdus mean?' asked Faith.

'My PIP says *"emerald",'* answered Morgana.

'So, it's like an emerald lake,' chipped in Skye, who was still rubbing his forehead.

'That's it!' exclaimed Julius, sitting up and slapping his friend on the back. Skye coughed and glared at him. Julius, oblivious to this, carried on: 'An *emerald lake* – don't we have one of those here, in Satras?'

The others looked at him, their eyes growing wide with comprehension.

'It would make sense,' said Morgana. 'It's the only *genuine* body of water on the Moon and it does have a rather emerald-ish colour to it.'

'So, who are these "*lovers*" she was going on about?' asked Faith.

They fell silent for a minute and stared out of the cafe window, which stretched from floor to ceiling and overlooked Satras's main courtyard below them.

'Right there,' said Skye suddenly, jumping up from his chair and pointing at the far shore of the lake that lay at the foot of the Hologram Palace. 'How did I not think of it before?'

'What are you on about?' asked Julius, peering out of the window. Then he spotted it – a statue of a man and a woman gently embracing, their lips lightly touching. He had surely seen it at least a hundred times, but never before paid much attention to it.

'The first time we went shopping at Going Spare, I went for a date with Pippa Coleman, didn't I?' answered Skye. 'Well, she met me there, under the kissing lovers.' He was beginning to blush a little now.

'*A date?*' parroted Morgana, and grinned at him. 'Well, you guys do have your little secrets, don't you?'

They all looked innocently in different directions; Skye had suddenly found something very interesting on the ceiling to stare at. They were spared any further interrogation, though, as Mario approached their table and began to clear up the glasses.

'Mr Mario,' asked Julius, turning to face him. 'What's the *actual* name of Satras's lake?'

Mario seemed a bit taken aback by the question and stroked his bushy moustache distractedly. 'Why, it's Emerald Lake. Only, those big pompous heads back in the day called it by its Latin name, which incidentally I can't pronounce.' He stopped for a moment, lost in thought, and then mumbled, 'Such a funny thing.'

'What's a funny thing?' asked Julius.

Mario shook his head. 'Oh, nothing. I was just thinking that it's funny how sometimes such beautiful things can come from the ugliest of people.'

'What do you mean?' asked Faith.

'Well, this entire place was Clodagh Arnesh's idea. Satras was her baby – the Palace included.' The cafe owner looked at them each in turn and, seeing how they were now hanging on his every word, continued. 'My ancestor Carmine, *may-he-rest-in-peace*, was given a special invite from Clodagh herself to leave his ice cream parlour in Naples and move his business to Zed. He had tonnes of pictures of her eating in here. Good for business, you understand. Well, back then it was. Quite often, she would pop in just to get an ice cream cone to take down to the lake, so she could eat it on one of those little boats. They've got some of the pictures stored away in the Curia's archives, as far as I know.'

He stopped and looked at them but they were still just staring back, dumbfounded, at him.

'Anyway, it's been nice speaking to you, but I've got ice creams to cream and milkshakes to shake,' Mario said, skilfully scooping up the rest of the glasses. He stopped for one further second, then mumbled something about strange kids and left.

Once he was gone, Julius leaned forward and said, 'It's incredible how easy it is to forget that Marcus Tijara didn't actually build Zed by himself,' said Julius.

'At least now we know where to go for the next clue,' said Morgana.

'Yes, but we need to figure out how to get back here on New Year's Eve without being seen,' added Faith.

However they were to do it, thought Julius, it wasn't going to be easy. Just before seven-thirty, they boarded the Intra-Rail back to Tijara, in time for curfew. As they approached the station, they noticed a group of men in official uniforms clustered outside the school entrance.

'Hey, what's going on over there?' said Skye, moving closer to the window.

'Looks like Security's out,' replied Faith.

And sure enough Julius could see Tijara's front-gate guards, the Leven twins, talking to the Chief of Security, Lieutenant Foster, who was a living nightmare for any student who dared to step over the line.

'Look, Freja and Cress are there too,' said Julius. 'And Professor Chan.'

As soon as the train came to a halt, Julius leapt out. There was a large crowd of students gathering at the entrance to the school. He pushed through them to the front of the throng, followed closely by the others. Two girls, who Julius recognised as 5 Mizki Seniors, were sitting to one side, crying on each other's shoulders while Nurse Primula attended to them.

'Skye,' called Julius, pointing at another girl, who was standing separately, a few metres away from them, by herself. 'Isn't she one of Ife's friends? We met her this summer during the camp.'

'You're right. It's Betty,' Skye answered. 'Let's go ask her if she knows what's going on.'

When they approached her, she seemed to recognise Skye immediately, and walked towards him with her arms open.

'Oh Skye, it's horrible!' she said, hugging him tightly as tears streamed down her face.

'What's the matter, Betty?' he asked.

'It's Ife,' she sobbed.

76

'What happened to her?' said Skye, now also visibly worried.

'We were on our way back to school, when these men jumped out from behind the hedge and pushed us to the ground. We didn't have time to do anything, it happened so quickly.'

'What do you mean? What did they do?' asked Skye.

'We ... we picked ourselves up and ... and we looked around, but Ife ... she wasn't there. She was gone!' And with that, Betty's tears became an uncontrollable torrent.

Skye, for once, didn't know what to say, so he just stood there, holding her. Julius felt his heart turn cold. He looked over at Grand Master Freja, who was standing, arms crossed, surveying the children. Julius had not seen him in six months, but it was noticeable how tired he looked. Just then, their eyes met and Freja motioned for him to come closer. Despite his surprise, Julius didn't hesitate and went immediately.

'Sir,' he said, bowing.

'Mr McCoy,' replied Freja, bowing back.

'Is this Salgoria's doing, sir?'

'We don't know yet, but we have to consider the possibility. In the meantime, I need you to remain sharp, and look out for each other. Remember last year, McCoy. Salgoria can be very determined when she wants something.'

'Yes, sir,' Julius said. There was a multitude of questions he wanted to ask, but as Freja seemed quite preoccupied just then, he pushed them to one side.

The Grand Master dismissed Julius, then walked back to his deputy and began speaking privately to him. Lieutenant Foster meanwhile, briskly ushered the students inside the school gates.

Julius knew that it wouldn't take long for the news to spread, so he was not surprised when all of the Tijaran Mizki pupils were called to assembly that same evening. It was Master Cress who entered the hall to address them and, as he did, all eyes were fixed firmly on him. He bowed to the students and motioned for them to sit.

'At this very moment, the Masters for all three schools are making this same announcement. As you have no doubt heard, one of our students was removed from these premises against her will earlier this evening. Ife Alika, a 5 Mizki Senior, was returning to school for dinner when five men attacked her party and, it seems clear, kidnapped her.'

A buzz of whispering erupted throughout the hall.

Cress waited for the students to quiet down before resuming. 'We do not know the identity of those behind this terrible act but, as a safety measure, we would like for all of you to be extra cautious and look after each other. Respect all curfews and keep your PIPs on standby, so your location can be pinpointed at all times. The Grand Master is at this moment talking to the Alika family, and requests that you all keep them in your thoughts during this worrying time.'

*

'This is bad,' said Faith, sitting down on Julius's bed.

After Cress had dismissed the students, they had wandered back to their rooms in eerie, near silence.

'They don't want to say it, but Salgoria is behind this,' said Skye. 'Remember what I told you last year, about those kidnappings? The Arneshians were to blame for them. Now they've started again.'

Julius was stretched back in his Lazy Boy, playing with a corner of his t-shirt. Of the four members of the Skirts, only Morgana and he

78

knew that Salgoria had in fact resumed her kidnapping ways much earlier – the previous year to be precise, when she had tried to nab Julius. For some reason, though, he still didn't feel ready to tell the other two about this.

'All those folks who got kidnapped, they were found dead,' continued Skye. 'She will die too.'

'We don't know that!' blurted out Julius. 'If it is Salgoria, she might have another need this time. She might need her alive.'

'Julius is right,' said Faith. 'It isn't much to wish for, but his guess is as good as yours. Better, actually.'

Skye nodded. There really was nothing they could do about it, except wait for more information. That night Julius didn't sleep much and, from the faint glow of Skye's PIP, he knew he wasn't the only one. He thought about Ife's family – what they must be going through – and hoped against hope that they would find her soon.

*

December was a joyous time for the students, as they were allowed to reunite with their families in Satras – the only time of year this happened. However, the normal heightened atmosphere of anticipation, which the holidays usually brought, seemed to have been considerably dampened. There had been no new developments in Ife's case, a situation that was not easing anyone's mind. Unfortunately, things were about to get worse, as the people of Zed were soon to find out.

On the evening of Sunday the 12th of December, Julius was having dinner with Faith when the mess hall screens switched from the Hologram Palace score charts to Zed News. This was an internal channel that reported on life on the Moon, exclusively for Zed's citizens. As the breaking news logo appeared, the students instantly fell silent. Morgana and Skye stood rooted to the spot in the middle of the hall, with their food trays still perched in their hands.

'This is Iryana Mielowa, reporting live from Satras Intra-Rail station. Tonight, at 19:00 hours, there was another kidnapping: 4 Mizki Apprentice Sharon Dally, from Sield School, was snatched from this very platform. Mrs Mayflower, a worker in the Hologram Palace and long time resident of Satras, was also attacked during the incident.'

Julius and Faith looked at each other, astonished.

'We understand, from Mrs Mayflower's account, that three men sneaked up on her and Miss Dally as they were waiting for the train to arrive. Mrs Mayflower managed to fight off her assailant, but was thrown across the ground where she lay, unable to aid the young girl as she was dragged away along the rail tracks. Although there are no confirmed leads as to who is behind this attack, the common consensus is that this episode is indeed related to the disappearance of Ife Alika two weeks ago. The possible involvement of the Arneshians is also being seriously considered, although in the minds of many this is already a certainty. Here now is a recording of Mrs Mayflower's statement as she was carried away to Satras Hospital.'

The image switched to a crowd of people gathered around a stretcher. Upon it, Mrs Mayflower was resting, clutching a handbag to her chest. There were photographers all around her, illuminating the platform with the flashes from their cameras. Several security officers were huddled around her, trying to hold back the eager reporters. Ms Mielowa, being the most intrepid of them, had managed to force her way through and push a microphone under the old lady's nose.

'They didn't want *me*!' Mrs Mayflower was explaining. 'One of them grabbed hold of me and started to drag me away, but one of the others told him to stop because they only wanted the girl. So the one who was attacking me said, "But she's a woman too", and the other answered, "She's far too old to be of any use to *her*". Too old? *Moi*? No manners these days, I tell you.'

At that point, a group of official Curia representatives stepped in, flashing their badges, bringing the interview to an abrupt end and hurrying the stretcher away.

The image switched back to Ms Mielowa. 'The Curia has, of course, recommended extreme vigilance from all residents of Zed. We'll be back with further news at midnight.'

'You are joking me,' gasped Faith, leaning back in his chair.

Morgana and Skye walked over to the table and sat down.

'How much you wanna bet the Arneshians are behind this?' said Skye.

'I bet Freja is going to ground us all, just in case anyone else disappears, and that means goodbye Satras,' said Faith.

'I get the feeling that I'm the one who'll be needing some protection,' said Morgana.

The boys looked quizzically at her, not understanding what she meant by that.

'Weren't you listening?' she asked. 'Mrs Mayflower said those thugs were after *women*. And one of the attackers also mentioned that old women were no use to "*her*".'

'*Her*? Salgoria, you mean? But you're right,' agreed Julius. 'Ife, Sharon – both female; both young.'

'And both students,' added Morgana.

'I'm not so sure that matters,' answered Julius. 'The only reason they didn't take Mrs Mayflower was because of her age.'

'True,' said Morgana.

'In any case, all we can do is not let you out of our sight when we're outside Tijara's walls,' said Julius. Right, guys?'

'Of course,' replied Faith instantly. 'And Morgana, you may want to talk to the girls in your dorm and tell them to stick together too.'

'I could volunteer myself for bodyguard duty for one or two of your female friends,' said Skye, winking cheekily. 'Like Siena and Isolde, for example.'

'What are you like?' she said, rolling her eyes in mock exasperation. 'What about looking out for me?'

'Only kidding,' he said. 'I have my assignment, Miss Ruthier. You will be well guarded. The Skirts stick together.'

'Absolutely. Best you remember that, young man,' she said.

Julius finished his dinner in silence, only half listening to their banter. He couldn't even begin to imagine what he would do if anything ever happened to Morgana.

THE MID-WINTER ORACLE

'It's an ugly statue and no mistake,' said Faith, looking up at the kissing lovers.

Julius and Morgana were also looking at the sculpture, their heads tilted to one side.

'That's because you haven't done any kissing yet,' said Skye. 'You'll have a different opinion one of these days.'

'Yeah well, find me a girl that can see past this skirt first, then I'll let you know if I've changed me mind,' answered Faith, sounding quite unconcerned about it.

Julius looked at the foot of the statue. There was a small slab of marble with a short phrase cut into it, reading: "To M. Forever yours, C."

'That's *so* romantic,' said Morgana, with a long sigh. 'I hope, someday, someone will do the same for me.'

'Zed to Morgana, please reply,' said Julius, clicking his fingers under her nose. 'How are we going to get here on New Year's Eve?'

'We'll need to sneak past the Leven twins and maybe Foster too. Plus, enter Satras without security asking why we aren't at the school ball,' said Faith.

'And don't forget about the kidnappings,' added Julius. 'They'll never let us out. Especially not you, Morgana. Also, everyone knows it's your birthday on the 31st, so it'll look weird if you're not there.'

'I knew you would say that,' she huffed.

'I know it's a pain, but I'm right, and you know it,' he said.

'Oh, all right,' she agreed. 'I'll stay behind, but only this once. And anyway, why would the game give us clues that require being out after curfew?'

Skye shrugged his shoulders and said, 'I guess it's the only way to test how *brave* someone really is.'

'For sure,' said Julius. 'And don't worry, Morgana, we're claiming this prize for *all* of the Skirts. You'll be playing your part anyway.'

'Speaking of skirts,' said Faith. 'I think I have an idea.'

'Which is?' asked Julius.

'I can foresee me skirt having a little malfunction, at around seven-thirty pm, on the last day of the year.'

'And?' said Skye.

'See, officer,' said Faith, pretending to plead with one of the Satras security guards, 'I was collecting me uniform for the ball when I fell into the lake and this skirt got waterlogged. So naturally, me friend here went off to find some help. But then a couple on a boat came along and gave me a lift so, when he got back, he couldn't find me. Then we both decided to look for each other, him at the bottom of the lake, me up on the shopping level.'

'That's very convoluted,' said Morgana, 'And a bit silly.'

'What if we come here as normal to get our uniforms and only one of us stays behind, hides and retrieves the message?' offered Skye.

'He's got a point,' said Morgana. 'The fewer of us missing, the better. It'll raise fewer suspicions back in Tijara.'

The boys looked at each other and nodded.

'I'll do it,' said Julius.

'No, I will,' said Skye.

'We'll draw straws then,' said Faith. He hovered over to a nearby juice stand and asked the owner for three long straws. They watched as he cut the end off one of them. Then he turned around quickly and, when he turned back to face them, the straws were all neatly lined up, sticking out of his clenched fist. He offered first pick to Skye.

He pried one out, instantly realised it was a long straw and cried, 'Shoot! That's so unfair!'

'Heh, heh, heh,' cackled Faith dramatically. 'It's just the two of us now, pretty boy.'

Julius looked at the closed fist and picked the straw on the left.

'Yes!' he cried triumphantly.

'Double shoot!' said Faith. 'Can you believe the luck of this guy?'

'Oh yeah, baby,' said Julius, doing a little victory dance just to rub it in a bit more.

'Just make sure you keep your PIP on at all times,' said Morgana. 'We want to see everything.'

'Besides, we'll need to be able to tell you if they find out you're not in school and you're in serious trouble,' said Skye.

'Seriously, though,' said Faith. 'You may want to think of an excuse in case they catch you.'

'I'll just say that the Oracle made me do it,' he said, grinning.

'That's a one-way ticket to the loony house,' answered Faith.

*

'What do you mean you're not coming?'

85

Julius was sitting by the terminal in his room. Skye was dozing in his bed, and he could hear him breathing through the partition that separated their room in two. It was the last Sunday before the midwinter break. That morning, Julius had received a message on his PIP from his mother, asking him to call her back after lunch. Julius had done so, and was now staring at the screen with an extremely disappointed expression on his face.

'I'm so sorry, honey,' said Jenny. 'Your father broke his leg and the doctor said he can't leave the house, let alone leave orbit.'

'How did he do that?'

'Do the words *chasing Michael* and *flight of steps* mean anything to you?'

Julius pursed his lips, trying to suppress a grin. 'He didn't see the steps?'

'Nope,' she said, exasperated. 'There were too many pairs of socks floating around the hallway, obscuring the stairs from view.'

'Jeepers. What is it with that kid and making his socks fly?'

'Who knows,' she replied. 'But, ever since you went away, Michael has been trying hard to fill your shoes, bless him. At least he hasn't set fire to the bed, like you used to do when you were little.'

'I don't remember that.'

'Whenever you had a nightmare, the bed would start smoking. We had to install a smoke detector in your room.'

'That bad, huh?'

'You were hard work all right,' she said. 'But I wouldn't want you any different.'

Julius smiled shyly. 'Well, why can't you just bring Michael and the two of you can visit at least?'

Mrs McCoy sighed deeply. 'Trust me, I would love to, but your

Dad's finding it very difficult to move about easily. And you know how terrible he is with cooking as it is. I wouldn't want him burning the house down.'

'OK then, why not send Michael to me, by himself? You could get a couple of days of peace and quiet with Dad. It sounds like you both need it.'

'I don't know Julius, he's still very young.'

'He won't get lost, honestly! Put him on the shuttle and I'll pick him up at this end. Where could he go anyway? Moon walking?'

'Funny man you are. What about the kidnappings? Tijara told all parents about it, even though, of course, we can't tell another living soul.'

'It's girls they're after. Michael will be fine.'

'Where will he sleep, though? He can't stay in Tijara at night.'

'Stop worrying, Mum! Look, why don't you ask Morgana's folks? I'm sure they'll be happy to take care of him.'

'That could work, actually,' said Jenny, relaxing a little. 'I'll ask them and let you know.'

'Thanks, Mum.'

'We'll miss you, darling. Take care now, and say hi to Morgana.'

'I will. Say hi to Dad.'

The video screen went blank. Julius was pretty sure the Ruthiers would be more than happy to bring Michael with them. Feeling a bit more content, and a little sleepy, he decided to follow Skye's example and have a short nap.

'*At least I'll get to see one of my family,*' he thought to himself as he drifted off.

*

For their last Telepathy lesson, on Tuesday morning, Professor Beloi told them to pair up as usual, and then spread them throughout the maze. This time Julius worked with Morgana, while Skye and Faith joined forces for a change.

'*Pay attention now,*' said Beloi's voice in their heads. '*Does anyone remember what a Scrambler is?*'

All hands shot up simultaneously, to the delight of their teacher.

'*Mr Kashny?*'

'A Scrambler is a device like a hair band. It was created by Clodagh Arnesh when she was a teacher in Tijara. When you wear it, it creates interference in your brain waves, so that no one can read your thoughts.'

'*That is correct. What else does it do? Miss Sundaram?*'

'It can confuse the mind of anyone who comes too near the wearer, sir.'

'*Very good. Today, you shall try to be reunited with your other half using Telepathy. However, I have fitted several Scrambler devices throughout the maze, with the sole purpose of hindering your efforts.*'

'Great,' muttered a depressed boy's voice to the left side of Julius, causing a few stifled giggles among the students.

'*Indeed, Mr Yuran,*' boomed Beloi's voice, making the Mizkis grab their heads in surprise.

'Sorry, sir ...' said Grigor Yuran, sheepishly.

Julius thought the task would be easy enough, despite the interference. However, it took more than twenty minutes before he was able to pick up even the faintest thought from Morgana. The Scramblers were viciously powerful, sending countless different signals through the air at the same time. No matter how hard Julius tried to focus on Morgana, he just couldn't reach her. Very occasionally, he caught a hint of her voice in the chaos and tried to follow it. He also tried sending powerful signals out to her, the equivalent of mind-shouts – but even that didn't always work. By the time the lesson ended, three hours later, not one pair had been rejoined, creating much frustrated chatter among the pupils the rest of that day.

The next few days passed uneventfully. Julius wasn't sure if it was just because of the missing girls, but a solemn atmosphere hung over the school, in stark contrast to the previous year. The teachers smiled very little, their faces often imbued with worry. As far as Professor Beloi was concerned, Julius wasn't sure what to think, given that he was very good at keeping his innermost thoughts to himself. Even Professor King, who was easily the most cheerful man Julius had ever met, was quite subdued. His embalmed reindeer, known to the students as Jeff, was parked in a corner of the classroom, looking sadly at the Mizkis through its glass eyes. Julius remembered with a smile how last year King had taken it for a crazy joyride above their heads, simply using his telekinetic abilities. The fact that he wasn't up to any similar tomfoolery this year was proof enough of his dampened spirit. The only teacher who seemed unaffected by the gloomy atmosphere was Professor Chan, who kept training them in the dojo at Olympic levels.

'I think this whole thing has made him worse,' said Skye, at the end of a particularly painful abs workout.

'If that's even possible,' replied Julius from the floor. He was just lying there, panting in exhaustion.

'Someone needs to push me back to me room,' said Faith, resting his head against the wall, his arms hanging limply at his sides. 'Even the skirt is refusing to move.'

'Fat chance, mate,' said Skye. 'We'll have to sleep here tonight.'

'Class, on your feet!' cried Chan.

'Professor, please,' pleaded Lopaka feebly. 'I think I'm going to pass out, sir.'

Professor Chan examined the students sternly. Every single Mizki was sprawled out somewhere. Julius thought that they looked like bodies left behind after an explosion. Chan seemed to have reached the same conclusion, because his expression softened a little.

'In my days, children were made of stronger stuff,' he said. 'Where you are, just kneel and face me, please.'

The students complied as quickly as their sore limbs would allow.

'We train hard because what's happening out there is hard,' said Chan.

Julius noticed a subtle shift in the mood at those words. The groans eased up a bit and everyone seemed to listen intently.

'Over the mid-winter break, you will spend a lot of time outside Tijara. I don't need to remind you how serious the situation is, so I am asking you to be particularly careful. The ladies should not be left by themselves at any time. Respect the curfew and, if you spot anything or anyone suspicious, report it immediately. You'll find that the security in Satras is greatly increased these days, although they may be wearing regular clothes so as not to attract attention. Understood, Mizkis?'

'Yes, sir,' the class replied in unison.

'Very well,' said Chan, standing up. 'You have worked well this year. Enjoy your break. Dismissed!'

The students stood and bowed to him before leaving the dojo.

'Did you hear that?' asked Morgana, once they were outside in the promenade. 'Increased security. Are you sure it's a good idea going after that Oracle thing?'

'We knew there would be security, right?' answered Julius.

'Yes, but a normal level of it. Not undercover officers,' she replied.

'I'm curious, Julius,' said Faith. 'I want to know what this Oracle is all about. But you're the one risking getting caught. It's your call, mate.'

'I'm curious too, truth be told,' said Skye. 'If you decide to go, I'll share the blame if something happens.'

'Likewise,' said Faith.

'Of course, guys,' nodded Morgana.

'Thanks,' said Julius. 'Then it's settled. I'll go as planned.'

Julius was touched by the show of support, but he sincerely hoped there would be no need at all to test their friendship.

*

It was a Zed tradition that during the week before New Year, all Mizkis were allowed 24 hours to spend with their visiting family. All games at the Hologram Palace were suspended, so that its holodecks could be used by the students and their guests for their main meals. It had been decided that, this year, the 2MJs would be hosting on the 26th of December. Morgana had told Julius that Michael would be coming up with her family and that they would have a traditional Japanese New Year meal. This news greatly excited Julius. For one thing, he loved Japanese history and culture, but he was also dying to wear his new kimono, a present he had received the previous year from Morgana's parents. Skye would be having the usual annual meal, hosted by the head of the Terra 3 space station. He wasn't particularly happy about their visit, though, and was showing all the visible excitement of a dead body. Faith, meanwhile, had decided that he would indulge his mid-winter craving for all things sun, sand and surf by taking his family for a virtual trip to Brazil.

On the morning of the last Sunday Julius, Morgana and her sister Kaori, headed to the Zed docks to collect their families. Julius's classmates were all there too, eagerly waiting for their relations. Minutes later, the Earth shuttle arrived and, when its doors opened, a river of smiling faces poured out onto the platform. Julius spotted the Ruthiers immediately. Alistair Ruthier was a tall man in his forties, broad of shoulders and rosy cheeked. Fujiko, his wife, was quite the opposite – a small woman also in her forties, with a face as smoothly perfect as a doll, and eyes as black as coal. It was easy to see which features Morgana had inherited from each of them: she had her dad's green eyes and physique and her mum's straight raven-black hair and delicate facial appearance.

'Hana-chan! Sakura-chan!' cried Mrs Ruthier as soon as she spotted her daughters.

Julius smiled as he heard the pet names. Morgana was Hana-chan, meaning "flower", while Kaori was Sakura-chan – "cherry blossom". Then Michael came pelting out of the shuttle, dodging a nearby family by a few inches, and ran to his brother. The hug he gave was as heartfelt as ever, but Julius noticed how he pulled away a bit quicker than normal, perhaps a sign that he was growing up and so becoming more self-conscious when it came to showing affection. However, there was no hiding his enthusiasm at being back in Satras. He was all big eyes and barely contained excitement as he stood there in front of his brother. Julius turned to Fujiko and Alistair, gave them a warm hug each and thanked them again for bringing Michael along.

'It is our pleasure,' she said. 'Besides, he was so excited about getting a chance to wear his new kimono!'

'Can you believe it, Julius?' said Michael, beaming. 'She got me one too!'

'I'll help you both to fit them properly tonight, before the meal,' said Alistair.

'We'll need the help, for sure,' answered Julius.

After collecting their luggage, they walked off together to the Moon-Hole Inn. It was the oldest of the hotels on the Moon capital and inside it was done up in the style of a large, wooden Swiss house. Its simple but charming interiors lent it a quaint, homely atmosphere. After checking in and receiving their room numbers at reception, they quickly dumped their belongings and headed out again towards the shopping area. Julius had told Mr and Mrs Ruthier that he wanted to spend some time alone with his brother, before they all met up again at the hotel to get changed for the meal. Of course, they were quite content with that, as they seemed just as eager to have some quality time with their girls.

Michael wanted to see all the gadget shops in Satras, lover of all things technological as he was. Julius was happy to oblige and took him to browse at Going Spare before proudly showing off his new PIP and shields, which left Michael positively green with envy. The meal was set to start at 15:00 hours, so Julius knew to avoid eating too much at lunch. With that in mind, they picked up a glass of freshly squeezed pomegranate juice each, along with a handful of falafels, and went down to the lake to eat them aboard one of the rowing boats.

'This lake is cool,' said Michael, touching the water with his fingers. 'It's so green and shiny.'

'Well, soon you'll be able to see it every day,' said Julius, finishing the last dregs of his juice.

'Yeah, I'll have to wait until the August session to do the test though, 'cause I'm not twelve until July.'

Julius thought he heard a little apprehension in his brother's voice. He looked at him closely, and sure enough he could see a tiny dark wisp floating above his head. 'You're not worried, are you Mickey?'

'A bit.'

'I was worried too, remember?'

'I know, but I'm not you, Julius. My skills are different, I don't even know if they're there sometimes. I mean, sure I'm great at making socks fly, but that's about it. You used to liquefy the bathtub!'

'I wouldn't be too concerned about it. Doctor Flip has always said that mind-skills come out at random times, and that adolescence can trigger certain abilities that may have been dormant before. I mean, there's this guy in my year, Barth – nice guy, and he has his moments, but he's a menace. His skills are nowhere near the class average, yet he's still here. I think you've definitely got more potential than someone like him.'

'Really?' said Michael, hopefully.

'Faith can tell you – he's his roommate. But just don't ask Morgana about him. Barth almost cut half her hair off with his shields.'

'And he's still alive?'

'Just.'

'Well, maybe you're right. I guess my skills will get stronger at some point.'

'Sure they will. You'll see.'

Julius thought for a moment about Michael's abilities. It was true that he had never noticed a wide variety of skills in his brother's repertoire but, then again, it was also true that different people developed in different ways. If nothing else, he was sure Michael would make an excellent technician and have a career in engineering, just like Faith. He looked at his brother again, and saw that the wisp above his head had turned from black to yellow.

'Ah, Michael-san,' said Julius, slipping into a mock Japanese accent, 'let us go get changed. Tonight, we wear kimono with honour, *neh*?'

'*Hai*, Julius-sama!'

They fixed each other with matching stern expressions and then broke into a fit of laughter. Calming themselves a little, they rowed to the side of the lake and disembarked. By the time they arrived at the hotel, they were in a great mood. At 14:00 hours, when they knocked on the Ruthier's door, Alistair answered – he was already magnificently decked out from head to toe in the traditional Japanese garb.

'Wow!' said Michael. 'You look just like a samurai!'

'Thank you,' he replied, and gave a polite bow. 'I've put the kimonos in your room, Michael. Let's get changed in there and leave the girls to do their thing.'

They went to the room next door, where Michael begged to be the first to get kitted out. Julius was happy enough to watch, as Alistair was so skilled at it that it was a pleasure to observe him. Michael was soon ready – his vibrant blue kimono making him look very smart indeed.

'Can I go show the others, please, please, please?'

Mr Ruthier chuckled. 'OK, go on then.' Once Michael had shuffled out of the room, he turned his attention to Julius. 'Your turn now.'

As Julius stood, arms in the air, being wrapped in the various layers, he tried to memorise the movements so he could attempt it himself next time.

'Very important,' said Mr Ruthier. 'Always drape the left over the right side. The other way is how you would dress a dead man for his funeral.'

'Good to know,' replied Julius.

'There now, you're ready,' said Alistair, tightening the sash and moving him over to the mirror.

'That's just! Thanks.'

They stood there in silence for a moment in front of their reflections, admiring the fine craftsmanship of the kimonos.

'I can't believe how grown up you are,' said Mr Ruthier. 'You know, it seems like yesterday that you and Morgana first met. You were just five years old then, when we moved in next door to you. Do you remember that day, Julius?'

Julius turned to face him and was surprised to see how worried he suddenly looked. Smoky wisps were pouring out from the top of his head.

'Kind of,' said Julius uncertainly, trying to recall. He hadn't thought about it in years.

'She was sitting in our front garden, playing with her doll, while we were unloading the car,' continued Alistair. 'Mr Johnson from across the street; his dog – I forget its name – got loose and ran across the road, barking like crazy. Fujiko had taken Kaori inside and I was carrying a chair. But you had seen everything and, as I turned my head, realising with dread that I would never get Morgana out of the way in time, there you came, striding across our lawn with your hand stretched out in front of you. I'll never forget how you shouted

96

at that silly mutt, "Get away from her!", and next thing the dog flew backwards, as if someone had fired it out of a slingshot. Then Morgana ran up behind you and gave you the biggest hug, and you both just stood there, without saying anything, watching as the dog yelped all the way back to Mr Johnson. The look on his face – it was priceless – but I was in too much shock to laugh at the time.'

As Julius listened to the story, the memory of it came flooding back to him. It was strange to think how, in that one moment, as he stood with this girl he had never met before hugging his back, he instantly knew that she was someone he wanted to have around him forever.

'There's something awful happening in Zed,' said Mr Ruthier, his tone becoming very serious, 'and I bet the Arneshians are behind it. You *will* take care of my girls won't you, son?'

'Of course I will,' said Julius, sincerely. 'They are my family.'

Alistair nodded, satisfied. 'Glad to hear it.'

Just then, the door opened and Michael entered the room.

'Ah, right on time,' said Alistair. 'Are the ladies ready?'

Michael shook his head. 'Not yet. They say they need five minutes, and that yes that does really mean five minutes, and that I look great, and we should wait for them downstairs.'

'Well, that's a lot of information for one sentence,' said Mr Ruthier, grinning at the young boy. 'But I think I got it all. Come on then, let's go.'

With that, they left the room and caught the elevator down to the hotel foyer. Julius felt quite proud that Morgana's dad was showing such trust in him, to look after her and Kaori. But there was no doubt in his own mind that he would do everything in his power to keep them both safe, no matter the cost.

There were various people, guests and staff, milling about in the foyer. When the girls arrived, ten minutes later, everyone stopped what they were doing and turned to admire them. Morgana was wearing a lilac kimono with a striking, red-and-white pattern design on it, which Julius liked very much.

'*Good thing Skye's not here,*' he said to her, using a mind-message, as they walked through Satras towards the Hologram Palace. '*If he saw you dressed like that, he'd be developing a crush on you right now.*'

'*Shut up!*' she answered in the same way, blushing slightly.

Julius grinned and observed with curiosity the admiring looks thrown in the direction of Morgana and Kaori by the older Mizkis. He had to admit, they did look beautiful in their kimonos, with their dark hair gathered up in picturesque swirls at the tops of their heads. Julius noticed a few of the students also looking at him, but he wasn't sure exactly why. Perhaps it was to do with the stories of the inorganic draw he had performed last year, or his Solo record, which had given him a level of unwanted fame in Tijara. Maybe it was for no other reason than the novelty of him being dressed in a kimono, escorting the two pretty girls to either side of him. Whatever the reason, he began to feel quite uncomfortable and hurried his steps toward the Palace.

When they arrived, the security guards invited them to use the door on the left. Morgana led the way downstairs, until they reached the lift that would take them to their holodeck. Kaori stepped in front of the metal door and gave the command: 'Computer – activate 4MA Ruthier.'

The door opened and they all stepped inside the lift. A few seconds later, the opposite door opened, leaving Julius and Michael gaping in wonder at the site beyond it.

'Welcome to Ritsurin-Kōen garden,' said Morgana and Kaori together, stepping out and turning to bow to the others.

'What a wonderful choice, girls,' said Fujiko, clapping delightedly.

'And it's all ours for the night,' added Kaori.

As Julius took a few steps into the garden, the crisp, fresh air hit his nostrils and awoke his senses. He breathed deeply, enjoying the smell of wet pine trees, his eyes basking in the brilliant, virtual landscape. A walking path wound its way around and over several koi-filled ponds and islands, which were all interconnected by wooden bridges. He ambled along behind the others, fully distracted by the beauty of the trees, until Morgana joined him.

'I knew you'd like it here,' she said.

'It was the perfect choice to inaugurate my new kimono. By the way, where is this exactly?'

'Takamatsu. It's in the Shikoku province.'

Julius nodded. They were now approaching a *ryokan* – a traditional Japanese house. It was a low wooden structure, raised up a few steps from the ground. Outside the doors were two pots, each containing three sawn-off bamboo shoots surrounded by pine tree sprigs.

'This is called *kadomatsu*, Julius,' said Kaori, pointing at one of them. 'It's a traditional decoration of the New Year Holiday. We place two of them in front of homes to welcome the *kami* – the spirit – of the harvest, so that the next crop will be bountiful.'

Julius absorbed every detail and piece of information he was given, eager as he was to learn more about this fascinating culture. By now he knew that, as he entered the house, he had to remove his shoes before stepping onto the *tatami*, a woven rush-grass mat used for covering the floor. Everyone wore *tabi*, the split-toed socks used for walking around inside the house.

99

Fujiko bowed to the holomaids that would attend to them, waited as they slid the *shoji* screen-door open and then entered the dining room. Julius followed her, stopping to bow slightly as he passed the maids. Inside was a low, short-legged table in the centre of the room, surrounded by several floor-cushions. Julius was directed to kneel between Alistair and Michael. As everyone settled, he let his eyes wander around the room. The paper screen walls enclosed them on all sides, except one that instead gave way to a large window overlooking a well tended Zen garden. It was surrounded by three red brick walls, the furthest of which had an alcove set into it, housing a hanging picture-scroll and a delicate flower arrangement.

'*Akemashte omedetō gozaimas!*' said Fujiko.

'*Tanjōbi omedetō gozaimas*, Morgana,' added Kaori.

Julius and Michael stared blankly at them, not understanding what had just been said.

'Happy New Year,' explained Morgana. 'We never seem to be together for that *and* my birthday, which is what Kaori was saying, so we use this occasion to celebrate both.'

'Well, happy New Year and happy birthday, then!' said Michael.

Soon, the holomaids brought them a hot towel each to wipe their hands and faces, along with some warm *sake* and *oolong* tea. Next came the food, which was laid out on heated plates at the centre of the table.

'During New Year,' explained Fujiko, 'we eat a special selection of dishes called *osechi*. Right now on the table you can see rice, boiled seaweed, fish cakes, mashed sweet potatoes with chestnut and sweetened black soya beans. But nowadays people will also have whatever other food they want. I've asked the girls to order some *sushi* and *sashimi* for you, Julius, since I know that you like them so much.'

'*Dōmo arigatō gozaimas*, Fujiko,' said Julius bowing his head. 'This is just!'

The meal continued through the afternoon in a festive atmosphere. It felt very much like it was really New Year's Eve, which Julius thought was probably a good thing, since he knew he was going to miss the actual party on the night, thanks to the Oracle-quest. For the present, though, he lost himself in the day. He knew that the food itself was generated by a magnetic field and that they were only able to eat it because of the energy-to-matter conversion, but he was still astounded by the quality and flavour of it.

After the meal, they took a stroll through the garden to digest and savour the tranquillity of the place. The Ruthiers wanted to hear about everything that was going on in Zed, and how each of them was doing in, and out of, school. Jenny and Rory McCoy had specifically asked them to check how everything was going with Julius, or as Jenny had put it: "Please make sure you tell him I say he must eat properly – no good him nurturing his mind-skills if he's going hungry." And so, after a good hour discussing the kidnapping situation, Julius was put through a series of questions about any possible ailments, injuries or mental fatigue he may have been suffering, which made Michael laugh a lot as he watched his brother being interrogated like that.

'Laugh all you like, bro,' said Julius, with a raised eyebrow. 'Next year it will be you under the microscope. Never mind Mum and Dad – the school is worse. They even keep tabs on how many times you go to the loo.'

'They do?' asked Michael, looking genuinely worried.

'He's kidding you,' said Kaori, leaning towards him.

Michael glared at Julius, who was grinning cheekily, and then pounced on his older brother. Next thing he knew, Julius found himself in a headlock and his scalp getting the full knuckle-rubbing treatment from Michael.

'Geroffme!' laughed Julius, trying unsuccessfully to shake his brother off without using his powers, and thinking to himself, *'Man, the little tyke's getting strong.'*

Although Morgana had witnessed their little wrestling matches many times before, they always made her giggle, especially this time with the comical sight of Julius getting bested by his little brother like that. In fact, it made her laugh so much that she had to sit down.

The rest of the evening was spent playing games and eating sweets inside the house. By the time they finally left the holodeck it was well past eleven. Julius, Morgana and Kaori insisted on accompanying their guests to the hotel. Julius saw Michael back to his room, to be sure he had everything he needed. Michael barely managed to get himself changed into his pyjamas, sleepily half-brushed his teeth and then slumped onto the bed and instantly slipped off into dreamland. Julius stood there for a few seconds, listening to his gentle snoring, and a tiny smile touched his lips. He switched off the light and closed the door gently behind him as he left the room.

'What a perfect evening,' he thought to himself, as he padded along to the Ruthier's room, where he stopped and knocked lightly on the door.

'Morgana answered – she was looking a little bleary eyed, obviously tired out from the long day.

'You ready?' he whispered.

She nodded and, a few seconds later, Kaori joined them out in the passageway.

'Mr Ruthier stuck his head out and said, 'Good night, son. And remember, keep your eyes open, OK?'

'I certainly will, sir,' answered Julius.

With that, the three of them headed back to Tijara for the night.

*

'It was great to see you, Julius,' said Alistair the following morning.

They were all standing on the dock platform, saying their farewells.

'You too,' said Julius. 'It was so nice to share your reunion with all of you. And thanks again for bringing Michael along.'

'That was our pleasure,' said Fujiko, taking a quick break from embracing her daughters. 'You know you two are like family anyway. Now come on, Ali – let's leave these fine young men to say goodbye to each other.'

She gave him a hug and then turned back to the girls, who were quickly swallowed up in a blanket of cuddles from their parents.

'Hey, bro,' said Julius, kneeling in front of Michael. 'Make sure Dad's leg heals fine. No more sock jokes for a while, OK?'

'OK,' he replied with a grin. 'I'll be careful.'

'Excellent. I'll see you in September, right here, on this platform. I'll come pick you up myself.'

'I hope so, Julius,' he said in a tiny voice, which was quite unusual for him.

'Come here,' said Julius, pulling him close. 'You'll be fine. You are a real McCoy, you hear me?'

Michael nodded, his face still buried in Julius's shoulder.

'We need to go now,' said Alistair.

103

Julius let his brother go, and watched as he boarded the shuttle. Morgana and Kaori stood by his side and waved to their family, until they had disappeared inside the ship.

'You're so sweet with your brother, Julius,' said Kaori, smiling.

Julius, who was entirely embarrassed about being mentioned in the same sentence as "sweet", turned a shade of crimson and headed for the nearest exit, trying hard to hide his face from her.

'I think it's lovely,' she said, ignoring his reaction. 'Well, I'm off, sis. See you for your birthday.'

Morgana waved to her as she left and then turned to Julius. 'Come on you, let's get back. And stop all that blushing or I might start thinking you have a crush on my big sister!'

Julius, now turning so red that he looked sunburnt, kept his head turned away and followed her back to the train.

*

On Friday the 31st, Julius woke up with a knot of anxiety in the pit of his stomach, which he was unable to rid himself of for the rest of the day. After lunch, he made his way into Satras with the rest of the gang, where they stopped by Twitch & Stitch to collect their evening suits for the New Year ball. He picked his up as normal knowing that, if he didn't, there would soon be word sent to Tijara. So, once out of the shop, he rolled up the new clothes and stuffed them unceremoniously into his rucksack. At six o'clock, they all headed over to Mario's for an ice cream.

'I've got a bad feeling about this,' said Morgana, sipping the last of her milkshake.

'You're not helping,' said Julius. 'Look, we said we'd do it, and this is the best way of going about it. I'll be careful and keep a low profile.'

'Let's synchronize our PIPs, guys,' said Faith. 'Time's a-tickin' and I need to get back and change. You know it takes me a bit longer. Julius, activate your video-cam option.'

Julius switched on his PIP and the familiar circular panel materialised above the palm of his left hand. With his right finger he scrolled through the menu options, until he found the video-cam, and selected it.

'I found a way to secure a channel just for us,' continued Faith. 'Select channel fourteen, Morgana's age.'

'Thanks, Faith. I feel ... remembered,' she said drily.

'My pleasure. Activate it now.'

Julius followed the instructions and was pleasantly surprised to see Faith's face pop into view on his monitor. He moved his hand in front of him, watching as the image moved over to Skye and then Morgana.

'It seems to be working,' said Skye, who had just activated his PIP. 'I can see what he's seeing now.'

'So can I,' added Morgana, peering at her own screen. 'Hmm ... my hair looks far too messy. Can't have that on my birthday, now can I?'

'We're all set then,' said Julius. 'Come on, let's get moving.'

He walked the others to the exit, which was now packed with students, then made his way back to the lake and hopped into one of the boats that was moored by the shore. Rowing out to the centre of the lake, he concealed himself beneath one of the many small bridges and waited for the Mizkis to return to their schools. The ball normally started at 20:00 hours, which meant that very soon he would be alone. He could see plenty of adults, with and without Zed uniforms, walking about, but none of them seemed to take any notice of him. Julius lay back in the boat, underneath the seats, selected an e-magazine on his PIP screen, and began his vigil.

*

'Julius, come in,' said Morgana's hushed voice.

Julius sat up, startled. He had fallen asleep without even noticing. He lifted his palm and blinked at the PIP, which was displaying an image of Morgana's face.

'Did you fall asleep?' she asked, concerned.

'Obviously,' answered Julius groggily. He felt sore all over from lying on the hard wooden floor of the boat for so long.

'It's almost midnight.'

'Really?' said Julius, suddenly wide awake. He checked his watch and realised he had fifteen minutes to go. 'Shoot! Any news from your end?'

'No. No one's noticed your absence. Mind you, we've kept a very low profile. Apart from Skye, who's been dancing with every girl he could find, of course.'

'No surprises there, then,' said Julius. 'Here's been quiet enough. There aren't many people about. Most folks are either in the Palace or in the bars upstairs.'

'How are you going to get near the stat ... ouch! Skye, watch those dancing feet of yours, will you?'

'Sorry. Where is he?' he heard Skye ask, then: 'Faith, come here quick!'

For a few seconds there was a bit of confusion as first Skye and then Faith squeezed their faces into view next to Morgana's.

'You could use your own PIP, you know?' said Morgana, getting slightly crushed between their heads.

'But this is much more cosy!' said Skye, merrily.

Julius shook his head, and said, 'Happy birthday, Morgana. What are you guys doing?'

'Making sure you don't fall asleep again, by the sound of things! And moral support, of course,' answered Faith. 'We snuck out into the garden. Are you still out on the lake? It's almost time. Hurry!'

'I'm afraid to sit up, in case someone sees me,' whispered Julius.

'Switch to video-cam mode and hold your PIP up,' said Skye. 'We'll check for you. A holoscreen will be less visible than your big head.'

Julius lifted his hand slowly above him, until the screen was sticking up over the rim of the boat.

'All clear, mate,' said Faith. 'I think it's time for you to pull a Jeff.'

Julius understood what was meant by that. He needed to use his telekinetic skills to move the boat near the statue, just like Professor King had done the previous year with his now infamous dead reindeer. First though, he would have to pinpoint exactly where the statue was. 'Where do I go, guys?'

'From your position, you need to go east,' said Skye.

'No, it's west,' added Morgana.

'Good job I'm the navigator,' said Faith. 'Go north.'

Julius, who was now totally confused, thought it would be best if he had a look for himself and so quickly popped his head up, checked where the statue was and then lay back down again.

'Guys, I'm going south,' he said.

'I knew that,' mumbled Faith.

'Shhh!' said Morgana. 'Let him concentrate.'

Julius focused his mind on the prow of the boat, as he needed to turn it to face in the right direction first. Once he had successfully done that, he willed the boat towards the statue. He had to move really slowly, so as to mimic the speed of a drifting object and not arouse any suspicion from anyone who might happen to be passing by. There was no sound from his PIP, as the others had gone deathly quiet. Julius could tell they were feeling as tense as he was. Occasionally, he would bring his hand up, so they could check he was moving in the right direction, and that no one was staring curiously at the boat.

'Slow down,' whispered Morgana. 'You're almost there.'

Gently, Julius brought the boat to a halt. He felt a slight thud against the keel as it bumped against the side of the lake and came to a stop.

'The statue's just there,' said Skye. 'Keep your head down and your PIP up. We'll watch what happens for you.'

'And I'll keep an eye out,' added Morgana.

Julius nodded. He pressed the record button on his monitor, propped his hand on his bent knee and adjusted its position so that they could see the foot of the statue. There were only a few minutes left, but it felt like ages to him as he lay there, trying hard not to move a muscle. Looking up, towards the ceiling, he traced the outlines of the various bridges that criss-crossed high above him, linking the upper tiers of Satras. He could hear various soft melodies drifting down from the different restaurants and bars, and his thoughts turned to food, which instantly made his stomach grumble.

Suddenly, Julius caught a hint of movement out of the corner of his eye, and he tensed up. He could have sworn that he had seen a shadowy figure peeking over the handrail of one of the bridges which passed just above the statue. But, as soon as he had looked up at it, the shadow had instantly retracted. His heartbeat quickened as he lay there, wondering what he had seen, but he didn't dare move. It could have been no more than a reflection from the water, or just someone passing by, he tried to reassure himself. After all it was New Year's Eve, so of course there would be people about. Since the figure hadn't reappeared, Julius forced himself to relax, although in the back of his mind he couldn't quite shake the feeling of being watched.

'Here she comes,' said Skye, excitedly.

Julius closed his eyes and focused only on her words. 'Well met,' he heard the soft voice of the Oracle say. 'I am glad you could join me again, here at our favourite spot. I am the second Oracle, and I will set you on the right path. My time is short, so hear my words. We shall meet again in fifty-five days from now, in the last five minutes of the day. Go to *Pèsaro* and touch the sea. The door that is revealed to you there will lead you once more to me. You will heed my words two more times. Remember, only the bravest can reach the end. Farewell, my bringer of life.'

Julius lay there for a moment, in case there was any more, but there was nothing to be heard except the intermingled music from the restaurants.

'The coast's clear, Julius,' said Morgana. 'Come on. Get yourself back to Tijara now.'

Julius quickly swung himself over the edge of the boat. He landed in the water, but here by the shore, the depth was low enough that his combat boots easily kept him dry. Moving stealthily, he zipped across to the far wall. Keeping himself close to it, he hurried towards the exit, hoping not to bump into any guards.

'Take the stairs,' said Skye. 'They're tucked away nicely. Besides, the lifts don't have any walls, so anyone would easily be able to spot you.'

Julius flipped his palm up and looked at the screen. He had almost forgotten about it still being on. 'Good thinking, mate. Surprised you managed to spot that with my PIP turned upside down and all.'

'Well, I've always been a bit different in the way I see things,' answered Skye with a grin.

Julius smirked. 'OK, I'm going to have to move fast now, so the view may get a little blurry. I want to keep my PIP on though. You make handy lookouts.'

'Quite right,' said Morgana. 'Now stop talking and get moving.'

Julius nodded and took the stairs in long strides, two at a time, almost running now. Once he reached the top of them, he crouched down behind a nearby pillar and scanned the broad terrace that overlooked Satras. It was empty. He was just beginning to edge forward when suddenly a mighty roar broke the air around him, and he leapt in fright. Then he heard the sound of raucous music, mixed in with cheering voices and realised that the bell must have struck twelve.

'Happy 2857, Julius!' he heard Morgana, Faith and Skye say in unison.

'Thanks,' he said, turning his screen upright again. 'Do you mind if I get out of here first?'

'Um, of course not. Sorry, mate,' said Faith sheepishly. 'Carry on.'

Fortunately for Julius, the security guard at Satras's main gate was so busy trying to hug a blonde female officer that it gifted him the perfect opportunity to slip past without being noticed. Not that Morgana and Faith were helping matters any.

'They're going to see him!' said Faith anxiously.

'He's turning! No, wait!' added Morgana.

'Look the other way! The *other* other way!'

'Wait a minute – she's not kissing him back!'

'Will you two shut up, or I really will have to turn this thing off!' hissed Julius, pressing his mouth against the monitor. 'They'll hear me for sure if you keep that up!'

'Sorry,' they both said, and fell quiet.

Once on the Intra-Rail platform, Julius waited for the train in the shadows of the nearby trees, only daring to emerge when it had come to a full stop and was about to leave again. In a flash, he leapt from his hiding place and darted inside, just before the doors shut.

'Good work,' said Skye. 'And now for the hard part.'

'Damn it!' cried Julius, slapping his forehead in frustration. 'Of course. How am I going to get past the Leven twins? We really should have planned this better. I'm dead now, for sure.'

'Well, before you go writing out your last will and testament, would you listen to us?' said Faith. 'It's not like we spent the night eating and dancing, you know.'

'That we did, actually,' said Skye. 'Especially dancing.'

'The point is,' interrupted Morgana, 'that we *also* figured out a way to distract the twins. So when you get off the train, hide somewhere until we tell you to move. And, by the way, put your suit on. We'll be quick. Over and out.'

Julius relaxed slightly, and once he reached the stop for Tijara, he did as Morgana had told him to. As he climbed off the train, he

111

spotted a convenient and suitably large clump of bushes, which he hid behind and began to undress. His suit was badly wrinkled, but somehow he didn't think people would take much notice of that. He was just about to get changed into it when he heard Morgana's voice yelling from the direction of the school entrance. He looked up in alarm, and without thinking twice, sprinted for the gate, clutching his suit, dressed in nothing but his underwear.

'Something's wrong. Oh, please don't let her be kidnapped!' He thought desperately to himself as he ran.

He could hear an almighty commotion of some sort coming from the foyer and, when he passed through the gate, he saw the Levens running towards the promenade. Julius sprinted after them, still oblivious of the fact that he was wearing next to nothing. When he reached the corridor he almost tripped over the twins who, for some reason, were lying on the floor. He managed to hurdle them, but landed in a puddle of water, skidded madly and careened face-first into the large fountain which surrounded the assembly hall, creating a tidal wave that soaked the floor. He sat up, feeling completely bedraggled – spluttering and spurting water out of his mouth. He wiped his eyes and saw Morgana, Faith and Skye standing under the waterfall, soaked from head-to-toe. As if that wasn't enough, just then Captain Foster entered the scene and stood there, arms folded, surveying the carnage in ominous silence.

Ten minutes later they all found themselves standing in Foster's office, waiting to discover just how bad their punishment would be. They each had towels wrapped around their shoulders and were trying to dry out as best they could. They looked like a line of well drowned rats.

'I have been working in this school for many, many years,' said

Foster, standing up behind his desk. 'But I have *never* witnessed a scene like tonight's. Would anyone care to tell me what you were doing in that fountain, *with or without* your clothes on?'

Julius, who had no idea what had happened in the seconds preceding his amazing entrance, decided to let this one pass. Besides, he had already done quite enough work for one night, so he thought it only fair that someone else do the explanations for this one.

'Sir, it was just an accident,' said Faith, putting on his best "responsible adult" voice. 'We were a little overexcited about the whole New Year thing, and so we thought we'd start the year off with a dare. So Mr McCoy, Mr Miller and meself challenged each other to a little *mind-swim* race in the fountain, to see who could do the fastest lap around the assembly hall. Very silly, I know. We apologise profusely for that.'

'And?' said Foster, clearly not satisfied with the story.

'I slipped and fell into the water before I was able to deactivate me skirt, sir. So Mr Miller jumped in to rescue me, so I wouldn't rust and sink to the bottom like a lost pirate's treasure. Then Miss Ruthier came looking for us, and seeing that we were clearly in distress, she jumped in to try help us as well.'

'*And?*' said Foster. Some of the edge had left his voice – he was obviously gathering some amusement from the situation.

'When our brave security officers heard the commotion, they rushed to see what was happening and slipped on the wet floor.'

Foster turned his head towards Julius, and then looked back at Faith. It was clear that he wanted an explanation for the half-naked student standing in his office. Faith swallowed, and nodded. 'Me Mum used to say that one should never go swimming with clothes on – me old crazy Uncle Jim used to do it all the time – anyway, Mr

113

McCoy must also have been taught that. Unlike me, he decided to put those words into practice. He's very wise for his age,' he finished with a nervous grin.

It was taking Julius all of his strength to keep from bursting into laughter. He could feel a tear squeezing its way out of his eye, while he struggled to control the muscles in his face. To top it all off, his empty stomach let out an almighty rumble that ripped through the silence for a good few seconds.

'So sorry, sir,' he said, looking down. 'Swimming makes me very hungry.'

And that was it. Foster gave them a week-long ban from Satras, for inappropriate behaviour, and an extra week for cheek.

Faith started to say something, but the Captain fixed him with such a stare that he quickly clamped his mouth shut again. 'Count yourselves lucky I'm in a good mood tonight. Now, leave! Get yourselves dried up before you catch pneumonia.'

Once outside, as they walked back to their dorms, Morgana elbowed Julius in the ribs. 'You silly sod, I told you we were going to distract the twins. You should have just slipped in through the gate while you had the chance. What on earth were you doing running around in your undies?'

'I *was* getting changed when I heard you yelling and I thought, well ... I didn't know what to think. I can't help it if you're such a great actor that you even fooled me.'

She smiled and put her arm around him. 'Well, I suppose I can't blame you for looking out for me, hey? Anyway, I'm tired now,' she said, yawning. 'I'll see you guys tomorrow. We can talk about what that Oracle said another time. We sure went to enough trouble for it.'

The boys waved goodbye as they went their separate ways.

'Come on,' said Skye. 'I've brought some food back to the room for you.'

Julius barely had time to get himself dried up, fed and into bed – he was fast asleep as soon as his head hit the pillow. All in all, it had been quite a night.

AN OLD FRIEND

'Fifteen days without games,' groaned Skye.

It was the first day of the year and, after a long lie-in, the Skirts had met under the oak tree, in the garden. Julius was munching on a slice of lemon and walnut cake, the last remnant of what had been a huge breakfast, even by Skye's standards. Now, with the entirely convincing midday sun shining down through the branches from Zed's shield, creating magical sparkling reflections on the surface of the stream, Julius felt finally and positively jam packed.

'I think we got lucky, actually,' said Faith. 'The Leven twins didn't even realise that Julius came from the front gate in the first place.'

'Narrow escape, if you ask me,' agreed Julius. 'I'll tell you what though, if the next clue turns out to be another curfew breaker, outside of the school's walls, I'm going to become very suspicious.'

'Speaking of the next clue,' said Morgana. 'I can't understand it at all. What's Pez ... Pesr ... and what sea are we supposed to touch?'

Julius activated his PIP and watched the recording he had made of the second Oracle. Faith, who was sitting by his side, leaned in to look.

'What's that word she's saying?' asked Julius? 'It starts with "P".'

'It sounds Italian to me,' added Faith.

'How do you know?' asked Skye in surprise.

'Me mum's family is Italian, remember, and this word sounds Mediterranean for sure. Let me check.'

Julius watched as Faith activated his PIP. Using a holographic screen meant a lot of finger-walking in midair, one of the peculiar things that Julius had observed about their new toys.

'Here it is,' said Faith, turning the screen towards the others. 'Lady and gentlemen, this is *Pèsaro*.'

'Are you sure that's what the Oracle said?' asked Morgana. 'I mean, that looks like a city ... on Earth.'

'In Italy, yeah. I'm fairly sure it is.'

'So, I take it this town is near the sea?' asked Julius.

'To be sure,' answered Faith. 'It's on the Adriatic coast.'

Julius looked at the others with a raised eyebrow and, judging from the silence, he knew they were all just as surprised as he was.

'That's that then,' said Skye. 'There's no way we can board a shuttle and head to Italy. End of story.'

'Yeah,' added Julius. 'That *is* a bit too much to ask.'

'Shame though,' sighed Morgana. 'I was enjoying this little treasure hunt. I guess we can check with the Hologram Palace and ask them what the prize was.'

'Hold on, guys,' said Faith, his nose remaining buried in his holoscreen. 'I don't think we need to go anywhere, except perhaps to Satras.'

'How come?' asked Julius.

'I know it's a long stretch, but hear me out. There's a connection between the town of *Pèsaro* and our local barber shop.'

'The *Barber of Seville?*' asked Skye, confused.

117

'Yes. The owner of the shop is this chap called Figaro Rossini, who told us that he's a descendant of *the* Rossini.'

'Who is ...' said Skye.

'Giacomo Rossini was a famous Italian composer. Centuries ago, mind you.'

'The guy that wrote the Barber of Seville!' said Morgana. 'That's a clever choice for his shop name.'

'OK, but I still don't see the connection,' said Julius.

'Rossini was born in *Pèsaro*,' concluded Faith.

Julius's mouth formed an O as he realised the meaning of this information. 'So the third Oracle could be *inside* his shop?'

'I think so,' said Faith. 'I can't really see how we're going to touch the sea, though.'

'Well, given that it's the only lead we have,' said Morgana, 'I think it's worth a try. We'll have to check the shop out as soon as this silly detention is over.'

Everyone agreed. Julius felt a tingling excitement creeping over him. Even if the lead turned out to be a dead end, he was glad they at least had *some* hope of finding the next clue. He was growing increasingly intrigued by the mysterious silver-clad lady.

*

As the lessons resumed that year, the students quickly slipped back into their routine. There was a strange sense of eagerness to learn in the air. Julius put it down to the two kidnappings. After all, none of them would want to be caught off-guard if it should happen again. There was a lot of talk in the boys' changing rooms about what they would do if they had to defend any of the girls from an assailant, and what mind-skills were best to use. There was no hint of false bravado in any of these discussions either. Julius genuinely believed that Mizkis were all about watching each other's backs.

He could only imagine what the conversations were like in the girls' dorm, given that they had the most to be worried about. He had been careful to keep a close eye on Morgana recently, and he knew that Faith and Skye had been doing the same. Whenever they were out in Satras, she was never left alone and even on the rare occasions when she went somewhere that they couldn't follow, like the ladies' room, there was always at least one of them close at hand, just in case. Julius wondered if she had noticed but, since she had not made any complaints about feeling "stalked", he had decided to not even broach the subject. Since Ife's disappearance, it also seemed like Skye had calmed down with his schoolboy crushes. Although he had only briefly become fascinated with her, during the previous Summer Camp, Julius knew her disappearance had affected him. A few times he had noticed Skye staring off into the distance, at nothing in particular, especially when he thought no one was watching. Once again, Julius had decided it was best not to bring it up, but to make sure his friend knew he was there if he needed to talk about anything. Julius wasn't particularly good with the whole bonding thing when it came to people who weren't his direct family, or Morgana. Regardless of that, he knew deep down that Faith and Skye were becoming close enough to him that they may as well have been his brothers.

On a Tuesday afternoon, after changing into his tracksuit, Julius headed for the dojo. Professor Chan motioned the students to enter and kneel in three rows before him. All eyes were turned to the wooden box at his feet, as today they would finally be given the famous Gauntlet.

'As promised, Mizkis,' began the Professor, 'today you shall receive your own personal Gauntlet. How many of you have used a Sim-Gauntlet in Satras before?'

Julius and the rest of the Skirts immediately raised their hands, followed by about half of the class.

Professor Chan nodded, then opened the top lid of the box and started handing the Gauntlets out to the students. Once he received his, Julius was pleased to see that it looked largely the same as the one he had used before in the Hologram Palace.

'During your Combat games,' continued Professor Chan, 'you aim and tighten your fist in order to shoot. It is the same with a real Gauntlet. Moreover, as the energy leaves your body, it will be coloured, normally in yellow, same as the ship catalyst's beam. Now, before you put them on, I want you to listen to me *very, very* – and one more time – *very* carefully, without touching anything until I tell you to.'

The class looked up at Chan, puzzled by the unusual request.

'There is a red dot at the beginning of the hard ridge, right above your wrist. That is the safety button. To make it active you need to press it with your finger. Each safety has been built with your own unique fingerprint programmed into its memory, so it will only work when it is being used by its rightful owner. The reason for all these precautions is that this device is *not* a toy. When you wear it, you must always check that the safety is on. A few years back, an actor was performing for our Zed officers in Satras. He was killed by a round of applause from an excitable individual who had forgotten to do this.'

Julius stared at Chan, horrified.

'I trust, 'continued Chan, obviously enjoying the facial

120

expressions of his students, 'no one here wants to kill their friend with a handshake, correct?'

The Mizkis shook their heads earnestly.

'I thought so. Put them on now and go line up against the back wall.'

Julius stood between Skye and Faith, while Morgana made sure that she was as far away from Barth as possible, without actually leaving the dojo altogether. Chan clapped his hands twice and, out of thin air, thirty dummies materialised – one to each student.

'Activate your Gauntlets now and, when you're ready, you can begin. To start with, just try to aim and hit your target.'

Julius watched as Chan moved swiftly out of the way, then he pressed the red safety button. The Gauntlet instantly began to vibrate and tightened slightly around his right hand. Making a fist, he took aim at the dummy's head and squeezed. Immediately, a yellow beam shot outwards and crashed into the chest of his target, propelling it backwards.

'Wow!' he cried, and turned to watch his friends.

'Try harder,' ordered Chan over the noise. 'I want to see those dummies crash against the opposite wall.'

Julius didn't need to be told twice. This time he focused harder and squeezed his fist closed even tighter. The dummy flew backwards as if hit by a meteor, striking the wall like a freight train.

'This is incredible!' yelled Barth, waving his armed hand about excitedly. 'Oops, sorry,' he then added, quickly lowering his hand after noticing how everyone had ducked down, covering their heads.

'Mr Smit!' shouted Professor Chan. 'If I so much as see you even vaguely pointing that at anything other than the dummy in front of you, you'll be taking its place while I use you for target practice! Is that clear?'

Barth gulped hard and nodded anxiously. His arm shot upwards like a bolt, pointed directly ahead of him. Sure enough, the next few beams he fired were deadly accurate, perhaps propelled by his fear of the Professor's wrath as much as anything else.

Fortunately, the lesson continued without any further incident. Julius was doing a good job of pushing his dummy back against the wall every time he tried, so Chan told him to try control his energy now, by moving the target back only a few feet at a time. Julius found this more challenging but, since controlling energy was also part of his training during Draw lessons, he figured this could only help.

'Good, Mizkis,' said Chan a while later. 'A suggestion though: it is all very good shooting with one hand when you, and your target, are standing still but, when you are moving around, as you would in a real combat situation, it is more stable if you do like so.' The Professor lifted his right arm in front of him and rested it on top of his left, wrist to wrist. 'This is better. Now try it.'

They all mimicked him and sure enough, by the end of the second hour, everyone was easily able to hit their mark. So, when they returned the following Thursday, Chan had them practising their Mindkatas, only this time using their Gauntlets. The 2MJs were positively abuzz with talk of it, so thrilled were they by this new gadget. Surprisingly, Morgana couldn't even stop talking about it during Pilot training that Friday – her favourite class. She was closely examining the Cougar's catalyst, asking if Professor Clavel would show her its inside. She wanted to know exactly how it worked and if there was any way it could be assembled onto a Gauntlet. Faith thought this a jolly good idea indeed, and insisted that they should find a way of doing so without delay. They were so obsessed with this idea that they didn't even notice Clavel trying to explain how there was a high probability that their brains would explode as a result of a reverse stream of energy, should their new invention overheat. Julius and the rest of the class listened with great amusement to this heated debate, while calibrating their own catalysts.

On Monday the 17th of January, the last bell rang, signalling Julius and his friends to rush from their Shield lesson as if the classroom had been set on fire. Two weeks away from Satras was a hard price to pay for any detention. Their eagerness was even more heightened because they were desperate to test their theory about the third Oracle. They headed straight for the Intra-Rail platform, where they boarded the train and were in Satras a few short minutes later. Julius led them towards the barber shop, navigating along the shortest and least crowded route among the maze of paths and bridges that was the main shopping area.

'Here we are,' he said, stopping outside the entrance to *the Barber of Seville*. The shop was empty, except for one man who was having his face slapped with aftershave. 'What are we going to say to him?'

'I'll ask him some questions about music,' answered Faith. 'But I think someone should get a haircut too.'

'Don't look at me,' said Morgana defensively. 'Especially not after the Barth catastrophe.'

'Fair enough,' said Julius. 'Skye will do it then.'

'Why me?'

'Because Julius and I have already had one,' said Faith. 'While you were busy kissy-facing that Pippa Coleman girl from Sield School.'

'All right then,' said Skye, resigned to his fate.

123

Faith opened the door and waited for the others to enter, before following them in. As had happened the last time he had been in the barber shop, Julius was immediately enveloped in a cloud of soothing aromas, from the smell of the leather on the swivel chairs, to the aftershave.

'Hello! *Benvenuti*,' cried Mr Rossini, with his usual joviality. 'Have a seat and I will be with you shortly.'

They entered quietly and sat down on the chairs lining the back wall. As they waited, Julius casually inspected the room with his eyes. One thing he had not noticed on his previous visit was that the shop also seemed to be a kind of small museum of barber history. As well as the typical shelves containing various hair products – razors, scissors and towels – there were also glass cabinets containing heavily rusted iron blades and old, dishevelled brushes. He noticed a single, closed door at the other end of the shop, and felt sure that they would have to check it out somehow, to see where it led.

'So, what can I do for you today?' asked Mr Rossini, bowing with a flourish to them.

'I would like a trim, please,' said Skye, trying to sound like he sincerely wanted one.

'Excellent. Come this way then.'

'Mr Rossini,' said Faith, following them to the chair. 'If you don't mind, could I ask you about your ancestor, the composer?'

'But of course!' Rossini answered, seeming very pleased. 'Ask away, my boy. I knew it when I saw you last time – you have a very keen ear for music. So, what would you like to know?'

Faith proceeded to ask the most bizarre questions he could think of, so as to keep the barber's mind focused on Skye's hair and the topic at hand. Meantime, Julius and Morgana strolled around the shop, acting as if they were merely looking at the curious displays spread around the room.

'*Morgana,*' said Julius, with his mind.

'*I can hear you,*' she said, walking over to him, still pretending to observe the items in the glass cases.

'*I don't see much in this room that could help us,*' said Julius. '*But there is a door in the back that we should check out.*'

'*I see it,*' said Morgana, glancing in that direction. '*I'll go. You keep him busy.*' Then Morgana turned to the barber. 'Sir, can I use your bathroom please?'

'Sure. It's in the back,' he said pointing towards the door with his head.

Julius grinned and walked towards the opposite end of the room, where he stopped in front of one of the cases, containing a particularly old foam brush which had very few bristles left on it.

'Mr Rossini,' he said. 'Why did you keep this old brush?'

The barber turned towards him, scissors in midair, and looked at the display. 'That "old brush", as you call it, belonged to Marcus Tijara, young man,' said Rossini proudly.

'No way!' cried Julius, pressing both palms against the glass.

'This business has been here since the beginning of Zed, and many important backsides have sat on these very chairs – well, the cushions have to be changed every fifty years or so, but the chair frames are the original ones.'

'*It's a bit dark in here!*' Julius heard Morgana's voice say in his head.

He moved away from the display with the brush and resumed his stroll around the shop. '*Use the light from your PIP!*'

'*Good idea.*'

Suddenly, Julius stopped. Through one of the glass cabinets he had spotted a framed picture hanging from the wall. He moved as close as the glass would allow, his nose pressed against it, and squinted his eyes. It was a panoramic image of a seaside town, with the sun shining down on a calm, blue sea. A shiver ran down his back.

'Mr Rossini?' he said, continuing to stare at the picture. 'What town is this?'

The barber turned his head, still holding a strand of Skye's hair between two of his fingers. 'Why, that's *Pèsaro*,' he answered. 'It's the birth city of my family, the Rossinis. It's in Italy, you know?'

Julius nodded politely, but his mind was miles away. This had to be it – the Oracle's clue. But what exactly was he supposed to do with it? He concentrated, recalling the lady's words in his memory: something about going to *Pèsaro* and touching the sea, followed by something else, about a door being revealed. Trying to act casual, he stretched his arm behind the glass case and placed his fingers against the portion of sea in the picture. Nothing happened.

'Great,' he muttered under his breath.

'*What was that?*' said Morgana, in his mind.

'*What was what? Are you OK?*'

'*Yeah yeah, I'm fine. But I heard a click just then, somewhere in this room, like when a catch is released.*'

Julius looked at the picture again: '"*The door that is revealed there to you will lead you once more to me*". *That's what she said. Hang on, I'm going to do it again. I want you to try and figure out where the sound is coming from.*'

'*OK,*' answered Morgana.

He pressed his finger against the blue sea again and again, each

126

time asking Morgana if she had managed to find the secret door. It took several attempts, but eventually she did.

'*Wait*,' she said. '*I can feel a draught coming from the floor – it's a trapdoor. I'm going to check it out quickly.*'

Julius couldn't do much more than wait and hope that no noise would filter through and alert Rossini. Five minutes later, Morgana reappeared in the shop, long strands of cobweb hanging from her hair and clothes.

As soon as Julius saw her, he grabbed her arm and dragged her out of the shop in a hurry, throwing a "We'll be back" in the direction of his friends. It took him a while to clean all the clinging threads off her, not least because she was jumping hysterically from one foot to the other, shaking herself as if she was covered in repulsive bugs.

'I hate insects! Especially in my hair,' she whimpered, trying to calm herself down.

'What, does it happen that often to you?' said Julius, grinning.

'I'm all right now,' she said, ignoring him.

Five minutes later, Faith and Skye walked out of the barber shop.

'What happened in there?' asked Faith, looking at the small pile of cobwebs and dust curls at Morgana's feet.

'Forget that,' she said. 'Let's move away from here.'

They walked over to the nearest bench, in the middle of one of the bridges, overlooking the lake.

'So I touched the sea in the *Pèsaro* picture,' said Julius, 'and it opened a trapdoor in the back room, which Morgana found.'

'It was in the corner of the room,' explained Morgana. 'It was half hidden by boxes, and judging by the layer of dust on the floor, it had been undisturbed for a while. So I had a look inside it. There was a ladder, which led down into a large empty room. It had no exits that I could see.'

'And you don't think Mr Rossini has been down there at all?' asked Skye.

'No way. I mean, the place was full of cobwebs and the air was stale. I could see a wall of dust in the light of my PIP and when I walked around the room I left the kind of footprints you would leave behind on the sand. I don't think anybody has been down there for at least a few years. We'll need to go back there one night, when the shop's closed.'

Julius stood up and shook his head. 'This is game over then.'

'What do you mean?' asked Skye.

'It's one thing breaking curfew ...' began Julius.

'... and another breaking and entering,' finished Faith.

Absolutely,' said Julius. 'Let's go speak to someone at the Palace. This is getting far too fishy.'

No one argued with him – they all knew he was right. You just didn't do these kinds of things on Zed. So, they made their way down to the Palace, hoping to find some answers.

As they entered through the gate, it became apparent that Mrs Mayflower had still not resumed her duties at the kiosk since the attack. Another woman was there working in her place but, seeing as they didn't really know her, they decided instead to speak to Mr Smith, the technician in charge of Flight games. They walked down to the right sector and approached his desk. He was busy signing in a group of 3MA students, so they waited in line for him to finish.

'Look who we have here,' said Mr Smith, happily. 'I haven't seen you guys since last year. What took you so long?'

'Hello,' said Morgana. 'We haven't abandoned you. This year we've just been trying our luck with the Combat games.'

'I know you are. The Skirts are already at the top of that scoreboard too, as you well know. I'm very impressed. So, are you here to fly?'

'Actually not,' replied Julius. 'We would like to ask you something, but I'm afraid it may sound a bit strange.'

'Ask away,' he answered.

'Is there some kind of bonus level built into the games?'

'What do you mean?' he asked, looking puzzled.

'For example, if you do really well during a Combat game, then a hologram appears with a puzzle and if you can figure it out, you get a prize.'

'Not that I know of,' he said.

'What about a treasure hunt?' asked Morgana, directly.

'No, sorry,' he said. 'But you know, an in-game bonus is actually a good idea. You don't mind if I run it by my colleagues, do you?'

'Be our guest,' said Faith.

'Mr Smith,' said Julius, 'are you sure there's nothing like that going on already?'

'McCoy, I don't know what you're trying to find out, but I'm telling you again, there are no bonus levels or treasure hunts present in our games. There never has been and I'm sure I would have been notified of any changes if they had been made, since I am one of the game programmers. Satisfied?'

Julius nodded and wandered off back to the arena, with the others in tow. Once there, they sat down in a quiet corner. None of them had said a word since they had left Mr Smith. Julius's mind was conjuring up all sorts of explanations. He really wasn't sure what to make of it.

'It's a prank, or an Arneshian stunt,' he said finally.

'Either way,' said Skye, 'shouldn't we tell someone? I mean, it doesn't seem likely that we can go meet the third Oracle now, does it?'

'I don't feel like telling anyone yet,' said Faith.

'I agree, actually,' said Julius. 'On New Year's Eve, the Oracle said she would meet us twice more. After Rossini's clue, there would be only one to go. Are we sure we want to give up now?'

'Of course not,' said Morgana. 'Besides, if we go to Cress now, he's going to find out about our last out-of-hours escapade and, if this turns out to be a hoax we'll have got ourselves into trouble for nothing.'

'OK, fine,' said Skye. 'How are we planning to keep this date with the third Oracle then? Because I'm telling you, I'd rather not get another detention. My mum has already "donated" one of my surfboards to a black hole, she was so angry about the last one.'

'That's easy enough,' said Julius. 'We're not going to be there at all.'

'I'm a tad confused,' said Faith.

'We're going to rig Rossini's basement with cameras, and watch the show from the comfort of our dorms,' said Julius.

'You know, McCoy,' said Faith, patting him on the knee, 'I thought you were dumb like a dumbbell, but I was wrong.'

'That's a brilliant idea, Julius,' said Morgana. 'It's agreed then.'

Julius couldn't help feeling rather pleased with his fine suggestion. All they needed to decide now was who was going to get the next haircut.

*

Early on Saturday the 5th of February, the Skirts left Tijara carrying a rucksack each. They got off the train at Satras station and headed straight for Pit-Stop Pete's shop, where they purchased ten night-vision mini-cameras, along with some cables and a few rolls of duct tape. Then they went to Going Spare, where Faith bought a special connector for his PIP, plus a handful of various other gadgets. Julius had no idea how all the pieces were meant to fit together, but that was Faith's area of expertise. From the moment they had decided to rig the basement, Faith's brain had gone into overdrive and he had spent the last three weeks devising the best way of building their surveillance system. Once he had finished his blueprint, his face had lit up with pride and he had handed the shopping list to them. Thankfully, between the four of them, they had enough Fyvers to allow them to buy all the stuff, and it was decided that they would proceed with their plan on the first available date.

'Here we go again,' said Julius, standing outside The Barber of Seville. 'Who's getting the haircut, then?'

'You are,' answered Morgana. 'Faith has to rig the basement, Skye has had one recently and, well, I'm a girl, so I don't need one right now, and certainly *not* from a barber.'

'OK, I get it,' sighed Julius. 'Come on, let's go.'

As they stepped into the shop, Mr Rossini stood up and opened his arms to them.

'My friends! What a pleasant surprise!' he cried.

'Good morning, sir,' said Morgana, smiling her most charming smile. 'The boys just can't get enough of you.'

'You honour me with your presence,' he said with a bow. 'Who will it be today?'

'Me,' said Julius walking towards the chair. 'Not too short please, but less wild.'

'Mr Rossini,' said Faith in a small voice, 'is it OK if I use your bathroom for a moment? It's me skirt, see, there's something wrong with one of the panels and it's hurting me leg quite badly.'

'But of course,' said the barber, looking at Faith with concern. 'Right at the back and take your time, brave young man.'

'Thanks, sir,' he answered. Then he collected everyone's rucksacks and disappeared with a "They're for me spare parts."

'Does he always have to carry those bags around?' asked Mr Rossini, after Faith had gone.

'Today he's travelling light, actually,' answered Julius, looking extremely serious, and leaving Rossini speechless. 'But let's worry about my haircut now.'

'And since we are here,' added Skye, 'why don't you tell us more about your famous ancestor, Giacomo Rossini?'

Mr Rossini looked like his birthday had come early; he was more than happy to indulge them, and started a long and colourful story that covered most of the 19th century and all of the 20th. However, by the time Julius was ready, Faith had still not re-emerged from the basement and so they allowed Mr Rossini to carry on with his musical history to cover the 21st century too. Although the barber had a knack for storytelling, Julius was ready to pass out there and then from sheer boredom. Just as he was beginning to despair, Faith joined them again, with a triumphant smile and four empty rucksacks.

'Thank you, sir,' said Faith, 'I really needed that.'

'Don't you worry. This shop will always be open to you and your friends. Well, come back and see me when your hair gangs up on you again.'

'Thanks. Will do.' said Julius as they left the shop.

Once they had put a safe distance between them and the barber shop, they stopped.

'All done,' said Faith. 'I was able to create a circular rig on the ceiling, so we've got all angles covered.'

'Good job you had the skirt so you could hover upwards,' said Skye. 'Because trying to pass a stepladder off as a repair kit for your skirt would have been a real stretch.'

They laughed and walked back down to Satras's main floor area. To celebrate their success, they decided to challenge each other to a Flight game, for old times' sake, an idea that yielded another top time record among the 2MJs of Zed.

*

The live feed from the cameras was only accessible through Faith's PIP, so it became quite common to see Julius, Skye and Morgana – individually, or together – staring into Faith's holoscreen at every opportunity. After a while, they even stopped asking him for permission and would sometimes just grab his hand as they passed him in the corridor, for quick peeks. At mealtimes, Morgana could be found sitting next to Faith, a fork in her left hand, which she used to distractedly eat her food, and her right holding up his hand so she could stare at his holoscreen. Sometimes she would pass his hand over, like a box of sweets, to Julius or Skye. Faith didn't seem to mind, strangely enough. In fact, he had got into the habit of leaving his PIP tuned into the surveillance channel and become adept at doing pretty much everything with his right hand only.

Thankfully, their classmates didn't seem to have picked up on this odd behaviour which, according to Skye, was probably because the Skirts were becoming known as a naturally odd bunch anyway. There was only one occasion, when Ferenc Orban and Lopaka Liway had asked them what on earth they were up to. They had merely been told that it was important, top secret experimental research on Faith's skirt, as authorised by Pit-Stop Pete, supreme maker of said skirt. Faith's serious look discouraged them from asking any further questions.

Julius soon grew certain, as did the other three, that there was no fear of Mr Rossini finding the cameras. In fact, they were pretty sure he didn't even *know* that there was a basement in his shop to begin with. Watching the feed so regularly was just a way of biding time, like the way a person would sometimes unconsciously keep checking their watch, as if that would hurry time itself.

Once though, Julius and Faith could have sworn they had seen a shadow moving in a corner of the room. They rewound the footage and checked it several times. Then they showed it to Morgana and Skye, not telling them what to look for, to see if they too would catch a glimpse of the mysterious shadow. In the end they had all agreed that something had indeed moved in front of the camera, but since it wasn't spotted again on any of the other footage, they let it go.

After what seemed an eternity, Thursday the 24th finally arrived. Julius was very excited and quite unable to concentrate for more than a few minutes at a time, which, funnily enough, turned out not to be a problem during that morning's Meditation lesson. Professor Lao-tzu had asked half of his students, including Julius, to wear Scramblers while trying to communicate with a partner. So when Barth, who had been paired with Julius, was unable to perceive even half a thought and was getting redder and redder from the effort of concentrating, it was attributed to the Scrambler's powers, rather than to the fact that Julius wasn't really trying at all.

Lunchtime was spent peering over Faith's shoulder for the usual checks of the "just in case" variety. Thankfully they had Martial Arts in the afternoon, so were kept seriously busy by Professor Chan and the fresh excitement of fighting with the Gauntlet. As they sat down for dinner that night, Faith decided that he needed to rest his left hand and kept his fist closed for the whole meal.

'So, where are we going to meet tonight?' asked Julius, wiping his mouth and leaning back in his chair.

'If it wasn't for the small issue of Morgana's gender, I'd say the boys' dorm,' said Faith.

'That's OK,' said Morgana, with a cheeky grin, 'I feel up for some mischief tonight. Besides, I've been left on the bench too much already. Coming over to your dorm is not going to be a problem.'

'What's the penalty if they catch you in a boy's room?' asked Skye, 'I'd just like to know for, um, future reference.'

Julius, Faith and Morgana stared at him in silence.

'Never mind,' said Skye, 'Just kidding.'

'Well I don't know what would happen, but I'm pretty sure it's not allowed. I'll be careful,' she said.

'I'll tell you what,' said Faith, 'I can feel a plan hatching. Meet me in the foyer of the girls' dorm at 23:30. Oh, and wear trousers.'

'OK,' said Morgana, looking suspiciously at him.

Julius decided that it was better not to ask. The others disappeared off, but he spent another hour relaxing in the garden discussing extravagant Ottoman rulers with Ferenc Orbán who, like Julius, had a passion for ancient history. Gustavo Perez and Yuri Slovich sat nearby, staring mystified at them, as Julius and Ferenc eagerly discussed whether Selim the Sot had *really* drowned after drinking too much champagne, and about how Ibrahim the Mad had lost his marbles after being imprisoned by his brothers for twenty-two years. They ended off with an animated debate on who had been the best sultan – Süleyman the Magnificent or Mehmet the Conqueror – before retiring for the night.

Later that evening, there was a knock on his door. 'I told Barth we were filling in our diaries,' said Faith, entering the room and closing the door behind him.

Julius was sitting at his desk, finishing off a letter home. 'Good,' he said, swivelling in his chair to look at Faith. 'I've checked, and all the 2MJs have turned in for the night. You shouldn't meet anyone from our year at least.'

'I'm really curious to know how you're going to sneak Morgana in here undetected,' said Skye, sitting up in his bed, where he had been lounging and watching a movie on his PIP. 'If it works, I might use it sometime in the future ... for another purpose.'

'Just make sure I'm not here when you do that, you hear?' said Julius.

'Of course. My brain is already plotting the perfect plan,' said Skye.

'Yeah, we know where your brain is all right,' replied Julius.

'That would be in your pants, in case you're wondering,' added Faith.

Julius and Skye couldn't help but snigger at that, and were still laughing as Faith made to leave. 'I'm gonna go wait in me room,' he said, pausing in the doorway. 'I'll keep a channel open, so you may wanna switch over when you're finished laughing.'

As soon as Faith was gone, Julius moved over to Skye's bed and plonked himself down next to him. Skye had turned to the open channel and Julius shoved him to the side so he could see the holoscreen properly.

'He's right, you know?' said Julius.

'What, you mean about my brain?' said Skye. 'I can't help it. Girls just have this effect on me. It's like I need them to know that they can count on me, that I can protect them. They're so different to boys; so adorable and ... uh, I don't know. It's difficult to explain, I guess.'

'Ah, we're just messing with you. We know you mean well. Besides, I reckon every girl needs a gent like you around. Although, I doubt most of them would be happy to share you with the competition.'

'Yeah, I've already learnt that lesson with Pippa,' said Skye. 'She got all jealous and upset, 'cause I asked her about her roommate.'

'When?'

'On our first date – the one by the lovers' statue?'

'You're kidding, right?'

'Nope. She just got into a huff and cut our date short.'

'No wonder! I mean, come on. I'm no expert at this dating stuff, but even I know that one at a time is the decent thing to do. You're some guy, you know that?'

'I agree,' said Faith's voice from the PIP.

'Me too,' said Morgana. 'I hope you knew I was online by the way.'

'Uh huh ... sure,' said Skye, clearing his throat and fidgeting nervously. 'No problem.'

'One bit of advice though,' said Morgana. 'Keeping your options open is of course an option, but I would highly recommend that you make that clear to whoever you're dating at the time, 'cause hurt feelings aren't funny.'

Julius stared at Skye with an expression that clearly said, "I told you so."

'Of course,' answered Skye, feeling glad that she couldn't see him blushing.

'Right, now, everyone shut it,' said Faith. 'Press the mute button. I don't want anybody hearing your voices. Morgana, I'll be there in a minute.'

Skye muted the sound on his holoscreen and the two boys watched as Faith left his room. To all of their amazement, they saw that he was carrying a wakeboard, which he placed on the floor in the middle of the corridor. He hovered over it, slipped his feet inside the straps and tightened them as much as he could above his boots. When he floated upwards, the board went with him.

'What the ... Hey! That's the board I use in the Palace for waterskiing!' said Skye.

'It'll be all right. He normally knows what he's doing,' said Julius, trying to sound reassuring.

'Yeah, normally.'

Faith continued his ascent, looking as if he was actually riding waves and enjoying the sun. When he reached the promenade, he continued in the same fashion towards the girls' dorm.

Julius saw Morgana's mouth drop open as Faith appeared in the foyer. She had been hiding behind a plant and emerged into the open as he stopped in front of her. Faith freed his feet and gestured for Morgana to sit down in the middle of the board. Despite the lack of sound on Skye's screen, it was clear from Morgana's hand gestures that she was saying something along the lines of "Are you out of your mind?".". Faith, in reply, pointed at his watch and made as if he was about to turn away. Morgana quickly stopped him, then stepped onto the board, gathered her legs up and buried her head between her knees.

'Tell me he's not really going to ...' started Julius.

Sure enough, Faith hovered above Morgana and gently descended over her, his conical skirt covering her like a tea cosy.

'He's unbelievable,' said Skye, sounding impressed.

'Yeah, and *she's* awfully brave,' added Julius. 'Let's hope he doesn't let one out, or we might have a blue, comatose girl coming our way.'

It took Skye a few seconds to realise what that remark meant, but as it sunk in, he howled with laughter, while Julius tried to keep his friend's hand steady so he could continue watching the PIP.

Faith, meanwhile, slipped his feet back into the straps and shakily took off again. He was swaying a little from the effort of keeping his balance but he soon managed to inch forward in the direction of the boys' dorm.

Skye had managed to pull himself together and was now glued to the screen again. In fact, he and Julius had grown so tense that neither of them had realised they were clutching each other's forearms. It was a bit like watching a silent horror movie, with Faith's various expressions their only indication of what was going on. Suddenly, he stopped in the middle of the promenade and stared intently ahead of him.

'What's happening?' said Julius.

'Is someone there?' asked Skye, tightening his grip on Julius's arm.

'Ouch! How should I know? I'm sitting here with you, remember!'

Faith looked around anxiously, then flew back into the girls' dorm foyer, and hid behind the wall.

That was when Julius and Skye managed to catch a glimpse of exactly what the problem was: three of the Professors – Morales, Chan and King – were taking an evening stroll through Tijara.

'They're really stuck now,' said Skye.

'We've got time. He just needs to be careful,' replied Julius, only half convinced by his own words.

Julius turned his thoughts to the layout of the school. All areas opened onto the promenade which encircled the assembly hall. Its black marble walls were in turn overlaid by the cascading water that ran into a fountain all around the base of the walls – the same fountain where they'd had their little incident on New Year's Eve. On the screen, he could see that the teachers had stopped between the entrances to the dorms, and were giving no sign of moving anytime soon. He knew they would have to distract them somehow, so that Faith and Morgana could sneak past safely.

'Skye, I think maybe you should go ask Professor Morales if she can help you with your Spanish.'

Skye didn't need to be asked twice. He leapt from the bed, stopped briefly in front of the mirror to smooth down his curls and dashed out of the door.

'I was kidding ...' said Julius. 'Oh, never mind.'

Two minutes later, Faith's camera zoomed in on Skye approaching the Professors. A few seconds after that, Julius was treated to a brief cameo of Faith staring into the camera and mouthing words that he took to be, "He's completely bonkers".

Whatever Skye had said or done, however, it seemed to have worked, as shortly afterwards Faith and his cargo were able to leave their hiding place and hover to a now empty corridor. When he turned into the foyer of the boys' dorm undetected, Julius let out a long sigh of relief.

140

He hurriedly opened the door and ushered the crazy surfer into the room, then closed it again as soon as he had scanned the corridor to make sure that no one had woken up and noticed.

'Let me out!' said Morgana, knocking on the inside of Faith's metal skirt.

'Just a moment, woman. I need to land first!' he said, setting the board down. He hastily loosened the straps and hovered upwards. As he did so, Morgana rolled out onto the floor.

'I thought I was going to be stuck in there forever,' she said, stretching and breathing in deeply.

'Where's Skye?' asked Julius.

'That man, honestly,' said Faith. 'He greeted everyone, apologised for the late hour and asked to speak to Morales about an urgent matter.'

'Which was?' asked Julius.

'Apparently his brother is about to marry some two-timing Spanish woman, and he has decided to save the family honour by writing a letter, in Spanish, warning her to change her "wily" ways or risk being exposed to the whole family.'

'What did she say to that?' asked Julius, his eyes widening.

'She just put a hand on his shoulder, told him how brave he was and how many girls would appreciate that kind of attitude when he's older.'

'What? Is she completely dumb?'

'You gotta give it to him. He's got the whole puppy-eyes routine mastered,' said Faith.

'Apparently so,' agreed Julius.

'Then she took him off to the canteen so they could sit down and talk about it,' continued Morgana.

'Well, if he misses the Oracle, I guess he can just watch the recording,' said Julius. 'Speaking of, shall we get ready?'

They all sat down on Julius's bed, with Faith in the middle so they could watch his screen.

'I got a little upgrade just for the occasion,' said Faith, smiling proudly and switching on his PIP. The screen appeared to be twice as large as it had been before.

'That's just,' said Julius, impressed.

'That's what you're getting for your birthday,' said Morgana to Julius.

'OK guys, here we go,' said Faith, holding his hand out slightly in front of him so the screen was clearly visible to everyone.

The image they saw was the main angle from the trapdoor into the centre of the room, which they thought was the likeliest place for the Oracle to appear. Just to be sure though, Faith had placed the remaining cameras in positions that also covered the four corners of the room. Those other views were now minimised to icon size at the bottom of the screen. The night vision light created an eerie atmosphere: everything had a curious green tinge about it. Specks of dust floated around like snowflakes, before falling into the vague outlines of the shoeprints left behind by Morgana and Faith. Their eyes were soon drawn to the centre of the room, where the dust had begun to swirl and converge.

'There she is,' whispered Morgana.

Slowly, the shape of the lady began to form in front of their eyes, her silver mantle tinged by the green light. She looked up, straight into the main camera, almost as if she knew that it was there. Julius held his breath in anticipation of the new message.

'Well met,' said the Oracle. 'I am glad you could join me again.

142

I am the third Oracle and I will set you on the right path. My time is short, so hear my words. He left Artemis speechless when he told her, "Be my bride"; or so Sir Pierre believed when he found her gift, and sighed. We shall meet again in fifty-five days from now, in the last five minutes of the day. You will heed my words one more time. Remember, only the bravest can reach the end. Farewell, my bringer of life.' She finished with a smile in their direction, and then slowly faded into nothingness.

'This one sounds tricky. We're going to need to analyse it word by-,' she began, and then stopped abruptly.

Julius turned his head to look at her. She was staring wide eyed at the screen, so he followed her gaze and froze.

The shadow of a man had appeared in the middle of the room, staring at the spot where the lady had been standing just seconds earlier. He took a few steps away from the main camera and then turned, slowly. Julius felt all the air rush out of his lungs and his jaw dropped open in disbelief as the face came into focus. 'Red Cap,' he whispered.

Red Cap looked around him, then up towards the main camera. They watched silently, still in shock, as he stretched out his hand and tore it loose. The feed disappeared. The remaining four quickly followed suit.

Just then, the door flew open and a flush-faced Skye stumbled into the room. 'What did I miss?' he asked, and was greeted only by their white faces.

'You'd better sit down,' said Morgana.

GASSENDI'S ROCK

'What happened?' asked Skye, who was obviously quite alarmed by the odd reception he had received. 'Did the feed fail?'

Julius, who was sitting on the bed in silence staring into nothing, promptly stood up and, without a word, left the room. He headed straight for the stairs, not caring if he bumped into the Grand Master himself. When he reached the promenade, he turned left and headed for the mess hall. The kitchen was empty, its surfaces freshly clean and shiny for the morning breakfast. He marched over to the hot drinks dispenser and ordered the first thing that came to mind: 'Hot chocolate. No sugar.'

He spilled a little and almost dropped the cup, his hands were shaking so badly. Fortunately, a hand reached out from the left and steadied it just in time. It was Morgana – she had left the room right after him and followed in silence. 'Go sit down,' she said. 'I'll bring it over.'

Julius wiped his hands with a paper towel and sat down at one of the smaller tables. Morgana joined him a couple of minutes later, carrying two cups.

'What's going on, Morgana?' said Julius, clearly upset.

'I don't know,' she said, gloomily. 'I don't know why Red Cap is back or what he's up to.'

'Do you think the Oracle is just one of his tricks? Have we been played for fools all along?'

'Maybe he's just involved with the kidnappings. That was, after all, why he was here last year.'

Julius took a sip of chocolate. 'What if he's come back for ... well, for me?'

'What, because you're a White Child?' she asked, looking at him with some concern.

Julius nodded.

'Could be. But, it doesn't *feel* like last time. It seems like they're only targeting girls. Also, we haven't had any sign of Red Cap since last April, or seen anything that suggests he's directly involved in this business. And the Oracle seems far too nice to be involved with the Arneshians.'

Julius thought about it. 'So you're saying that Red Cap just happened to stumble into that basement by mistake?'

'Not by mistake. But ... he could have followed us, maybe.'

Julius knotted his eyebrows. 'When I was lying on the boat, by the lovers' statue, I had this feeling like I was being watched. Then I saw a shadow moving, on the bridge above me.'

'There you go,' said Morgana. 'It was our friendly holo-psycho. He heard the Oracle's clue and decided to check it out, especially because *you* were involved.'

'You could be right, you know. Still, I'm pretty sure Red Cap has something to do with these kidnappings, but it doesn't seem like they have anything to do with the Oracle.'

Morgana looked at him, sipping her drink in silence. Julius could tell she wanted to say something, but left her to talk when she was ready. Sure enough, a moment later she put the cup down and looked up.

145

'Listen Julius, what about the guys? Don't you think you should tell them about this White Child business? It would make things easier if they knew.'

'Maybe, but it doesn't seem necessary for others to know about this.'

'"Others"?' said Morgana, flushing slightly. 'I'm not talking about just anyone here, Julius. It's Faith and Skye, our friends. A few months ago they risked their lives on Kratos with you, remember? You owe them an explanation.'

Julius was taken aback by her reaction, but he knew she was right. He had postponed this chat for far too long. He would much rather have kept it a secret, but they *had* risked life and limb because of him. What's more, with Red Cap back in the picture, it was entirely possible that Julius might be in danger again, and his friends too by association, so at the very least he needed to warn them. 'All right, all right, I'll tell them tomorrow.'

'No! Tell them now.'

'Tell us what?' said Faith, hovering over to the table, followed by Skye.

Julius motioned for them to sit and took a deep breath. For the next while, there was no other sound in the mess hall other than Julius's own voice. The more he said, the lighter he felt, as if an invisible weight had been lifted from his shoulders. He told them all about the conversation with Freja, the day the Grand Master had revealed his true nature as a White child. Then he recounted how Queen Salgoria had been kidnapping highly skilled Zed officers in order to splice their DNA together with the Arneshian's own genes, and how those experiments had failed, causing the deaths of so many in the process. Then he moved onto the bits they didn't know about

146

the attack on Zed the previous year; the plot to kidnap him, led by Red Cap, in order to use his special DNA and that of an Arneshian to create the perfect being. He finished off by telling them of Freja's warning to be careful, in case Red Cap came back for him, no matter how unlikely that had seemed at the time.

'A *White Child*,' said Faith in astonishment. 'Well, paint me red and call me a beetroot.'

They chuckled at the quip, and immediately felt the sombre mood lift a little.

'McCoy's a White Child. Who would have thought?' said Skye, obviously pleased. 'He is a little pale, it's true.' He grinned at Julius, who punched him on the arm.

'Actually, we should have at least suspected as much after that Draw stunt he pulled on Kratos,' said Morgana, who seemed relieved now that Julius had shared the whole story with the other two.

'Guys,' said Julius, 'you have to swear you won't tell a soul.'

'Of course, mate,' said Skye. 'But I reserve the right to call you WC.'

'You do that, and I'll tell every girl on Zed that you still wet the bed.'

'OK,' said Morgana, standing up. 'And on that note, I think I can call it a night.'

'I'm shattered too,' said Faith. 'Let's discuss the situation another time, guys. I think a major piece of news like that is enough for one day.'

Julius followed them back to the dorm, feeling tired but much happier. The anger he had felt when he had seen Red Cap on the screen had almost completely dissipated. Morgana had been right, after all. It was much better now that the others knew everything he did. However, he had his doubts about how that would make things any easier. Being a White Child wasn't necessarily a burden, but he wondered if it would make the others look more to him for leadership. It wasn't a thought he was entirely comfortable with. As much as he valued having them around, when it came to making decisions, he still felt like a Solo player.

*

During the last few days of February, Julius found himself fighting an internal battle: should he tell Freja about Red Cap, or not? The others had not said very much on the topic, but he was certain that they were considering the consequences as he was. There was no mistaking what a big decision it was, and he didn't feel like making it alone. So, on Tuesday the 1st of March, he called a meeting under the oak tree, in Tijara's garden.

'I think you all know what we need to decide, guys,' he said. 'Do we tell Freja?'

'I say no,' said Faith.

'No for me,' said Skye.

'No,' said Julius.

'Ditto for me,' added Morgana.

Julius looked at them each in turn, feeling strangely relieved at the unanimous vote. 'If we told Freja, we would have to explain why we had surveillance cameras in Mr Rossini's basement, which could get us all into a lot of trouble. And, with Red Cap thrown into the picture, I could see me being completely grounded and out of action, for my own protection. Not to mention being totally cut off from the rest of the treasure hunt. Red Cap escaped me once already and I really don't want to give him another chance to do it a second time.'

'OK, so what reasons are there for why we *should* tell him?' continued Morgana.

'Because of Ife and Sharon,' said Skye. 'If Red Cap is tied to the kidnapping, and chances are that he is, then we really ought to.'

'This information could save their lives,' agreed Morgana.

'They'll never allow us to continue with the treasure hunt,' said Faith. 'Especially since the Hologram Palace staff doesn't even know anything about any in-game bonus.'

'Shoot,' said Julius, slumping back on the grass. 'We're trapped.'

Lacing his fingers together, he placed the back of his hands over his eyes and breathed deeply. The cold grass was doing a good job of soothing the tense muscles in his neck, while a few of the longer blades tickled his ears pleasantly. He remembered Freja's words from the previous year. He had asked Julius then to trust in his new family – the Tijaran family.

'We have no choice,' said Julius, sitting up.

'No, we don't,' said Morgana. 'Not when there are lives at stake.'

'We tell the whole story,' said Skye, 'and we share the consequences.'

*

As they arrived at the senior staff area, they bumped into Master Cress, who was just exiting his office.

'Sir,' said Julius, bowing. 'We wish to speak to Grand Master Freja.'

'He's busy right now, McCoy. Is there something I can help you with?'

149

Julius knew that Freja trusted Cress completely, but he wanted to talk to the Grand Master directly. There was sure to be some form of punishment because of their treasure hunt, so he at least wanted the chance to tell the story face to face. 'We wish to speak to him directly, sir, if you don't mind.'

Cress looked at them, puzzled. 'He's in a meeting and I ...'

'It's about Red Cap, sir,' Morgana blurted out, interrupting him.

Cress's face instantly took on a look of concern. 'Very well. Wait here. I'll call you when he's ready.'

Julius sat down in one of the armchairs that lined the corridor, while Master Cress disappeared into Freja's office. Waiting for Freja was never a pleasant experience. No matter the reason for seeing him, Julius always felt like a naughty boy who had done some terrible mischief and was duly about to be punished for it. The wait didn't last too long, thankfully. Five minutes later, Cress opened the door and invited them in.

Freja's office was made up of two rooms, separated by a large archway. The main door opened onto a living room, which was furnished with three grey leather sofas facing a long, glass-top coffee table. There was a trolley with bottles and glasses on the other side of the room, no doubt for use when he was entertaining guests. To Julius's delight, the walls of the room were obscured by several large bookshelves housing a seemingly endless amount of books. This was a precious sight indeed, since books made of real paper had become extremely rare over the course of the last 500 years. The books themselves were shielded by transparent protective panels, making Julius feel as if he had just stepped into a museum like the ones his parents loved so much, back on Earth.

As they reached the main part of the office, the bookshelves gave

150

way to mounted pictures, shelves laden with trophies and various other objects, which Julius did not have time to examine properly. Behind a large mahogany desk at the end of the room, stood Carlos Freja, in typically pristine uniform and sporting his usual impenetrable gaze.

Julius and the others stopped as they drew near, and bowed their heads.

'At ease,' said the Grand Master, extending his hand out in front of him. 'Sit, please.'

Four chairs had already been set out for them, so they quickly obeyed. Julius was aware that Master Cress had sat down on a chair behind them and that, as he had foreseen, he would be listening to their news.

'I have a recording you should see, sir,' said Faith, activating his PIP.

'Send it through, Mr Shanigan,' said Freja. He motioned for Cress to join him and, activating his own PIP, he placed his left hand in front of him for them both to watch.

Julius sat in silence as the video was transferred to Freja's device and then carefully studied. The voice of the Oracle resounded clearly in the stillness of the office, her latest clue unresolved. Then, after a brief silence, they heard the sound of footsteps on a squeaky floor board, and the noise of the camera being ripped from the ceiling, which signalled the end of the recording. Freja and Cress looked quite stunned, a little too much for Julius's liking. Freja stared intently at Cress for a moment and Julius was sure that a mind-message had just been passed between them. It had been so quick and unexpected that he had only caught a brief hint of what sounded like a murmur.

'I think you ought to explain some of the background to this

151

video, Mizkis,' said Freja. 'Tell me everything – I want every last detail, even if you don't think it's important.'

Faith began to tell the story, starting with how Julius had sensed something in the cave, to the scanner in the chamber and the first Oracle that had appeared there. Freja looked at Julius intently as he listened to that part, but said nothing. Faith continued on, as the Grand Master switched his gaze back to him, recounting everything that had happened up to and including New Year's Eve. At that point, Freja looked at Julius and said, 'We were wondering where you had *really* been that night, Mr McCoy. Weren't we, Master Cress?'

'And it does explain the performance that you put on for Captain Foster,' added Cress, raising an eyebrow.

Julius sunk into his chair, reddening and hoping that Faith would hurry up and finish. The story then turned to all of the events surrounding Mr Rossini and his barber shop, ending with the appearance of Red Cap in the basement.

'Sir,' said Skye, 'We don't think that the Oracle has anything to do with the Arneshians, but we do feel that Red Cap is tied to the kidnappings.'

'We came to you because it was the right thing to do,' said Julius, 'but, now that Red Cap has seen the Oracle, we wish to see the treasure hunt through before he does. Please don't take it away from us.'

'In the light of what we have just seen, I cannot grant such a concession lightly, Mr McCoy.'

'Sir, please,' said Julius, trying hard to sound determined, rather than confrontational. 'She said that we will only see her one more time before the end. We've come so far. Let us finish this.'

Freja searched him with his grey eyes for a few seconds. 'I will consider your request.'

Julius sighed in relief. It wasn't a "yes", but it was certainly better than an outright "no".

'There is also another matter to consider,' said Cress. 'That of your trespassing on private property and, of course, breaking curfew.'

'*Here we go,*' thought Julius. '*That's another detention for sure.*'

'We shall take into account the various factors that have prompted your actions,' continued Cress. 'You will be informed of our decision in due course. Dismissed.'

They bowed and left the room in single file, feeling quite surprised that they had escaped without having the books, and a few shelves thrown at them, at least for the moment.

*

Once they had gone and the door shut behind them, Cress turned to Freja, looking incredulous. 'They *really* didn't recognise her.'

'Surprising, isn't it,' said Freja, leaning back in his chair.

'I know we don't teach History and Politics until third year, but I had to admit, I was quite astonished by their ignorance.'

'It's been a long time, Nathan. Besides, she did look rather young in that video. Their misplaced trust in the Oracle may just give us the advantage we need though. It's probably better if they *don't* know who she is.'

'Are you going to let them continue the hunt then?'

'Yes, I am. This discovery is an unexpected victory for Zed. Besides, I suspect that we need to follow this lead to the end if we want to find the missing girls. The two paths lead to one shared destination; there's no doubt in my mind about that. There's also that scanner they mentioned. It could be nothing – an activation device of some sort – but I just wonder ...'

Cress waited for him to finish, but he seemed lost in thought. 'Maybe we should take over from here then. It could be dangerous for them.'

Freja looked at him and shook his head. 'I fear that, if we do that, we'll lose the scent. For whatever reason, they were the ones who found the hologram – I have a feeling that we need to let them see this one through. Besides, McCoy is like a hound that has just smelled blood. He will not stop until Red Cap is finished.'

Cress nodded. 'They certainly have done well with the clues so far.'

'Indeed,' said Freja, a little smile curling one corner of his mouth. 'They showed remarkable wit to overcome those obstacles. Tell them to continue and to report all progress on the next clue to you directly. We'll take some extra precautions too.'

'I understand. And what about the other matter?'

'Captain Foster has already dealt with the infringement on New Year's Eve. I'm sure you'll find the correct recourse for their inappropriate behaviour towards Mr Rossini.'

Cress nodded. Freja eased back in his chair and passed his hands over his face, his gaze fixed on nothing in particular.

'You look tired, Carlos,' said Cress.

'I am, Nathan,' sighed Freja. 'I spent most of the day in a videoconference with the Curia, the other Grand Masters and the family of the missing girls.'

'How are they coping?'

'Well enough, given the circumstances,' said Freja. 'I mean, the Curia asked them not to disclose news of the kidnappings to any journalists, while the Curio Maximus is practically blackmailing them with a guilt trip: if they talk, there's a chance their daughters could be harmed in retaliation. Then there's us, promising that we'll do everything in our power to get them back but, given our previous record, the chances are *not* in our favour.'

Cress watched as Freja walked over to the water fountain and poured himself a glass of water.

'I want McCoy under constant surveillance, Nathan,' said Freja, turning to him. 'I know it sounds awful but, as a White Child, *he's* the one we can't afford to lose. Do what you must.'

*

'Detention or not,' said Skye, once back in the promenade, 'we did the right thing.'

'Of course we did,' said Morgana. 'If there's even a small chance that our video can help Freja find the girls, then it's worth it.'

Julius nodded. He agreed with them, of course he did, but apparently Red Cap still had the power to get under his skin. Last year, Freja had told him to let it go, that he was only a hologram, a slave of Salgoria's. But, for Julius, that wasn't so easy. Since his reappearance, Red Cap's face had haunted his dreams almost every night. Sometimes, in those dreams, Julius didn't manage to escape and was captured at the end of a futile struggle.

'I really hope they'll let us finish,' said Faith.

'I don't care what he says,' said Julius, 'because this time, if Red Cap crosses my path, I won't let him get away.' There was enough anger in his voice to stop the others dead in their tracks. 'I'm not kidding.'

155

They believed him, and none of them found anything to reply.

*

The following Monday afternoon, the 2MJs were finally treated to their first class of Martial Arts, in which they would be able to fight using both a shield and the Gauntlet. Professor Morales was waiting at the dojo entrance, welcoming the students with her usual smile, while Professor Chan stood by her side with furled eyebrows, a double act that the Mizkis had become quite accustomed to. Faith had been calling them "the odd couple" since November, due to the plainly evident difference in the two teachers' personalities. Morales's natural bubbliness could hardly be more in contrast to Chan's serious nature. It seemed that the more she smiled at him the closer his eyebrows got to each other, creating a mono-brow effect.

'Oh boy,' whispered Faith, looking at Chan. 'He's wearing his constipated face again. I foresee severe pain of the muscles and cracking of the joints for tonight.'

'You know what?' said Morgana, observing the teachers closely. 'I think he fancies her.'

'Who? Morales?' asked Julius, horrified.

'Why? What's wrong with that?' said Morgana. 'She's an attractive woman.'

'But, but ... they can't,' stuttered Julius.

'Why not?'

'They're teachers,' he answered, as if that should clearly prove his point.

'No-uh,' said Morgana, shaking her finger under his nose. 'They are as human as you are.'

'Julius is right,' added Skye. 'Besides, she's in love with me. I'm far more charming than Chan.'

'Is that right?' said Morgana, chuckling.

'How do you know he likes her?' asked Faith, genuinely curious. 'I mean, it looks more like the opposite, actually. He never smiles at her, or even looks her in the eye.'

'That's *exactly* it,' said Morgana, knowingly. 'Pretending that you don't care for someone normally means the opposite. You want to arouse their curiosity as to why you don't like them, which in turn makes them think about you, often with astonishing results. I'm not saying it's a good method, but it has been known to work.'

'Wow,' said Faith, 'Remind me to ask you a couple of questions later on.'

'How do you know all this stuff?' asked Julius.

'WC,' said Skye, nudging Julius in the ribs, 'she's a woman. Of course she knows this stuff. It's a genetic thing. It's how they wile their way into our hearts.'

'Don't call me WC, or I'll tell Chan he's got competition, and then he'll use his constipated secret move on your a ...'

As Skye grabbed Julius into a head lock, the door of the dojo closed. The students immediately faced the teachers and bowed.

'First things first, Mizkis,' said Chan, 'I want you to use a Sim-Gauntlet for today's lesson. Since you'll be practising against each other, I really would like to avoid burying anyone tonight.'

As the students walked over to the shelf, Chan moved to the centre of the room, clapped twice and quickly moved his hands up and to the side. To their general astonishment, the dojo stretched itself instantly, turning into a much larger and wider room.

'I want fifteen students on the left and fifteen on the right of the room,' called Chan. 'Professor Morales will give each of you a coloured armband that contains a sensor. Anytime you are shot by one of the Sim-Gauntlets, the sensor will go off and you must step to the side of the main floor area immediately. Keep in mind, this exercise is about teamwork. Now, go to your stations and get ready.'

Julius and Morgana were each given a yellow armband, while Faith and Skye got red ones. The two teams moved to opposite sides of the dojo, where they were given a few minutes to prepare.

'Morgana,' said Julius, talking quickly. 'We need to stick together. My left shield will cover my side and front; my right one will do the same when I'm not shooting, but I can't protect my back. You'll have the same problem, so we walk back to back. That way, we'll be able to cover all directions. Why are you smiling?'

'Your eyes shine when you organise people,' she said, straightening her armband. 'You'll make a great captain one day.'

Julius blushed slightly and, not knowing what to say, he stood up and gave her his hand. Morgana grabbed it and jumped to her feet. She didn't add anything else, but he could see a little smile curling the corners of her mouth.

'Mizkis, activate your shields,' cried Chan.

A dull, electric noise ran simultaneously through the dojo, as all the shields came online.

'I want a clean fight,' added Morales. 'May the best team win.'

Her words had barely left her lips when the Mizkis began to advance toward the middle of the room, letting out battle cries as they went. Morgana moved quickly into position at Julius's back, ready to fire on anyone who dared approach them. Soon the dojo had transformed into a confusing battlefield, with students shooting at each other without any clear plan or tactic. The armbands of those who got hit flashed brightly before emitting a shrill beeping sound. As Julius dodged a few attacks and shot three of his classmates, he was strongly reminded of his test at the Zed Center almost two years before, where he had managed to prove his worth to the Lunar Perimeter selection panel amid the chaos of children trying to survive long enough to get through.

'Barth!' cried Morgana suddenly, grabbing Julius's t-shirt. 'Let's go get him.'

For a moment, Julius thought that she wanted to shoot Barth just to get him out of the training, as a safety measure. Then he spotted him, and understood that Morgana meant to rescue him. Barth was kneeling in the centre of the dojo, his shields on, desperately trying to protect himself. No one had made a move against him, which was surprising given that he was such an easy target. But Julius knew why: it was part of the Zed honour code – you didn't kick someone who was already down.

'All right,' he said to her, over his shoulder. 'Let's blast our way over there.'

She gave him the thumbs-up and they began to move rapidly sideways. Julius's right shield and Morgana's left one had created a wall to protect them, while the opening gap was covered by the quick bursts of light from their weapons. They shot at anyone who crossed their path, sometimes jumping over students who had been hit and were now trying to get to the sidelines by crawling on all fours. They saw others who had also been eliminated trying to get clear by ramming their way through the crowd.

'Barth, get up!' cried Julius, towering over his classmate.

'It's not safe,' said a little voice from under his shields.

'Barth Smit!' shouted Julius over the noise. 'You stand up right now and join us, or I'll shoot you myself.'

Morgana threw a look at Julius that clearly said, "Like that's going to help."

'I can't!' said Barth.

'Yes you can,' said Julius, a little more gently this time. 'We're covering you. Just use your shields to protect your open side. You'll be fine, honestly.'

Barth glanced up, looking pretty shaken, but gradually he started to shift towards Julius's legs and stood up cautiously.

'Attaboy,' said Julius, nodding his approval. Barth smiled and, just then, inexplicably decided to scratch his head. As he did, his shield lifted upwards, leaving Julius's entire right side unprotected. He looked up and, too late, saw that Faith had him in his sights. It all happened so fast that he could do nothing to prevent it. Faith grinned and squeezed his fist, the shot hitting Julius square on his hip.

'Sorry mate!' cried Faith, before retreating towards the few survivors left in his team.

Julius stood, looking with resignation at his flashing sensor then, without a second glance at Barth, made his way towards the sidelines.

'Come sit here,' said Lopaka, with a big grin. 'Man, that sucks. I can't believe he got you shot.'

'It's Barth,' said Julius, plonking himself on the ground by Lopaka's side. 'I should have known better.'

'Don't worry, no one's gonna think any less of you. You did the decent thing, trying to help him.'

'It was Morgana's idea, actually. I would have probably just left him there, but Morgana's different. Her heart's in the right place.'

'She's got a few other things in the right places too,' said Lopaka, watching her shoot her way through a group of Mizkis.

'Excuse me,' said Julius, with a comical look of shock on his face. 'I don't think I wanna hear any of that.'

'Oh, come on,' said Lopaka, nudging him in the rib. 'I don't know if you've noticed or not, but a few of our Mizki ladies are growing up fast. It's kinda hard to miss. Besides, why does it bother you? Are you guys going out?'

'*What?!*' said Julius, now looking even more shocked. 'No way! She's like my sister, honestly. And I really don't need to picture any of her round bits in my mind, thank you very much.'

'So you *did* notice she's got round bits,' teased Lopaka, undeterred.

As Julius's face continued to grow redder and redder, he realised with horror that Morgana was presently walking towards them, laughing happily, with one arm around Siena's shoulders. Julius's eyes took on a mind of their own and gave the two girls a proper once-over. Embarrassed, as he had never been before, he suddenly stood up and scurried over to Faith and Skye, hoping that by the time he reached them his colour would be back to normal.

*

Later that night, as the Skirts headed along the promenade towards the mess hall, they were approached by Master Cress.

'Mizkis,' he said. 'The Grand Master has granted your request.'

Julius felt a wave of relief wash over him at that news.

'You shall report directly to me on this matter,' continued Cress. 'And, in case you haven't noticed yet, your next meeting with the Oracle will fall during your Spring Mission. You have until the 20th

161

of March to figure out the next location.' Cress bowed quickly, and then headed back towards his office.

'Jeepers,' said Julius, turning to the others. 'We only have thirteen days left.'

'We'll work it out,' said Faith. 'I'm sure of it. But not right now, please. I'm feeling Chan's workout effects right down to my pinky toes. That is, if I could feel my pinky toes.' With that, he left, whistling to himself as he hovered away, leaving the three of them standing there in awkward silence.

Julius looked at the others with a shrug of his shoulders. 'It's Faith. That was normal for him.'

*

In the days that followed, Julius found himself busier than ever. Between homework, making a record of each lesson in his diary and the occasional visit to the Hologram Palace for a quick fight with the Skirts, there was not much time for anything else. It was only when Professor King reminded the students that he needed their choices for the Spring Missions by the end of the week, that Julius realised how urgent it was to put their heads together and identify the next location, as that would obviously decide where they went for the break. So, on Tuesday the 15th of March, he rallied the others together to spend the evening working on the clue.

'Come on, guys,' said Skye. 'Let's go talk over some dinner. I'm starving and I think Felice has made *gnocchi con burro e salvia* tonight.'

'What, you speak Italian now?' asked Julius in amusement.

'Felice likes to speak it, and *I* like Felice,' explained Skye.

'Well, whatever this *con burro salivation* thing is you're talking about, it sounds yummy,' said Faith. 'Besides, I think better on a full stomach.'

Julius nodded in agreement. He was tired, but the afternoon's training had also left him rather famished. Plus, he needed to remind himself of the details of the last message because, with all the recent events, it had grown quite hazy in his memory. And so, after they had wolfed down the quite delicious gnocchi, Julius felt ready to absorb himself into a discussion about the riddle. First, though, they had to stop Skye refilling his plate for the fourth time.

'Honestly, you're going to explode if you don't stop,' said Julius. 'These things tend to expand once they hit your stomach.'

'I just have two left, and then I'm done,' said Skye, swallowing the last mouthful. 'Mom always told me that I have the metabolism of a hummingbird, and that's 100 times faster than an elephant's.'

'Yeah,' added Faith. 'And, by the look of things, I bet you ate the damn bird and the elephant too, just for good measure.'

Julius threw his head back and let out a burst of laughter, quickly followed by Faith and Morgana. Skye threw him a look of mock indignation, but couldn't keep a straight face for long.

'You're funny, Irishman,' said Skye, wiping a tear from the corner of his eye. 'I'll let you live another year.'

'Thank you, Oh Royal Bottomless Pitness. And now, if you've done eating, we should probably crack on with solving that clue.'

'Right, let's go to the garden,' said Morgana, standing up. 'It'll be quieter there.'

Julius brought his food tray back to the rack, grabbed a glass of fresh apple juice and headed for the oak tree, followed by the others.

163

Once they were all seated, they activated their PIPs and settled down to watch the recording.

'He left Artemis speechless when he told her, "Be my bride"; or so Sir Pierre believed when he found her gift, and sighed.' As the words faded into the night, Morgana pressed a spot on her holoscreen, activating a holographic keyboard.

'I need to take some notes,' she said sitting up properly. 'This is definitely the hardest one so far.'

'We need to figure out who these Artemis and Pierre characters are,' said Skye.

Julius activated the Zed personnel database. So far, all the clues had led to lunar locations and he strongly believed this one would turn out to be no exception to that. He typed the name "Pierre" into his keyboard and pressed enter. For a few seconds he watched as page upon page of information scrolled rapidly in front of his eyes. When a series of pictures sprung into view, he touched the screen to slow it down. Carefully, he scanned the names under each photo, all of men named Pierre who had either worked or studied on Zed at one point or another over the years, going back as far as the year 2620.

'I've got at least 300 Pierre's here,' said Julius. 'But without any point of reference they're quite useless to us. We need to narrow it down a bit.'

'And I've found no trace of a woman called Artemis,' added Faith.

'Guys, let's read the riddle properly,' said Skye. 'It looks to me like a guy called Pierre asked this Artemis to marry him, right? So, shouldn't we be searching for *a couple* with those names, rather than two separate people?'

'No,' answered Faith, squinting at his screen. 'Not Pierre.'

164

'What do you mean?' asked Morgana.

'Faith's right,' said Julius. '*Someone else* asked Artemis to marry him. Pierre is just the person who found her gift.'

'OK, well what's the gift then?' asked Skye.

'How about this: when you ask for someone's hand in marriage, normally you give them an engagement ring, right?' said Morgana. 'A ring with a stone in it.'

'So you're thinking that, for some reason, Pierre found Artemis's engagement ring here on Zed,' said Julius. 'This is mental. Surely the Oracle can't be expecting us to pry into the private life and history of every single Pierre that's ever passed through here.'

'OK then,' said Morgana, 'let's do a search with these names, within Zed, but *not* in the personnel files. Maybe we need to think outside the box a little.'

Julius shrugged his shoulders and activated the search engine on his PIP. He typed in "Artemis" and waited, not feeling overly optimistic about what the results would be. Sure enough, three pages of random information appeared, all containing the name. He ran his eyes over the main titles of the various articles, trying to spot anything that stuck out from the rest, which wasn't easy given that he wasn't exactly sure what he was looking for. However, on the last results page, one particular heading caught his attention: something to do with ancient Greek mythology. Julius suddenly became very alert. He was already well aware that Artemis was a Greek name, thanks to his passion for Earth history, which had started when he was just a young child. His father, being a bit of a fanatic himself, had taken Julius to visit a different museum each weekend, and explained to his son how the story of Earth's people was passed on through what they left behind. Rory's enthusiasm had affected him

165

so much that, as soon as Michael was old enough to walk, Julius had insisted that he come along on their little field trips too. For his seventh birthday, his dad had given him a book of stories about ancient Greece and its gods, which he had read over and over again.

'I know who Artemis is,' he announced to the others, with a hint of satisfaction in his voice. 'We're sitting on it.'

'What?' said Skye, looking puzzled.

'It's the moon,' explained Julius. 'In Greek mythology, Artemis is the goddess of the moon, among other things.'

'Get outta here,' said Faith.

'I'm serious. The Romans called her Diana, and she also was the goddess of the moon. Besides, it doesn't look like there's ever been any actual person with that name in the whole history of Zed,' finished Julius.

'How can someone propose to a goddess?' asked Skye.

'And how can someone propose to the moon?' added Faith.

Julius shook his head. 'I'm not sure, but that's my best guess.'

'OK,' said Morgana. 'Let's run with it. If the Oracle used Artemis as a nickname for the moon, then this Pierre guy is somehow linked to it. Not to Zed, but the moon itself. Let's see if we can find a link in the database within the history of the moon.'

Julius lay down next to Faith and let him do the searching. Faith's right hand moved quickly over the holoscreen, selecting pages and moving icons in and out of view with quick swipes of his fingers.

'Hold it!' cried Faith, suddenly.

Julius sat up, his gaze drawn to the article that his friend had enlarged on the screen.

'Pierre Gassendi,' said Faith, with a broad smile. 'He's a French chap who named a crater here on the moon, called ... well, called *Gassendi*.'

'Guys, have a look at this picture of the crater,' said Julius excitedly.

Morgana and Skye crawled quickly over beside them and peered at the screen.

'It's the engagement ring!' gasped Morgana. 'Read what it says, Faith.'

'"Gassendi – named after Pierre Gassendi, French astronomer, 1592-1655. Large lunar crater at the northern edge of the Sea of Moisture. From above, the crater resembles a *diamond ring*. Gassendi is currently linked to the Zed Lunar Perimeter via a subway system. Gassendi has been an active mineral research facility since the construction of Zed."'

'So it was a meteorite that married Artemis,' said Skye. 'Go figure.'

'Exactly,' said Morgana. 'It gave her a precious *gift* and, centuries later, Pierre discovered the crater, which was eventually named after him. I think we've got it.'

'Makes sense to me,' said Faith. 'Let's run it by Cress though, and see what he reckons. We'll need to check if we're actually allowed to spend the Spring Mission in Gassendi.'

It was getting late, so they decided it was best to leave it until the next day. It was agreed that Julius would go see Cress during their lunch break. As he walked back to his room, Julius felt a deep sense of satisfaction spreading through him. Solving the riddles was pleasing enough, and knowing that they had the blessing of the Tijaran Grand Master was a great relief on top of that. Despite this, there was a part of him that couldn't quite understand why Freja was actually allowing them to continue with the hunt, especially now that Red Cap had made a comeback. Still, more than anything, he

167

was determined to repay the trust that Freja had shown in him and reach the final Oracle. And if Red Cap decided to get in the way, he would just deal with him too.

*

The following day, Julius wanted to catch Cress before he went for lunch so, straight after his Draw class, he hurried to the Master's office. Now, standing outside, he knocked on the door and waited.

'Come in,' he heard a muffled voice say, and the door slid open.

Julius stepped in and bowed.

'McCoy, have a seat,' said Cress, beckoning to a chair in front of his desk.

'Thank you, sir.'

'I take it you solved the riddle.'

'We think so, sir. The location of the next Oracle is in Gassendi.'

Cress raised an eyebrow, looking surprised. He then tapped a space on the holoscreen set into his desk, which opened up a document. With the tip of his finger, he slid it across to Julius.

Julius dragged the virtual document towards him and rotated it so it was facing the right way up. He realised immediately that it was a list of locations on the moon: Gassendi was the first name on it.

'You mean you figured the same thing, sir?' asked Julius, his eyes growing wide.

'Well ... naturally, we did a little research of our own,' explained Cress. 'The Grand Master loves a puzzle, you see. Gassendi was at the top of both of our lists. So, with yours, that makes three exact same guesses. I think we can safely assume it must be where the next Oracle will appear.'

Julius nodded, feeling quite pleased that they had all arrived at the same conclusion.

'Speak to Professor King about the Spring Mission. You will sign up to join the Gassendi crew. And, if any of your fellow students should ask, you're going there to study up close exactly how a mineral research facility works. We don't need a crowd following you. Understood?'

'Yes, sir.'

'You may go now,' concluded Cress, bowing his head briefly.

Julius bowed back, stood and left the room with a smile on his face. All in all, things were falling into place very nicely.

*

On Sunday the 20th of March, Julius and the rest of his classmates queued outside Professor King's office at midday. The Mizkis had been given a list of potential destinations that Friday and told to carefully examine all missions before deciding. Julius knew that, from the following year, their subjects would become much more specialised, in line with the specific career they would choose for themselves. This mission then, together with the Summer Camp, was vitally important because it would provide them with a taste of what was to come. Obviously this was not the case for Julius, though, seeing as the choice had been made for him once they had figured out the Oracle's clue. Not that he was complaining – after all, he was already pretty sure what he wanted to be once he left the Academy.

He glanced at his friends, who were lined up in front of him. The four of them must have looked rather out of place in that queue. It seemed that they were the only ones who were quietly waiting to be called, while all around them the rest of the Mizkis were noisily exchanging last minute information in the loudest possible manner.

'Morgana, finally!' cried Siena Migliori, pushing her way over to them.

'Hey, Siena – everything all right?' said Morgana.

'Yeah, all good. Except, I can't decide where to go this spring. What are you doing?'

'Errr ... mineral research facility of some sort ... boring really.'

'What? I thought you'd want to go to Flight School or something. Anyway, what about you guys?' she asked, turning to the boys.

'Same,' answered Julius, looking distractedly at his feet.

'Yeah, we're going there too,' said Skye, waving his thumb at himself and Faith.

'Well, where is this hot spot then?'

'It's called Gassendi,' answered Morgana. 'I'm not sure you'd like it.'

'Morgana Ruthier, is there something you're not telling me?' said Siena, eyeing her suspiciously.

'No, no! Honest. It's just that we ...'

'We've been given detention,' whispered Faith, hoping she would buy the lie. 'Please don't tell anyone.'

'*Again?*' said Siena, with a smile. 'OK. I'm not even gonna ask.'

'Sorry,' continued Morgana. 'But this place is *really* dull and just outside the perimeter.'

'Yeah,' added Julius. 'We don't even get to leave orbit. I don't think you'd like it.'

'I suppose,' said Siena, looking down at the list she was holding in her hands.

Julius watched as she inspected the document, holding his breath. In the meantime, the queue was slowly moving forward, and Morgana was trying her best to recommend other "nice places" to her. Eventually, they arrived at the desk, where Professor King was making the bookings.

Siena marched over ahead of them. 'Five for Gassendi, please,' she said with a triumphant smile. 'I'd rather be bored with you lot than be by myself.'

'*Five for Gassendi?*' asked Professor King, furrowing his brow and looking at her in surprise. 'I didn't even know Gassendi was on the list. Why on earth would you want to spend two weeks there? I thought you lot were more the pilot or fighter types; not the artsy ones!'

Julius looked at the others, quite at a loss for words. He had hoped that Cress would inform the Professor in advance, but that was clearly not the case. And what exactly did King mean by "*artsy*"?

'Sir,' said Faith, 'we decided that, before we completely rule out a career in a lab, we should really experience it first.'

Professor King stared at him, looking entirely unconvinced. 'I see. So, what's the *real* reason?'

'They got detention, and I'm accompanying them out of the goodness of my heart,' whispered Siena, leaning in close to the desk.

'Ah!' said King, raising his left hand. 'Say no more. Five tickets for Gassendi coming right up!'

*

Over the course of the next four weeks, Julius poured over the schematics of Gassendi every day, hoping to identify a likely place where the Oracle would make her appearance. However, without physically being there, this was easier said than done, so in the end he was forced to leave it be until he actually got there. The time couldn't pass quickly enough though, he and the rest of the Skirts were so distracted by the anticipation of what the final Oracle would reveal to them. They were so excited that they didn't even remember to think about what they would actually be doing during their mission.

Unfortunately for them, Master Cress had not forgotten about their *real* detention – the one they were due for trespassing on Mr. Rossini's property. It turned out to be working shifts in the barber shop, by way of punishment. They were to spend three full weekends as apprentices for the barber, who was extremely happy to receive the extra help. Master Cress had not mentioned the genuine reason for their detention to Mr. Rossini – an omission that Julius and the others were relieved about. After all, they had grown quite fond of the barber, and so it would have been a shame to lose his friendship.

Eventually, the day of their departure finally arrived. Julius eagerly packed his rucksack and remembered for a moment what he had been doing the previous year.

'*At least this year I won't have to get up at a silly hour on my birthday,*' he thought happily to himself.

JULIUS'S WORST FEAR

'This train is really something,' said Faith, sounding completely awestruck.

'It sure is,' replied Morgana in a similar tone.

Julius threw a glance at Skye and said, 'Here we go again.'

Watching Morgana and Faith slaver over the latest technology was something that Julius and Skye had grown used to and, judging by the knowing smile on Siena's lips, it must have been normal for her too.

Currently, they were sitting on the shuttle to Gassendi, waiting patiently to depart. The seats themselves were very comfortable, furnished as they were in supple leather. There were six of the chairs in total, set side by side in two rows of three each. These were fixed onto a clear, glass platform beneath their feet. Skye and Siena were to Julius's right; Morgana and Faith behind him. They had been told that the trip wouldn't take long at all but, according to Cress, it was a ride worthy of the Hologram Palace. Now, as Julius sat taking note of how there seemed to be no cabin enclosing the train, no tracks on the floor and only the entrance to a well lit tunnel stretching out into the distance in front of them, he wondered if maybe it was time to get a little worried.

'You should have seen Morgana's face last year, the first time she saw her dorm room,' said Siena to Julius. 'I thought she was going to short-circuit the entire floor, the way she kept pushing every button in the room.'

Julius grinned and nodded his head – he could imagine her expression well enough. To be fair, though, this was a remarkable train, entirely different to the Intra-Rail System they normally used. In fact, so far, *everything* was different about this Spring Mission. Last year, there had been the threat of the Arneshians, which had forced the Zed Grand Masters into sending all junior Mizkis to the colonies for their missions. Not that any of them had ever actually left in the first place, given how all hell had broken loose as soon as they had reached the Tijaran dock.

'*Well,*' thought Julius, '*I'll be seeing somewhere new this time.*'

'Seatbelt check, Mizkis!' an operator called out from the platform to his left, making Julius jump a little.

'Yessir!' shouted Morgana enthusiastically.

'Can you make it go fast, please?' pleaded Faith.

'Not sure you'd like that, kid,' answered the operator, a burly man who had the appearance of someone who would rather be on holiday somewhere with actual sunshine.

'Just this once,' implored Morgana.

'Don't do it on my account,' added Skye, turning to the man and shaking his head vigorously.

The operator sniffed and half-smiled. 'Don't you worry kids, this thing will go fast enough, so you'd better buckle up.' With that, he wandered off back to the control station.

Julius gulped, quickly tightened his seatbelt and gripped the armrests of his seat. As he breathed in, the surface beneath his feet began to vibrate and they lifted slowly into the air, until the train was centred in line with the middle of the tunnel entrance. They hovered there for a minute, while an electromagnetic field began to form around their seats, starting from the bottom of the vehicle, spreading to either side and in front of them, and finally up over their heads, creating a cocoon of sorts. As the blue energy threads uncoiled around them, Julius felt every hair on his body stand to attention. At the same time, their seats started to tilt slowly back.

'This is amazing!' cried Morgana.

'I know! Me heart might explode!' added Faith.

Julius had just started to turn around to say something to the two weirdoes behind him, when the train suddenly shot off. The acceleration was so strong that he was slammed straight back into his seat.

'WAAAHHH!' he shouted, unable to manage anything else. This was accompanied by a surround-sound chorus of screams from his own row and some joyful hollering from the back.

Julius couldn't see very much, save for flashing lines of white light streaming past his head. He felt as if he was trapped inside a bolt of lightning, which had somehow been harnessed and funnelled into an energy conduit. Sharp bends and twists flashed past him at a pace more appropriate to a ship at warp speed than to a public transport vehicle. He was starting to regret the eight pancakes he had wolfed down that morning.

Mercifully, the train began to slow and gradually came to a halt, easing to a complete stop beside a long platform to their right. The energy bubble around them made a static, crackling noise and faded away. Julius unbuckled his seatbelt and turned to the others feeling that, if his eyes got any wider, they would pop like two tiny balloons.

Every hair on their heads was standing on end, and tiny sparks of static were fizzing all about them.

'Um Skye, you look a bit green,' said Julius, eyeing his friend suspiciously.

On cue, Skye bent over and threw up between his knees.

'Aah, man!' cried Julius, lifting his legs as quickly as he could.

Siena fiddled desperately with her seatbelt buckle and only just managed to get free and escape the tiny, spreading pool of ooze. Morgana followed suit but, as she leapt out onto the platform, her legs wobbled and she stumbled on her feet, landing unceremoniously in a heap on the floor. Faith had quite simply passed out where he sat. It took three security officers to drag the five of them out of the train station and into their rooms, where they lay in embarrassed silence for a while.

When Julius felt steady enough to stand without holding on to the bed, he tottered over to a large glass desk in one corner of the room and sat down on the small chair in front of it. A bottle of water and a tray of glasses had been placed there. Julius gratefully filled one of the tumblers to the brim and gulped back several mouthfuls.

The living quarters were designed in much the same way as their dorm rooms back on Zed, except that they were quite a bit larger, so more people could fit inside. There were four beds in total. Faith and Skye lay sprawled out on two of them nearest to Julius's bed, which was set next to the far right wall.

'Wha ... where am I?' groaned Faith from his bed.

'You passed out on the train, which you deserve; and that there is your new bed for the next two weeks, which you *don't* deserve, quite frankly,' answered Julius.

'I can't help it that I got excited about the ride. I thought it was gonna be fun,' groaned Faith feebly.

'I'm *walking* back to Tijara. Never again,' groaned Skye, carefully sitting up in his bed.

'Bleah!' said Julius, pulling a face. 'I can smell your breath from here. Brush your teeth, man. It's the least you can do, seeing how you almost puke-washed my boots before, *and* Siena's.'

'Oh man. I forgot about that. That's *so* embarrassing.'

'Yeah, but it could have been worse,' replied Julius, who was beginning to feel a little sorry for Skye now.

'How? My star-rep is officially ruined.'

'Julius is right,' said Faith, hovering over to the table, swaying a little as he went. 'You could have thrown up on yourself; or on *her*; or peed your pants *and* thrown up; or all of the above.'

'Now that you put it that way, I guess ...'

At that moment, there was a knock at the door.

'Come in,' said Julius.

Morgana walked into the room, still looking a little pale. 'Not a word, please.'

'Yeah, it's better that way,' answered Julius, pouring her a glass of water.

'Siena is resting, so I figured now's a good time to have a talk about the Oracle.'

Julius nodded and activated the desk computer. As soon as the menu lit up on the glass surface, he searched for a map of Gassendi and opened the file. As seen from above, the research facility created a figure of eight, with the upper circle proportionally much smaller than the lower one.

'Just like an engagement ring,' commented Morgana.

The entire building was enclosed within a metal dome and each section was conjoined by long tunnels. The sleeping quarters were in the eastern portion of Gassendi's main body.

'We'll need to go there and try to find the exact location,' said Morgana. 'We can't do it now though. We're supposed to meet the head of the facility, Ms Davies, to get our duties for the mission, and we're already late as it is.'

'They won't mind us exploring Gassendi, surely,' said Faith.

'Yeah, but Siena will be with us,' said Skye.

'A little telepathy goes a long way,' said Julius.

'All right then,' said Morgana, 'but we need to do it sooner rather than later. We only have two days left till the Oracle's message.'

They all nodded in agreement. Morgana hurried off to fetch Siena and, together with the boys, they headed to Ms Davies's office. Julius was getting quite curious as to exactly what kind of research went on in Gassendi. All he knew was that they mined moon rocks for one purpose or another.

*

'Welcome to Gassendi, darlings!'

The tall, elegant lady who met them as they entered the office caught them all off guard with her casually exuberant greeting. She opened her arms wide and said, 'Please, sit down and be my guests.'

Julius couldn't help but smile. Almost everyone had manners here, but she seemed to be a step beyond that. With her posh English accent, long blonde hair and sophisticated gestures, she reminded him more of a movie diva than a Zed teacher.

She perched herself on the desk and leaned on one arm, legs

crossed, her right foot dangling freely. 'I have to confess, I am surprised by your presence here. For years, not even one student has chosen Gassendi. Now I have *five*. I was starting to worry about my lab. Why, without any new blood to replace us old cronies, there would be no future for mind-art.'

'Mind-art?' blurted out Faith. Then quickly he added, 'Beggin' your pardon, madam.'

'Of course,' she answered, passing a jewelled hand through her wavy hair. 'Gassendi is the artistic hub of Zed. And you, my darlings, are our new sculptors in the making.'

Julius's jaw dropped, and his wasn't the only one.

'Are you surprised that I should know of your hidden talents?' continued Ms Davies. 'Master Cress did say you were rather shy when it came to discussing your passion for mind-art.'

'Did he?' asked Julius.

'Indeed, and you know what else he told me?'

'Surprise us,' said Faith, looking worried.

'That it's someone's fourteenth birthday tomorrow!'

'You don't say,' answered Julius unenthusiastically.

'You'll have a fabulous surprise, darling,' she said, pointing at him.

'I can't wait.'

'Marvellous. Now, if you follow me, I shall give you the tour of our little cradle of inspiration.' She sprung lightly off the table and headed for the door, followed by five dubious faces.

Ms Davies led them along several illuminated corridors, calling their attention to the left and right every now and then – to the workshops, as she called them – where men and women in lab coats were staring at blocks of various sizes and moving around them as if they were performing some kind of tribal dance. Julius noticed a couple of men in blue overalls milling about as they moved along the corridor. They were young, well kept and definitely didn't appear to be artists.

'Ms Davies,' he said, catching up to her as she walked. 'Who are those official looking guys I saw? They didn't seem like they were teachers or anything.'

She stared down at him, looking a little confused, and then her face lit up as she realised who he was talking about. 'Oh, don't worry about them, dear. They're security guards sent over from Tijara a couple of days ago. There's another two about somewhere. I personally didn't see the need for them, but they insisted. I guess this whole dreadful business with the kidnappings has made them extra cautious, seeing as you all are going to be staying for a while.'

'Makes sense,' he said, trying to sound blasé. 'Can't hurt to be careful.'

'Quite right,' she said, nodding approvingly. 'A wise boy you are.'

After a few minutes, she stopped next to a small platform, where a middle-aged man was preparing to create something.

'Every working space,' she explained, accentuating each sentence with extravagant waves of her hands, 'is surrounded by protective force-fields, so that pieces of the lunar rock don't go zipping off about the room and harming others; this field can actually trap those pieces too. Mind-art requires years of practice, darlings, and *serious* fine-tuning of your White Arts. Essentially, what a regular sculptor would do with a hammer and chisel, you are doing with your minds. Even creating something as small as the petal on a rose requires carefully dosed energy bursts, or you risk blasting the whole thing off. What a tragedy that would be, hmm. Now, watch him.'

The artist on the platform was carefully studying the slab of rock. Julius took note of how the man's gaze intensified, and knew this was the same kind of focus someone would have when they were about to use their mind-skills. Suddenly, a small piece of rock flew off the slab and became trapped inside the force-field in front of where they were standing, making them all jump back in surprise. When Julius looked again, a perfectly sculpted nose had appeared, so elegant and fine that it looked almost real.

'Follow me, darlings,' said Ms Davies.

They resumed their tour, and Julius realised that they were now heading towards the smaller, upper portion of the building. As they approached a split in the corridor, Ms Davies took the path to the right.

'This is a *very* special section of Gassendi,' she explained. 'There is only one room here – the most important of them all.'

She stopped in front of a large doorway. Two sets of stairs fed off to either side of it, curving steadily upwards on an inward arc. They peered inside the room, which was a softly lit, empty area encased within a huge glass dome. Through it, they could see the stairs continuing their ascent, until they met to form what appeared to be a landing overlooking the glass bubble.

'Notice how wide the landing area is up there – that's where observers can stand – and how the stairs almost *embrace* the centre workspace,' said Ms Davies. 'In every generation, only two people are authorised to work using real lunar rock inside here. I, as the chief of Gassendi, am one of them.'

'I don't understand,' said Julius. 'What are the other workers using then?'

'It's a synthetic replica of the lunar rock. It's so similar that the untrained eye cannot tell the difference.'

'But why?' asked Skye.

'We can't very well keep drilling the Moon forever, my dear boy. Zed was built some 233 years ago. Imagine the size of *that* hole! Besides it keeps the artists on their toes; they know that only the greatest of them will claim the ultimate prize. This room is as precious as the diamond it represents.'

'Come again ... madam?' said Julius eagerly.

'Surely you know about Gassendi's shape, don't you, darlings? The engagement ring?'

They nodded.

'Well, this room is at the exact centre of the diamond ... if this really *was* a ring, that is.'

Julius's face lit up, and he threw a satisfied glance at the others.

'However, right on the opposite side of the main body, there is also a smaller circular room, inside a lesser crater; almost as if it were another diamond crowning Gassendi: a tiny, twin diamond.'

Julius's heart sank at those words. Surely, this is where the Oracle's clue was leading them, but which of the rooms was the right one? It was definitely going to complicate matters. It seemed odd to Julius that it hadn't been in the plans they had studied earlier. Perhaps they were out of date.

'Can we see the other one, please?' asked Faith.

'Sure,' answered Ms Davies, looking a little surprised. 'There isn't much to see really but, if you wish, you can even do your training in there.'

Julius's ears perked up. Knowing that the second room was not off limits to them certainly helped things. On the other hand, the presence of the two possible locations meant that they would undoubtedly need to split up.

'Come along then. Let's have a quick look at the other room. Time's marching on and we've so much to do, darling ones.' With that, she strode onwards and they hurried after her.

They moved along a corridor, which veered off right. It ended and met the beginning of another passageway, which led off to the left and then straight again. It was quite apparent that these walkways cut through the middle of the crater that Gassendi was situated within. Julius made a quick mental note of the route, which seemed simple enough, but he knew how easy it was to get lost in unfamiliar surroundings.

A few minutes later, they came to a doorway on their right. Ms Davies stopped and said, 'Well, there you go. As I said, not much to see.'

They looked inside. Indeed, the room was quite unremarkable, not much more than a circular space and nothing else.

'Happy?' she asked.

They nodded and followed as she led them back along the corridor. The next couple of hours were spent being introduced to the various artists who worked on Gassendi. They were largely eccentric types, but they all seemed friendly enough, and quite happy to see a new batch of students taking an interest in their craft. Ms Davies paired each of them with a sculptor, before taking them to the mess hall for lunch.

'Your training will start this afternoon, darlings,' she said. 'Your tutors will pick you up from here and take you to your work stations. As artists, we don't follow a strict working routine, but you are encouraged to train beyond your school hours. So, if you feel the need to sculpt at midnight, be my guests.'

'Great!' cried Morgana, her face lighting up. 'I mean, you never know when inspiration will strike you.'

'That's the spirit,' said Ms Davies with equal enthusiasm. 'I can feel it. You will do very well on Gassendi. Let me know if you need anything.' And, with that, she left them to their meal.

Julius wished they could talk freely about all the news they had just gathered but, with Siena sitting at their table, it wasn't possible and, given that their tutors were due to pick them up shortly, he knew that all planning would have to wait until the evening.

*

Julius's tutor was a man in his fifties, by the name of Walter Treat. Walter had spent the last thirty years of his life training in Gassendi, hoping that one day his luck would turn and he would create the ultimate masterwork that would gain him a place among the lunar rock sculptors.

'But don't feel sad for me if it doesn't, boy,' he said with a wink. 'I get to live in a fantastic place, doing the work I love, surrounded by likeminded people who always understand how I feel. And, believe me, that is a rare thing in life.'

Julius smiled, warming to Walter's optimism and passion for art. As someone who loved history, Julius had seen a few masterpieces in his life, and appreciated the intrinsic value of each of them. So, when he was placed in front of his first block of fake rock, there was no doubting that he would give it his best shot. To his surprise, the afternoon flew by, and it was only when Walter pointed out that it was past dinner time, that he stepped back to admire his sculpture. He crossed his arms and tilted his head to the right. Walter joined him and did likewise.

'I take it you meant to give it four legs, right?' asked Walter, delicately.

'Of course,' said Julius, trying to sound convincing.

'In that case, well done. You've just created your first four-legged, armless human being.'

Julius grinned, thanked Walter for his help and headed to the mess hall. Faith, Morgana and Skye were sitting at a table in the corner so he joined them.

'Hey, where's Siena?' he asked.

'She went to bed early,' answered Morgana. 'To tell you the truth, I'm tired too, but I waited for you so we can talk about the Oracle.'

Julius sat down. 'Sorry, I got caught up creating a masterpiece. I'll get something to eat later. Thanks for waiting though.'

'No prob,' said Morgana.

'Looks like Cress sent some reinforcements this time,' he said.

Morgana raised an eyebrow at him. 'What? Oh, the security guards. Yes. Do you think they'll complicate things?'

Julius shook his head. 'Don't think so. I'm sure they've been briefed to help us – don't see why they would stop us from doing what we came here to do.'

'Yeah,' agreed Faith. 'Sounds about right. Anyway, looks like this time it's pretty straightforward. We're free to roam around at any time, which means no need for sneaking about.'

'We've been *so* good at that up till now,' said Skye, sarcastically. 'Always seems to end in a detention. Seriously though, we'll have to split into two groups so we cover all possible areas.'

'Julius, how about you and Skye take the smaller diamond crater, on the other side, while Faith and I take the main one?'

'I don't know,' said Julius. 'Maybe I should take the main room, just in case.'

Morgana glared at him. 'In case of what? In case that's where she appears? You always get to do the fun part, Julius. Besides, there's a 50-50 chance. Knowing my luck, you'll get the room where the Oracle is.'

Julius looked at her and began to say something, then thought better of it. Morgana was a relaxed person but, when she made her mind up about something, she wasn't to be trifled with.

'OK, OK. Easy, tiger,' he said with a grin. 'Anyway, so I take it you and Siena are sharing a room?'

'Yes, but she normally falls asleep early. It won't be a problem coming out at night.'

'Then it's settled,' said Faith. 'We meet at eleven, here in the mess hall. Have your PIPs ready to record.'

'Tomorrow I'll let Master Cress know about our plan,' added Morgana. 'But right now, I'm off to bed.'

Satisfied now that they were organised, the boys were finally able to relax. Julius grabbed some food – grilled sole with a double helping of new potatoes – while Faith and Skye checked the latest Hologram Palace scores on their PIPs. They were suitably pleased that their records for team Flight and Combat were still unbeaten among the 2MJs, and chatted about possible tactics for future games until they could no longer keep their eyes open. Then they shuffled back to their bedroom and turned in for the night.

*

On the morning of his birthday, Julius woke up much earlier than

186

he would have liked, with the unsettled feeling of someone who has just had a particularly bad dream. He checked his PIP and saw that it was only seven in the morning.

'That's the worst present ever,' he mumbled.

He lay there, looking at the ceiling, a sense of anxiety gnawing at the pit of his stomach. He knew why, even as he recalled the details of his nightmare. In it, Red Cap had been on Gassendi, in one of the workshops. Julius had tried hard to recognise the room, but it kept eluding him. Red Cap was sculpting something, assisted by Walter Treat. Julius wanted to shout at his tutor to stay away, Red Cap wasn't a friend, but no sound escaped his lips and he was unable to move, because he was trapped inside one of the protective force-fields. Walter had given the Arneshian a hammer and a chisel to use on an authentic block of lunar rock. But, as Julius watched, he realised that the surface of it wasn't grey, as it should have been. Instead it was transparent, like glass.

Red Cap chipped away, bit by bit, until he had finished and proudly held out his creation in the palm of his hand, for Julius to see. It was a sphere, and inside it something was moving and wriggling about, like a tadpole. Red Cap looked up at Julius and said, 'It shall be mine.'

Julius tried to shout again, harder than before, but still nothing could be heard inside the containment field. He was powerless to do anything as Red Cap walked away, escorted by Walter. That was when he had woken up.

As far as he could recall, he had never had premonitions before, and he wasn't the type to get scared easily just because of a bad dream. Yet, the reality was that Red Cap really had been back in Zed and obviously knew what Julius and the others were up to. There

187

was every possibility that he would pop up in Gassendi too. They would have to be extra careful this time.

Since sleep was no longer an option, he decided to get up and treat himself to a nice breakfast. It was past eight o'clock when the others joined him, singing their usual tone deaf version of *Happy Birthday*, much to the amusement of the various staff members who were dotted about the mess hall. Ms Davies, true to her word, delivered his "fabulous present" as promised: permission to work inside Gassendi's special room for the day. He was overcome by a sudden, irrational fear that he would somehow end up stepping on the Oracle by mistake and making an almighty mess of the entire treasure hunt. He smiled nervously, aware of what a huge honour this was, and thanked her. She seemed convinced enough and left him to finish his breakfast.

Morgana, though, noticed his distress. When he told her what the problem was, she quickly reminded him that people had been working in the room for years already, so it was unlikely he could cause any damage that hadn't already been done. Besides, it would be a perfect opportunity to see if he could spot anything out of the ordinary about the place. It was enough to convince Julius to go in and he spent the day chipping away at a brand new slab of synthetic rock, or "listening to the block", as Walter liked to say. He sincerely believed that all blocks already contained an idea, which was a bit like their soul. By listening carefully to it, the sculptor was the *medium* who freed that idea, rather than its *creator*. This, he said, was the true path of an artist. By the looks of his sculpture at the end of the day, Julius wasn't entirely convinced that the idea he had just unleashed on the world made very much sense.

Later that evening, at dinner, Julius was treated to a lovely custard and nut birthday cake with fourteen candles, ordered especially by Morgana from Felice Buongustaio. But the *real* surprise of the day was that each of his friends had sculpted something just for him.

'Here,' said Siena, placing her present on the table in front of him. 'It's not great, but I know how you like history, so I made you a little replica of the *Duomo* in Siena, the cathedral of my city, in Italy.'

'Wow, this is really good,' said Julius turning the rock in his hands. 'It must have been difficult to make all those spires at the top. You did great. Thanks.'

Siena was visibly pleased when she sat down. Next, Skye and Faith stood up together.

'Ours is a linked present,' said Skye. 'I give you my home, Terra 3. May you be my guest one day.' He handed Julius an object resembling an elongated spinning top.

'Thanks man. I'd really like that,' answered Julius, gratefully accepting the gift. 'By the way, what's this flat tongue sticking out on the right?'

'That's my surfboard – the one my mum always threatens to chuck out of the airlock.'

'And here's me present,' said Faith. 'You'll be needing one of these if you're gonna go visit ol' mad goose Miller's home, that's for sure.'

Faith handed him a beautifully carved spaceship, in a model he did not recognise. It reminded him of a shuriken, the throwing stars that ninjas used, only the wings appeared to be much thinner than was normal. Julius could see that his friend had also done his best to create the entry hatches, the engines and the portholes.

'I invented it especially for you,' said Faith, with a hint of pride in his voice. 'When I've come up with a cool name for it, I'll let you know.'

Julius looked at him in amazement. 'Mate, you may be bonkers, but you're also a genius ... deep, deep down ... very deep down.'

'I'll take that as a compliment then!'

'And to complete the series,' said Morgana, stepping forward, 'here's your very own *Maneki Neko*!' She handed him a small, grey cat with an upright paw – a symbol of good luck in Japan.

'Good thinking, Morgana,' said Julius. 'Given the Red Cap situation, we could do with some luck, I think. Thanks.'

'What red cap?' asked Siena.

Julius stared blankly at her for a moment, silently cursing himself for the slip.

'Skye lost his cap,' said Faith, quickly.

'My favourite red one,' added Skye, trying to sound upset. 'It was Julius's fault, as usual.'

'I gave Julius the lucky charm, so he could find Skye's hat again,' finished Morgana

Siena looked quizzically at each of them in turn and Julius was convinced she hadn't bought any of it. Then her face relaxed and she turned to Morgana. 'Good thinking, girl.'

'By the way, McCoy,' said Skye, handing him a microchip, 'this is a voucher for Going Spare as well, since we'd agreed we would all use that shop for our birthday presents.'

'Thanks guys. This is just. Come on, let's have some cake.'

As he sat eating a slice, it dawned on him that his birthday had passed without any major crisis or disaster, as had happened the previous year. Tonight, he would chat to his parents from his room, as opposed to from the infirmary lounge, pleased to report that he was still in one piece. He smiled, happily enjoying the company of his friends, his earlier nightmare forgotten.

190

*

When the morning of the 20th of April finally arrived, everyone at the breakfast table, except Siena, felt slightly on edge. Julius knew they were all thinking about that evening, when the last Oracle would be revealed to them. He could see greyish wisps emanating from their heads, and knew it was a sign of the anxiety they were feeling. He looked down at his hands and saw a thin layer of the same colour covering his skin. He was glad that the others couldn't see this. Somehow, he felt that he needed to at least appear calm, despite how nervous he was. He had not shared his dream about Red Cap with them, as he didn't think it necessary to add any extra worries into the mix.

The best that he could do to make the day go by quickly was keep his mind occupied on his sculpting, and chatting to Walter a little in between. There was nothing more to plan – everyone knew their tasks. So, when at last eleven pm came, they met in the mess hall for a final chat over a cup of hot chocolate.

'Did you stroke the cat, Julius?' asked Skye, half seriously.

'Nope. Is that bad?'

'Basically it means that, if something happens to one of us, it's your fault,' said Faith.

'Thank you. Thank you kindly, sir,' said Julius bowing his head. 'I feel so much better now.'

'Don't mention it. I aim to please.'

Morgana looked at Faith with a raised eyebrow. 'I think it's time for us to leave.' And with that, she dragged him towards the exit.

Julius was smiling but, as they were about to disappear behind the corner, a sudden anxious thought hit him and he called after them. 'Faith, take care of Morgana, all right.'

'Roger,' he answered. 'Although it's more likely it'll be the other way around.'

Morgana hesitated for a minute, turned and looked curiously back at Julius. Then she smiled at him and disappeared around the corner.

'We should go too,' said Skye.

Julius nodded and together they headed towards the smaller crater. The corridors were eerily quiet at night, making Julius acutely aware of their footsteps echoing in the empty workshops. He was too used to the bustle of Satras, which never stopped, day or night, so he found this contrast a little unnerving. There was something a little odd about Gassendi too, beginning with the fact that it was not the kind of place one would expect to find in a military base.

'Why would Marcus Tijara want an artistic studio on Zed?'

'Kinda odd, isn't it?' said Skye. 'My dad says that, if you aren't that good a fighter, this is where you'll end up.'

'Seriously?'

'Nah. At least I don't think so. Besides, my tutor told me it was Clodagh Arnesh who got this place up and running, just a month before she was banned from the lunar perimeter.'

'That woman built an awful lot of Zed, it seems.'

'The girly stuff, you mean,' said Skye, sounding a little annoyed. 'Let's see, there's the ice cream parlour, the barber shop, the statue of the lovers and ... oh yes, an art club.'

'You're wrong, mate. You told me yourself she didn't become famous for her fluffy bunny collection.'

'Did I say that?'

192

'Well, not the bunny thing but, yes you did. You know just like I do that her brain was a match for Marcus Tijara himself.'

'I know, I know. But don't you go defending her because of the *good* stuff she did. She isn't a hero!'

'I wasn't ...'

'When you grow up on a space station like I did,' cut in Skye, 'the Arneshians aren't a topic for polite conversation, you know?'

'I know, but I didn't ...'

'Maybe on Earth it's easy to forget, but out there they're always on your mind. They could blast us all to smithereens without Earth, or Zed, even knowing it!'

Julius stopped in his tracks, waiting for Skye to finish. 'You done?' he asked.

'Yes,' he replied, lowering his voice. 'Sorry, I guess.'

'Never mind that. You're right, Skye. I have no idea what it feels like living out in the middle of the galaxy, far from Earth and Zed. But I'm here for the same reason you are: the Arneshians are traitors and as long as they want to control us, they are our enemies, no matter how clever they are or how many things they invent. I'm not defending Clodagh Arnesh, but you've got to know your enemies if you want to beat them.'

'Did Freja tell you that?'

'No. It was Master Isshin actually – before he went berserk and tried to kill us all last year.'

Skye smiled and held his right hand out to Julius. 'Ah man, I didn't mean to take it out on you. Sorry, but I can't stomach those traitors.'

Julius nodded and gripped his hand. He couldn't argue with that. 'Listen, last year you did a good job convincing me that the Arneshians couldn't even pee without us knowing about it, remember?' he said, lightly. 'What's with the sudden change of opinion?'

'That was before Zed nearly got wiped out last summer,' said Skye, starting to move again.

Julius took a few steps, and then stopped again suddenly. He cocked his head to the side, listening carefully.

'What's wrong,' whispered Skye. 'You hear something?'

Julius stood for a few seconds more and then began to walk again. 'I don't think so. Probably just the nerves.'

They walked the last few metres in silence and, when they reached their destination, they quickly checked that the area was clear. Once they were sure no one else was around, they sat down inside the small circular room, at opposite ends. Julius activated his PIP and made sure it was pointing towards the centre of the room, where he thought it most likely that the Oracle would appear, and Skye did likewise. Then, they waited in silence.

The minutes seemed to pass by way too slowly. Julius could feel himself getting tired, as his body began to relax, slumped against the wall. He looked over at Skye, who was also clearly growing sleepy, judging by the way his head was resting on his knees. Julius made an effort to focus and found his mind wandering back to his nightmare from the other night. His memory of the dream had been a little fuzzy when he had first woken up, he had been so disturbed by it, but now little details were coming into focus. He thought about the room he had been in, and the more he remembered, the more familiar the place seemed.

Suddenly, he sat bolt upright, his eyes widening in dismay as he was struck by the revelation that the room in the dream was indeed

Gassendi's special workshop – the heart of the main diamond. A feeling of deep dread crept over him, banishing any hint of sleep from his head. Was he waiting in the wrong place? And why had he let Morgana persuade him that she should go to the main room, which was much more likely to contain the Oracle and quite possibly the danger of Red Cap appearing there too? His unease was growing stronger by the minute and he stood up.

'Whatsa matter?' mumbled Skye, startled out of his nap.

'Something's not right,' said Julius.

'What? According to my watch we still have a minute to go.'

'I don't think it's *here*,' said Julius, pacing around the room. 'It's gotta be in the main room.'

'Relax. Morgana and Faith will get it.'

'It's not the Oracle I'm worried ab- '

Julius's words died in his throat as the sound of a scream pierced through the night.

'Morgana!' he shouted, and ran out of the room, closely followed by Skye. The sound of several sets of running footsteps echoed behind him. He turned his head, not breaking pace, and saw Skye just behind him, with two of the security guards further back.

'Come on!' shouted Julius.

Just then, another scream filled the air.

'That's Siena!' cried Skye.

A brief thought flashed through Julius's mind: *'What's Siena doing with them?'* But he let it go – there was no time for that now.

Gassendi had appeared to be such a small compound the other day, but now it seemed to stretch endlessly ahead as they rushed frantically along the pathway. Julius bounced off the wall as he swerved around a bend, he was running so fast, all the while reaching out desperately with his mind to Morgana, but there was no answer – not even a hint of her thoughts.

As they turned the last corner and the door to the main workshop came into view, a cold shiver ran through Julius as he saw what was happening. An ominous figure, unmistakably that of Red Cap, was standing in the middle of the room with his back to the door. The two guards they had seen the other day were standing to either side of the door, looking in but not moving. Morgana, Siena and Faith were all immobilized, floating in midair at the far end of the room, their arms pressed against their sides as if they were bound by some invisible rope. Their fearful eyes followed Red Cap's every movement. Julius had only a few seconds to take all of this in. Had he had longer to stop and properly assess the situation, he might have hesitated. But right then, seeing them like that, he felt a bright rage surge through him.

'What are you doing?' he shouted at the guards as he drew closer. 'Get him!'

They turned and the one to his left shouted, 'McCoy, wait!'

But there was no waiting – he charged and leapt at Red Cap, aiming to grip hold of his back and pummel him with as many physical and mental blows as he could manage. But, instead of flying through the atmosphere as he should have, he stopped in midair, as if he had hit an invisible bed of jelly, and hung there, in the middle of the doorway.

Everything after that seemed to happen in slow motion. He tried frantically to move but every effort was in vain, as he remained trapped and powerless. He heard Skye's voice from the corridor behind him, but it sounded muffled and far away. Then it dawned on him: Red Cap had activated the protective force-field that the Gassendi artists used during their work, so preventing anyone from reaching him. That's why the guards hadn't rushed in, and Julius had leapt straight into the trap. He cursed inwardly as he hung suspended, forced to watch helplessly, exactly like in his nightmare.

Red Cap ignored him; his right hand was held out at his side, palm facing towards Faith and the girls. It was clear that, whatever he was doing, he was controlling their bonds and keeping them from intervening. The Oracle floated in front of Red Cap, delivering her message. Julius saw her lips moving but couldn't quite make out anything that was said. She finished, and his heart sank as he saw a small hole open up in the ground at her feet, and a little container rising up from within it. Red Cap leaned over and picked it up. His hand disappeared momentarily – Julius's view was blocked by Red Cap's back – and, when it appeared again, the container was gone.

Julius cried out in frustration. Red Cap, possibly attracted by the muffled noise, straightened up and half-turned, keeping his right hand pointed at the others. He edged towards Julius and drew his face close. Julius knew those despicable features far too well, the memory of them etched deeply into his mind. The cruel mouth; the harsh, square jaw line; most of all, the mocking eyes. The panic Julius had been feeling a moment ago subsided and violent anger flared up in him again. But there was nothing he could do to stop the Arneshian, and they both knew it.

'White Child, you're late,' said Red Cap, shaking his head like a disappointed parent. His voice was still slightly muffled but Julius could just about hear every word he said. Then his eyes shifted, focusing on something behind Julius. 'Too bad they can't help you.

Time to go now, but make sure you come and find me – we'll have a little party.'

Red Cap moved towards the rear of the room, where Morgana, Siena and Faith were still hanging like flies in a spider's web. Julius became aware that someone must have raised the alarm, as several of the teachers and the two security guards were trying to push through the force-field, then pulling away quickly as they realised it was impossible to do so. Out of the corners of his eyes, he could make out people standing on the two stairwells and the observation deck at the top, staring helplessly down at them.

'Stop him!' he tried to shout. 'Somebody! Help them!'

Red Cap lowered his right hand and the three hostages fell to the floor. Without waiting for them to stand, he scooped up Morgana and Siena, one under each arm. Tightening his grip on them, he lowered his head, as if lost in concentration. Faith leapt up and tried to rush at him but Red Cap kicked him – he flew back and landed in a heap. The girls looked pleadingly at Julius. Panic and fear were etched all over their faces, as they struggled frantically to get away from the Arneshian hologram, but there was nowhere to go. The last Julius saw of them was Morgana's terrified eyes staring at him. Then they vanished into thin air.

CLODAGH ARNESH

Julius's throat was burning. Dr Walliser had wrapped a Heal-O collar around his neck, to soothe his voice box, and told him not to speak for an hour. Faith and Skye were also sitting in Gassendi's infirmary, more for moral support than anything else, since neither of them had actually suffered any injuries during the incident. Both Grand Master Freja and Master Cress had arrived on the first transport to Gassendi, as soon as word had been sent to them of what had happened, along with the doctor.

'I'm done,' said the physician to Freja and Cress. 'The boys are fine, but a few hours' sleep will go a long way right now. I gave them something to help them relax.'

'Thank you, Doctor,' said the Grand Master. 'We will join you shortly.'

Dr Walliser bowed his head and left them alone in the room.

'Gentlemen,' said Freja. 'Losing two more students was not in our plans. We are deeply saddened by this and we have informed the girls' families. Be assured, none of you is to be held responsible for tonight's events.'

Julius looked up at Freja and, unable to speak, sent him a mind-message. '*Sir, we need to find them. We can't just stay here!*'

199

'Mr McCoy,' said Freja, nodding in Julius's direction, 'says we should begin our rescue mission now. We are in full agreement there.'

'We've already been briefed by the guards we sent to watch over you,' said Cress. 'Two of them were up on the viewing area, keeping watch but, when they tried to rush down to stop Red Cap, he activated the force-field. He must have overridden the control box somehow – he's a smart holo, certainly the smartest I've come across. No matter,' he continued, shaking his head. 'We must be smarter. We will begin by retrieving and examining the recordings from each of your PIPs, plus the footage from the surveillance cameras in the room. That will hopefully help us determine the best course of action.'

The boys nodded. The mood had lifted a fraction – it was a relief for them having the heads of Tijara there, taking charge of matters.

'However,' added Freja, 'while we do that, I must ask you to remain here until I call for you. You need some rest and there is nothing you can do in Tijara.'

'But, sir-' began Skye, standing up.

'Mr Miller, this is not a request. It is an order!' said Cress.

'Yes, sir,' answered Skye, backing down.

Julius stepped towards Freja. *'Please, sir,'* he told him. *'Don't keep us waiting too long. Morgana ... she ...'* He had to stop, as a wave of emotion threatened to overwhelm him.

Freja put his hand on Julius's shoulder. 'I know. We will do everything we can for the girls – we will not rest until we have them all back.' He turned on his heels and, followed by Cress, exited the room.

Julius looked at Faith and Skye. Even if he could speak, he didn't

200

know what to say and was suddenly feeling very tired. The shock of the night's events was hitting home hard now, leaving him quite unable to think of any clear plan.

'We all need some rest,' said Faith, gliding past in the direction of the door. He looked truly wretched.

Skye put his hand on Julius's arm and squeezed. 'We'll find them.'

Julius moved his head up and down a couple of times. Just then, he didn't want to think about anything – only forget his pain for a few hours in the arms of sleep. They trundled off to the dorm in silence.

*

In all, Julius managed a good eight hours of sleep, thanks to Dr Walliser's medicine. His voice was also back; his throat was a lot better and his mind felt much clearer. Of course, his first thought when he woke up was of Morgana. How would he be able to face Kaori or her parents, especially after the promise he had made to Mr Ruthier not too long ago? It was a sickening thought but, despite this, he felt strangely calm. *'We're going to find her!'* he said to himself, and he believed it. He had to.

An hour later, he met Skye in the mess hall. He was sitting at one of the tables, drinking a cup of coffee.

'Hey,' said Julius, sitting down.

'Your voice is back,' said Skye, pouring some coffee for him from the flask next to him.

'Yeah. Have you seen Faith?'

'He's right behind you,' answered Skye, looking over Julius's left shoulder.

Faith had just entered the hall. He hovered over and sat down at the table. He was still looking downcast.

'Are you all right?' asked Julius.

'I'm sorry, guys,' said Faith. 'It's all me fault. I should have stopped him. I should have seen him coming!'

'Faith, don't,' said Julius. 'I don't think any of us could have done better.'

'Yes, but I was there with them. I was supposed to protect them,' continued Faith, miserably.

Julius shook his head. 'Freja is right. It's not our fault. Let's just concentrate on finding her ... them.'

'You heard his order,' said Skye. 'We can't leave Gassendi.'

'Yes, but we *can* start our homework, right?' said Julius, tapping the PIP chip under his skin.

Faith nodded. 'I can pull up the CCTV footage from the room too. It shouldn't be too difficult to access it from here.'

'Great,' said Julius. 'Let's go to our room. I don't want to attract any more attention.'

'Sure,' said Faith. 'You know, it's strange we haven't heard anything from Ms Davies yet. I wonder what Freja told her about all of this.'

'That reminds me,' said Skye, standing up, 'she wants to see us, before we do anything else. She came by when you guys weren't here. I don't think she knows about the Oracle. As far as she knows, we were working late and the girls were just victims of the Zed kidnappers.'

They headed over to see her and indeed, when they entered her office, there was nothing in her behaviour to suggest that she knew any differently. Julius even concentrated on her aura, looking for any tell-tale wisps of colours that would indicate her being suspicious, but all seemed normal, save for a slightly grey wisp above her head that showed that she must have been quite upset about what had happened.

'I am so sorry, my darlings,' she said.

Julius noticed that her eyes were bloodshot.

'I feel responsible for what has happened, as you were all guests in my facility. Yet, as the Grand Master says, we cannot control fate itself. It seems he was right.'

'Madam,' said Faith. 'I know it may sound a strange request, but could we take a look at the footage from last night?'

Ms Davies looked at them for a few seconds before answering. 'I don't see why not. I already made a copy for the Grand Master yesterday. You can have one too.'

Faith thanked her, activated his PIP and moved closer to her desk. She pulled the file up from her desk computer, pinching it delicately between her fingers, and pushed it towards Faith – it floated in mid-air for a second before it got close enough to the PIP's receiver and was sucked into it like water down a drain.

'Thank you, madam,' said Faith, stepping back.

'You're welcome,' she replied. 'At the very least, this kidnapping has absolutely confirmed the involvement of the Arneshians.'

Julius looked quickly at Skye and Faith, then back at the teacher, putting on a puzzled expression. 'What do you mean ... madam?'

'Well, that holo with the funny red cap obviously worked for the Arneshians. He was talking to Clodagh Arnesh, after all.'

Julius gaped at her, suddenly feeling as if someone had just dropped a boulder into the pit of his stomach.

'What?' asked Skye.

Ms Davies looked at them in surprise. 'Clodagh Arnesh. You *have* heard about the founder of the Arneshian Empire, right?'

'We know who she is. I meant, was she there? Where?' asked Skye impatiently – he appeared to be so flabbergasted that he had completely forgotten about all protocol and formalities.

'Right in the centre of the room, my dear. Where else? It was only her holographic representation obviously. She *is* dead after all.'

Julius felt his whole body grow heavy and he slumped down onto one of the chairs in front of Ms Davies's desk. 'The lady in grey: the hologram – that was Clodagh Arnesh?'

'Of course! I know her face well. It was a young Clodagh though. I would say from right around the time she left Zed.'

'Thank you, Ms Davies,' said Faith, sounding rather shaken.

'That's quite all right. I'm not sure how much it will help though. You'll have to excuse me now, darlings. I have urgent matters I have to attend to. Incidentally, if you need the day off, I quite understand.'

*

'How thick can we possibly be?' said Skye, his face buried in his hands.

They had returned to their room in complete, astonished silence. The realisation of how big their oversight had been was just beginning to sink in.

'It was them from the start,' said Faith, who was hovering back and forth distractedly. 'The Oracle, the kidnappings, Red Cap, it was all the Arneshians. We've been played for fools.'

'Freja must have known,' said Skye, lifting his head up and shifting uncomfortably on his bed.

'Damn right he knew,' said Julius, drumming his fingers on the table. 'And so did Cress, but they didn't say anything. For some reason, they let us carry on believing that the Oracle had nothing to do with the Arneshians. Why?'

'You'll have to ask next time you see them,' said Skye, shrugging his shoulders. 'But, if Freja believes this hunt is worth finishing no matter the cost, he must reckon it can help us find the girls. You can be sure of that.'

'So what do we do with this tape?' asked Faith. 'We gonna take a look?'

'Sure,' said Julius. 'I want to know what she said.'

Faith switched on his PIP. He swiftly transferred both his recording and the CCTV footage into the desk computer. Once that was done, he plucked the virtual file from Ms Davies between his fingers and shifted it into the middle of the room. 'Computer, activate file. On screen,' he said. The tiny folder suddenly expanded and transformed into a holographic projection screen. Julius sat back in his chair and took a deep breath. Seeing Morgana like that again wasn't going to be easy.

When the video started, it was quickly apparent that the camera had been positioned just above the door, inside the glass dome, looking towards the centre of the room. Faith and Morgana were standing by the back wall, looking rather excited, with their PIPs activated. Suddenly, though, their expressions changed – fear and panic were written on their faces as two more figures came into view, and Morgana screamed - it chilled Julius's bones hearing it again. Red Cap was holding Siena in a headlock and, when he reached the middle of the room, he shoved her at Morgana, who just about managed to steady her. At the top of the image, the two guards emerged from the shadows on the viewing platform and ran down the stairs to the left, rushing to get to the entrance of the room.

Red Cap produced a controller of some sort and pointed it at the door. Immediately, the force-field sprung into life at the edges of the dome.

He turned around again, just in time to see Faith thrusting his right hand outwards, clearly preparing to hit Red Cap with a mind-blast. It was already too late though – as the holo lifted his right hand up, the three of them were lifted off the ground and bound by whatever energy-force the Arneshian was using.

'See, Faith,' whispered Julius, 'you did all you could.'

Faith looked down and didn't answer. Julius switched his attention back to the video, where Red Cap was standing in the centre of the room, with his back to the exit. 'Where's McCoy?' he said. 'You were all supposed to be here. Wasn't the clue clear enough for him? And who's this little eavesdropper?' He pointed his left hand at Siena.

'Kiss me metal skirt,' said Faith defiantly.

Red Cap sniffed derisively at him. 'No matter – I'll find a use for all of you, don't you worry.' Then he stepped back and waited.

When Clodagh Arnesh appeared a minute later, he bowed deeply. Julius looked closely at her, almost as if he was seeing her for the first time. There was no denying that she was an incredibly attractive woman but, where before that had seemed quite normal for a harmless Oracle, as they had believed her to be, now it didn't feel right at all. In fact, it seemed completely wrong to Julius that the person responsible for so much hurt, and two centuries of hostilities, should be so strikingly beautiful.

'Well met,' said Clodagh's smiling hologram, 'I am the last Oracle and I will grant you what you seek. To you who have found me and accompanied me on this journey, hear my words, for my time is short. On the exact date of my birthday, deliver my most precious

206

possession to the wandering heart of Ahriman. Remember, only the bravest can reach the end. Farewell, my bringer of life.'

There was a muffled noise from somewhere out of shot, and Faith, Morgana and Siena turned their heads to face a point slightly to the left of Red Cap. Julius knew that it must have been when he had become trapped in the force-field. Unperturbed, Red Cap picked up the Oracle's treasure. From the elevated angle of the camera, Julius was now able to see what the Arneshian holo had done with it: his hand disappeared inside his belly and then reappeared without it. That was when he had turned towards the door, where Julius was hovering out-of-shot, like an insect trapped in a drop of water.

'Stop the video, please,' said Julius. 'I don't want to see the rest.'

Faith did so immediately, and let out a deep sigh. 'Well, at least it picked up what the Oracle said, right?'

Julius leaned back in his chair and closed his eyes. He forced the image of Morgana's terrified face out of his mind for a moment and focused instead on Clodagh's words. 'When is this birthday of hers, then?'

'We can look it up, but I'm sure Freja will know that already,' said Faith, searching the database on the desk computer. 'Here it is. According to this record, she was born on the 15th of May at 20:37.'

'We have 24 days left then,' said Julius. 'I'm willing to bet that Freja will want us to finish the Spring Mission in Gassendi. Mind you, I feel horrible saying this, but I don't think I'm ready to face Kaori as it is.'

'Well,' said Skye, 'there would be nothing else for us to do until then anyway.'

'I wonder if the clue means that we have to go to Ahriman, as in the *Halls* of Ahriman,' said Faith, who was looking a bit worried.

'It's the only Ahriman I know of,' said Julius, who was also quite nervous at the thought of it. 'Although she did talk of the *wandering heart* of Ahriman. Maybe it's not there?'

'Guys, before you start researching,' said Skye, 'know this: everything to do with Ahriman is top secret. You'll find no information on anything related to it.'

'Do we know *anything* about the place?' asked Julius.

'Other than it's used to scare kids, not really,' said Skye. 'It belongs to the Arneshians, and they build ... things there, I know that much.'

'Me dad always said that, if you break the law, that's where they'll send you,' added Faith.

Julius had heard that one before, from his own dad but, given that he now knew it belonged to the enemy, he doubted very much that earthlings would ever really be sent there.

'Well,' said Faith, 'that pretty much ends our hunt and leaves us totally at the mercy of Freja. If he decides to leave us out of it, there's nothing we can do about it.'

As much as he hated to admit it, Julius knew that Faith was right. He couldn't see them being allowed to return to Tijara until the end of the mission, or Freja even necessarily calling to update them on the situation. All they could do was wait and talk to the Grand Master on their return. And, if Freja decided to leave them behind, they would just have to find another way.

*

The journey back was mercifully not as bad as their trip *to* Gassendi. Either the technicians had noticed the absence of the girls or they merely didn't want to deal with another pool of regurgitated

208

breakfast. Whichever it was, Julius was grateful for the smoother ride. Over the last few days, his mind had been running amok with visions of Morgana's family waiting for him on the Zed dock platform, dressed in full samurai garb, their katana swords at the ready. As he got off the transporter and entered the main dock area, he mentally prepared himself for a barrage of insults and accusatory stares. However, all he found was Kaori, sitting alone on a bench, looking completely crestfallen. He stopped in his tracks, not sure what to say or do. Faith and Skye patted him on the back and waited quietly behind him.

'We're here, mate,' said Skye.

Looking up and spotting them, Kaori jumped up and ran towards Julius, who braced himself for a blow. But, instead, she opened her arms and threw them around him, gripping him tight as a flood of tears gushed out of her. Julius stood there with his arms by his sides, and allowed himself to be hugged, surprised and relieved that she wasn't angry at him.

'It's not your fault, Julius,' she said, as her sobbing eased a little. She turned her face first to Faith, and then Skye, 'None of you.'

Julius sighed, as all his earlier anxiety melted away. Now, feeling slightly awkward, he managed to raise his hands to her shoulders, not quite sure whether he should stroke or pat them. In the end, he just rested his hands gently on them, waiting for her tears to stop.

'Come with me,' she said to them a minute later.

Julius exchanged a quick glance with the others, and they nodded. They followed her and hopped onto the Intra-Rail. As they reached Satras, Kaori told them to get off. The buzz of noise as the door opened was in stark contrast to the quiet environments of Gassendi that they had grown used to over the last few weeks. In his present state of mind, Julius didn't really appreciate it. Kaori led them along the path beside the lake, past the Hologram Palace, until they reached an opening in the lunar rock. Julius had noticed it before, but had never thought to check inside it. It was a small grotto, with four wooden benches facing what looked like an altar of sorts. On its surface someone had placed a small projector pointing upwards, so that the pictures of the girls who had been kidnapped were displayed above it. Morgana was portrayed wearing her kimono, in a picture that Julius recognised as being from last December's annual meal. Her smiling face was lit up by the trembling flames of several holographic candles. The amount of mementos and small items laid out there was a little overwhelming – there were cards and good luck charms of all varieties, from students and staff alike, spread all across the surface of the shrine.

'Mrs Mayflower started it,' explained Kaori, sitting down on the front bench. 'She called it "The Wall of Remembrance".'

Julius took a seat next to her, while Faith and Skye sat down on the bench behind them.

'I didn't even know this grotto existed,' said Julius, quietly.

'It's always been here, as far as I know,' said Kaori, 'but the memorial started after Sharon Dally was taken.'

Julius sat silently, lost in his thoughts for a moment. The grotto kept the outside noise of Satras muffled, almost as if its walls were soundproofed. He appreciated the peacefulness of the place, and was deeply touched looking at the signs of friendship left there by so many different people. 'I'm sorry, Kaori' he said quietly. 'If only- '

'Don't, Julius,' she replied instantly. 'I know you well enough to believe that everything you could have done, you did. My parents believe that too. What we need to concentrate on now is getting her back; getting them all back! Morgana's a strong girl – she'll hold on until we get there.'

Julius held her gaze. Kaori was right: there was no time for regret or guilt now. He would get her back, no matter what it took. Failure was not an option.

*

That night in the mess hall, each of the 2MJs came over in turn to where Julius, Skye and Faith were sitting, to show their support. Although they still had to keep the real reason for their presence in Gassendi a secret – the excuse that it had been a detention still seemed the best one at that stage – they did still answer a few questions about what had happened during the kidnapping.

'Man, that must have been scary,' said Lopaka afterwards, shaking his head. 'You guys could have been hurt.'

Julius nodded absently, but said nothing. The mood around the Academy was understandably muted. The usual banter and mealtime commotion was at a minimum. Recent events, especially coming after last year's attack, had made the students quite edgy. It seemed that there was no completely safe place on Zed anymore. The disappearance of Morgana and Siena had also left Evita Suarez and Jiao Yu without roommates, so Evita had moved in with Jiao for moral support. It was just until the girls were rescued and returned safely to Zed, they assured each other. Everyone held firm to that hope, despite their fears that they would never see the missing girls again.

'Julius,' said Barth quietly, once the majority of the Mizkis had left. 'You'll find a way to get them back, right?'

'I will,' he said. 'You can count on it.'

Barth smiled, looking reassured. 'We'll see them soon, then. I know you'll succeed.'

'Thanks Barth, but ...' He paused in midsentence as an image of Red Cap's leering smile flashed into his head.

'But?' asked Barth.

'Nothing,' said Julius, pushing the image out of his mind. 'We'll get them back – that's all there is to it.'

*

On Monday morning, all classes resumed as normal. Julius, Faith and Skye headed to their Shield lesson. As soon as all of the students had filtered into the classroom, Professor Morales called them to attention.

'Mizkis,' she said, 'I can't tell you how saddened I am by the disappearance of your classmates. This is a tough time for all of us. But I *can* tell you I have no doubt that our Grand Master will do everything in his power to get them back.

'In the meantime, though,' she continued, 'we will train twice as hard. Girls, it's no use pretending you aren't targets for the Arneshians now. Our advantage is that they seem to think you are *easy* targets. You are not! If they come for you, make sure you give them plenty of resons to regret it.'

Julius was heartened by the way the girls all nodded their heads firmly in agreement. It was obvious that they had been in need of words like this from a strong woman like Morales. In fact, they seemed to take her message a little too much to heart because, as soon as training began, they set about the boys as if they were Arneshians. The lesson proceeded at a ferocious pace, girls against

212

boys, except for Julius and Skye, who were set to work together, to compensate for the fact that the girls were now two short.

'Calm down!' cried Ferenc Orban, as the session neared its end. He had been paired up with Leanne Nord, a stout, blonde Canadian girl, and was presently trapped in a corner, kneeling under his shield, trying to fend off her increasingly fierce attacks.

'No! I have to train hard and you ... will ... not ... get ... me!' she said through gritted teeth, punctuating her words with frightening bursts of energy.

Immediately, Professor Morales had to step in and release the poor boy from his predicament. 'Excellent job, Ms Nord,' she said, leading Leanne away. 'You've got that move properly sussed out.'

'No nasty Arneshian's going to kidnap *me*,' she declared, scrunching her forehead and swatting her fringe away with one hand.

'Yeah, and no one's going to ask you out either,' added Skye, under his breath.

Julius kicked him on the shin, and Faith slapped his hand on Skye's mouth, but neither of them could restrain their grins either.

'Ouch,' complained Skye, stroking his leg.

'Shush – you deserved that,' said Julius, wryly.

'I think that's enough for today, Mizkis,' said Morales, who was standing at the head of the classroom. 'Well done, all of you. And remember, look out for each other, OK.'

As the students were packing up for lunch, Professor Morales received a call on her PIP. Julius was just gathering his things when he heard the teacher's voice in his head: '*McCoy, Miller and Shanigan – stay behind please.*' Startled, he looked up and noticed Faith and Skye doing the same.

Once the rest of the class had gone, Professor Morales called the three of them over. 'The Grand Master wishes to speak to you all now, in his office. Dismissed.'

They bowed and left the room. None of them said anything, but Julius sensed that they were all thinking the same thing: surely Freja was calling them in to reveal the plan for rescuing the girls. They were so full of anxious excitement that, by the time they reached the staff offices, they were practically running.

Julius knocked on Freja's office door and, once again, it was Master Cress who opened it to greet them. 'Come in, Mizkis. Go through – the Grand Master is waiting for you'

They headed into the main office, where Freja was sitting behind his desk. Three chairs were laid out in front of it. '*There should be four,*' thought Julius, and lowered his head as a knot formed in his throat.

'Did you watch the footage?' Freja asked, once the boys had bowed and seated themselves.

'Yes sir,' answered Faith. 'Ms Davies let us look at it.'

Julius looked at Freja directly. 'Permission to speak freely, sir.'

'Granted,' replied Freja.

'I take it there's a reason why we weren't informed of the true identity of the Oracle, sir.'

Skye shifted uncomfortably in his seat, and Faith elbowed Julius lightly. Evidently they didn't think it was appropriate to question the Grand Master in this manner.

'Does it bother you, Mr McCoy?' replied Freja, nothing in his voice indicating that he had taken the question as being impertinent. He held Julius's gaze, observing him in his usual calm manner. 'Or rather, would it have made any difference to the way you approached your hunt, had you known that Clodagh Arnesh herself had created it all and there was a good chance this was all linked to the kidnappings?'

Julius thought about it for a few seconds. 'I still wouldn't have backed down, but I also wouldn't have ...' He stopped, unable to finish.

'Wouldn't have what?' said Freja. 'Let Miss Ruthier come along? I believe that, Mr McCoy. I also believe, however, that Red Cap still has a lot of influence on your behaviour, to the point where you lose sight of logic and, of course, control of your mind-skills. Had you known that he had been sent by Queen Salgoria to oversee the kidnappings and to personally take care of the Oracle's hunt, wouldn't that have affected you?'

'Maybe, sir,' answered Julius, still looking at Freja directly. 'But, like you said, I wouldn't have put Morgana in harm's way either.'

'Mr McCoy, I thought you knew Miss Ruthier better than that,' answered Freja, raising an eyebrow. 'You would not have succeeded. Miss Ruthier is just as headstrong as you are when it comes to finishing a job. You cannot make those decisions for her.'

Julius didn't answer, but inside he knew that Freja was right. Morgana would never have let him go to Gassendi without her. She was a Skirt through and through, as she had demonstrated last year, when they had first challenged Red Cap and his cronies in the Zed hangar. He had tried to send her away then to get help and she had almost ripped his head off for even thinking of protecting her like that. So yes, Freja was definitely right: Morgana would have insisted on going with them, no matter what he had said.

'But *you* could have stopped her, sir!' said Julius, staring intently at the Grand Master. Beside him, he heard a sharp intake of air from Skye.

Freja sighed and sat back. 'Don't think that doesn't bother me, McCoy. But there was a lot I had to take into consideration. We already had two girls missing and it seemed that you four had stumbled onto possibly the only clue that might lead to their whereabouts. Certainly those Oracle messages weren't meant for you. If I had started interfering and sending members of staff instead, Red Cap might have figured out that we were onto him and seriously jeopardised the mission. Our advantage, I thought, was that he *didn't* know that you had told us about your *treasure* hunt.'

Freja stopped momentarily and looked at Cress, who was standing behind the boys. 'Of course, we had hoped that the guards we sent would be able to protect you. They were some of our finest men – but it seems none of us accounted for the force-field, or for Red Cap being one step ahead of us. We *won't* make that mistake again.'

'That's right,' said Cress. 'And now, Mizkis, let's move on to what we called you here to discuss. What did you make of the Oracle's last message?'

'Not much, sir,' answered Skye. 'We know that Clodagh's birthday is on the 15th of May at 20:37 and that whatever she gave to Red Cap has to be returned to her on that exact date. As far as the location is concerned, we're not too sure. Ahriman is an Arneshian facility and all information on it is classified, so surely you know more than we do about it, sir.'

'Thank you, Mr Miller,' said Master Cress. 'This is all correct, except for one particular. Clodagh mentioned "the *wandering* heart of Ahriman" and that is *not* within the Halls of Ahriman.'

'You know where that is, sir?' asked Julius, hopefully.

'We know far too well where that is,' answered Freja, gravely. 'I myself was there once. The wandering heart is *Angra Mainyu*.'

216

Realisation dawned in Julius's mind, and quickly gave way to cloying fear. He remembered the name from a conversation he had had with Freja the previous summer. He noticed that Skye's knuckles had turned white, his fists were so tightly clenched, and a dark, wispy cloud was seeping from the crown of his head.

'I don't understand,' said Faith. 'What's an Angry Mineyew?'

'Angra Mainyu,' said Julius, flatly. 'It's the Arneshian lab where they experimented on those kidnapped people years ago.'

'It's where they found Bastiaan Grant's body,' said Skye.

Faith slumped back in his chair.

'When we boarded Angra Mainyu,' continued Freja, 'we became aware that Salgoria's ultimate goal was to create a perfect being by mixing the DNA of a powerful Arneshian, like her, with that of a White Child.' As he said these last two words, Freja quickly switched his gaze from Julius to the other boys.

'They know,' said Julius, aware that the Grand Master was trying not to draw attention to the fact that Julius was just such a person. 'It was best that I told them everything.'

Freja nodded. 'So, of course, this is why she tried to kidnap Mr McCoy last year. As you are aware, that attempt failed, and Salgoria's plan it seems, took on an unexpected new shape.'

Freja got up and walked over to the window of his office, which overlooked the school entrance. There, he crossed his arms and stood silently. The three boys were barely aware that they had leaned forward in their chairs, eagerly waiting to hear what this new plan was.

'It was our initial decision,' said Freja, 'that you should have no part in the last mission aboard Angra Mainyu,' said Freja, still staring out the window. 'Although we are well aware of your abilities

217

and willingness to help, you are young and not even fully trained.'
Julius was about to say something, but Freja raised his right hand,
indicating for him to remain quiet. 'I said it *was* our initial decision,
Mr McCoy. You see, the last Oracle is preventing us from leaving
you behind.'

Julius looked at Skye and Faith, who appeared to be as confused
as he was.

' "*To you who have found me and accompanied me on this journey,
hear my words*",' said Freja, quoting Clodagh's message. '" *To you who
have found me.*"'

'I'm not sure I follow, sir,' said Julius.

'Well, it's that part of her message, plus a couple of other things.
When you first told me about the way the first Oracle scanned you
before she appeared, it made me think.'

'About what, sir?' said Skye.

'That kind of technology has been around for some time; the
retina scanners outside your rooms work on a similar basis. Except,
the one that you found doesn't seem to have been programmed to
identify any one particular person: it seems that it was more like a
tagging device – the molecular signature of whoever was there would
then have been stored in its memory banks. I'm guessing it's a way of
ensuring that the person who started the mission was the one there
at the end.'

'Wait a minute,' said Faith. 'Beggin' your pardon, sir, but none of
the other Oracles used scanners.'

'True,' said Freja. 'That's very observant of you Mr Shanigan;
except, they wouldn't need to. The three Oracles that followed must
have been programmed to activate at the assigned times once the
first Oracle delivered her message.'

'Why go to all that trouble though?' asked Julius. 'And how do we know the last Oracle will use a scanner too?'

The Grand Master moved back to his desk and sat down again. 'Think about it: if the last Oracle could be easily activated, the Arneshians surely would have found it before now. As we already know, they've been using Angra Mainyu, on and off, for some time. It follows that Clodagh must have put some safety measures in place to ensure that whoever was going to claim her prize would have to show their worth by jumping through a few hoops before that. Those were very specific clues too. They certainly weren't meant for you Mizkis.'

'If they weren't meant for us, sir,' said Faith, 'then why wasn't the scanner programmed to only respond to an Arneshian?'

Freja smiled enigmatically. 'We don't think it was meant exclusively for Arneshians either.'

'Then who?' said Julius.

'Ah,' said Freja, 'we're not a hundred percent sure yet. We've got an idea about that, but we have to check a few more things before we can say for sure. There's one other telling factor, which I'm sure you can guess, Mr McCoy. Something Red Cap said to you on Gassendi.'

Julius stared at him and then his eyes grew wide as he began to understand. 'He said I must come and find him. At first I thought he was just taunting me, but he was giving me a message, wasn't he? He knows that I ... we need to be there.'

Freja nodded his head. 'You were right the first time, Mr McCoy. *You* have to be there. In the Gassendi footage, Red Cap seemed upset by your absence. One of the first things he asked was where you were. When things went wrong, he grabbed Miss Ruthier because he couldn't get to you, knowing you would do everything in your power to get her back. It goes against my better judgement, but there is no alternative: you must go.'

'Wait a minute!' said Skye, standing up. 'What about us – Faith and I? We're not letting him go on his own.'

'Sit down, Mr Miller!' cut in Master Cress.

'Sorry, sir,' said Skye, obeying the command. 'But ...'

'But nothing,' Freja interrupted. 'There's no need for you to be there. The first Oracle only scanned Mr McCoy.'

'But there could have been other scanners, sir ...' argued Skye.

'Yeah, yeah – I'm sure I saw one of those things scanning us too,' chipped in Faith, unconvincingly.

'Please, sir,' said Julius. 'There *could* have been some other tagging device we didn't know about. Before the first Oracle appeared we saw more than one light in the cave. We can't afford to go all the way to Angra Mainyu without them and find out that they needed to be there too. Plus, remember when the Arneshians tried to invade us: I wouldn't have got anywhere without them – I need them.'

'That tells me more about you as a person than their *actual* need to be there, McCoy,' said Freja, sitting back in his chair and looking at Cress. For a minute, the boys sat in anxious silence. Then Freja sighed and sat forward. 'Very well.'

'Yes!' exclaimed Skye and Faith in unison, then quickly controlled themselves again.

'There's something else,' continued Freja. 'Since Red Cap now has Clodagh's gift, it means that we cannot finish this without him either.'

'Red Cap ...' said Julius, under his breath. 'Do you think he was there right from the start, sir?'

'Indeed,' said Freja. 'He was sent for the Oracle by Salgoria and it was only by a fortuitous chance that you four stumbled upon it during your game. I'm pretty sure he must have been there when you received the first message, even though you didn't see him. So he must have been following the clues and plotting to grab hold of you on Gassendi, Mr McCoy.'

'That means that Morgana is definitely still OK then, right?' said Julius. 'He won't harm her because he needs her as bait.'

Freja nodded. 'I think so but, more than that, I think all of the girls are still all right. Their kidnappings are definitely linked to this Oracle business.'

'Sir, what do you think Salgoria is up to?' asked Julius.

'All in good time, Mr McCoy,' replied Freja. 'We shall depart on the evening of the 14th of May. The Grand Masters of Sield and Tuala will also be onboard, as this matter concerns them greatly. There will be a briefing on the way, once we leave Zed. It's safer if you don't know too much at this stage.'

'Mizkis,' said Cress. 'I trust you understand the need for complete silence on this matter.'

They all nodded.

'Very well. You are dismissed,' said Cress, bowing his head.

Once outside the office, they walked along the promenade towards the mess hall.

'What do you think?' asked Julius. He was still quite wound up from everything that had been discussed – he felt a pressing need to clear his head and see what the others made of it all.

'Well, Freja obviously knows the score and has a plan,' said Faith. 'That *is* good news.'

'The *other* good news,' said Skye, 'is that we're going too.'

221

'Yeah,' said Julius. 'That is *great* news. And we're going in with all three Grand Masters, no less.'

'I wish Freja had told us something about the plan though,' said Faith. 'This way, we're left guessing for the next twelve days.'

Julius agreed with Faith, but unfortunately there was nothing any of them could do about it. He would just have to endure the anticipation as best he could. One thought in particular kept popping into his mind, though, no matter how hard he tried to restrain it. Last year, Freja had told him that the previous time they had boarded Angra Mainyu all they had found were notes and the bodies of the kidnapped victims, a fact that the Grand Master had been careful not to mention this time. '*Remember, they need Morgana. She'll be OK,*' he kept reassuring himself. But, even if that was the case, what about Siena and the other girls? There was no guarantee of their safety. All Julius could do, however, was hope that they weren't too late already.

*

To their relief, the days passed by mercifully quickly. Julius, Faith and Skye guessed that the other teachers must have been told what was happening by Freja because, in all of their lessons, the three of them had every possible defence and attack application drilled into their brains. None of the Professors had openly admitted as much to them, although Professor Chan had offered them extra classes to teach them several new katas, and Professor Beloi had offered them unlimited use of the labyrinth in the evenings, to help strengthen their mind-channels. They had willingly accepted and were not at all surprised when, during these extra classes, they were also joined by random members of staff. Thankfully, they had been discreet enough not to attract any unwanted attention from the other Mizkis. When Saturday the 14th arrived, Julius was pumped up and raring to go, like before a big game. He found it impossible to sit still and spent most of that morning pacing up and down in his room. Eventually, he was growing so impatient that he decided he needed to do *something*.

'I need to get out of here. I'm going to go to Satras,' he said to Skye, who had been working away on his computer and doing a good job of ignoring his restless friend.

'Yeah, good idea,' replied Skye. 'Let's take our stuff with us – no sense in coming back here before we leave.'

They quickly packed a few essentials into a couple of light backpacks, including their own Gauntlets, which Professor Morales had insisted they take with them. Fifteen minutes later, they were out the door, and stopped by Faith's room to fetch him. He had been tinkering away on his skirt, which Julius guessed was probably more to do with keeping himself occupied than making any real adjustments. En route, he typed out a message on his PIP and sent it to Kaori, asking her to meet him in the grotto. Although they had sworn to keep the mission secret, Julius had filled her in on what he knew a few days before. He figured she deserved that much and, besides, he knew she could be trusted not to talk about it with anyone else.

When they arrived at the grotto, Kaori was sitting waiting on the front bench. She turned around as they entered and smiled weakly at them.

'You look tired, Kaori,' said Julius.

'It'll all be over soon,' she replied. There was no uncertainty in her voice. 'When do you leave?'

'Shortly,' said Faith. 'We need to be at the docks in twenty minutes. Cress told us to board the ship before everyone else, just in case someone sees us and wonders what's going on.'

Julius opened his pack and pulled out the *Maneki Neko* that Morgana had made for him back in Gassendi. He walked over to the altar and placed it there, next to the other gifts.

'Don't forget to stroke it,' said Kaori.

Julius did so. Regardless of whether he believed in luck or not, it was still something that Morgana had given to him, and touching it made her feel a little nearer, somehow. Julius sat down next to Kaori, and Skye moved over to the altar. He placed something on it that Julius couldn't see, but he guessed that it must have been for Ife.

Faith had nothing to leave, but he did stop in front of the altar for a second and stroked the cat, lightly. 'I'll take the luck of the Irish, and the Japanese, just to be sure,' he said, turning to face them. 'Come on now – we need to go, or we're going to miss the flight.'

As they made to leave, Kaori hugged each of them in turn. 'Good luck, all of you,' she said, a single tear spilling down her right cheek. 'Thanks for being such good friends. Morgana couldn't have wished for more.'

Julius squeezed her hand quickly and then ducked out the opening of the grotto. Together, the three boys headed up to the Intra-Rail stop outside Satras. They were soon at the Zed docks, where a strangely subdued Captain Foster was waiting for them. He led the way towards the shuttle pod that would be taking them into orbit, where they would be rendezvousing with the ship that would be taking them to Angra Mainyu.

'Mizkis,' he said, as they were boarding. 'Good luck.'

They all bowed, grateful for the gesture. A few minutes later, the shuttle took off, leaving the Lunar Perimeter far behind.

'Nice,' said Faith some time later, staring wide eyed out of the porthole beside him. 'Check out our ride.'

Julius, who had been lost in his own thoughts, unstrapped his seatbelt and crossed over to where Faith was seated. He leaned and looked through the window. They were just coming into dock alongside a large spaceship. Its outer hull was pitch black, like the open space around it. Several small lights were fitted against its shell, marking the outline of the ship. It looked much like a Cougar, except many times bigger, but it still retained the flat, raindrop shape of the smaller, one-man version. Their shuttle floated smoothly in through a large rectangular opening at the back of the ship and came to rest beside a long platform within the dock. They hurried over to the shuttle exit, eager to get a proper look at the inside of the spaceship, the first proper naval vessel that any of them had ever been on.

The hatch opened and, as they stepped outside, they were greeted by a Zed officer: a tall, stocky man whose name badge read "John Hardy". He bowed as they stepped onto the platform. 'Gentlemen, welcome aboard the Ahura Mazda.'

THE LOVERS' SHADOW

The officer escorted them to their quarters, which he had informed them were located on the upper deck. While they were walking, they passed several officers in the long corridors of the ship. Like John Hardy, most were quite tall and looked like they were at least a good twenty years older than the boys. All of them carried the air of seasoned professionals, completely at ease with each other and their surroundings – Julius knew that they had most likely been out here in space for who knows how long. The Ahura Mazda was probably more like a home to them than wherever they had originally come from. Certainly, as they drew closer to the upper section of the ship, where the main crew lodgings were situated, Julius immediately noticed how each of the berths had been decorated with personal items and pictures.

They reached the end of the corridor and Hardy stopped in front of a door on the right wall. 'These are your quarters for the next two days. The mess hall is back the way we came. You can get your food there from 19:00 hours. The Grand Master wants to meet you at 20:00 hours. Don't be late.'

They bowed as he left, and stepped into the room. It was nothing glamorous – not much more than a cubicle with bunk beds on both sides and a small lavatory area at the back. Julius dumped his backpack on the floor next to the door and threw himself onto the lower left bed. He was suddenly feeling quite tired – it had been a long day and the adrenaline that had made him feel like a caged tiger earlier on had faded away. The worries he had been carrying with him ever since Morgana's kidnapping were also starting to take their toll. It seemed that Faith and Skye were in need of some downtime too, because they both followed suit – Faith took the lower bunk opposite Julius and Skye the one above it – and were soon navigating their PIPs in silence.

Without realising it, Julius dozed off and was woken an hour later by Skye. 'Come on – I'm so hungry I could eat darkness. Let's get something from the mess hall before our meeting.'

Julius sprang up. He felt better – well rested. 'I really must have needed that,' he said, washing his face in the small sink at the back of the room.

'I bet the food here isn't as good as in Tijara,' said Skye, gloomily.

'Here we go again,' said Faith, pushing him out of the room. 'If it isn't girls, it's food. If it isn't food, it's girls, and so on and on and on, forever and ever and ever and ever ...'

Julius chuckled and, closing the door behind him, followed them down the corridor. They found their way to the canteen easily enough. As they entered, every one of the officers turned towards them, making the boys stop dead in their tracks. Julius looked around self-consciously.

'Who the heck are these guys?' growled a man, sitting at one of the long tables to their right. He had a long, jagged scar running along his left cheek.

'Don't you know – that's for that babysitting job you applied for,' answered a curly-haired man to his right, which was greeted by a smattering of laughter.

'What's *he* wearing?' continued the first one, pointing his fork at Faith.

'Your sister's Sunday best, that's what I'm wearing,' answered Faith indignantly.

The scar-faced man's eyes grew wide, and a threatening hush fell over the room. Then he let out a booming laugh, quickly followed by everyone else in the room. Julius breathed a sigh of relief – for one instant he had been sure they weren't going to make it out of there alive.

'Knock it off, Kelly,' said a female officer, who was sitting next to him.

'All right, all right,' he said, wiping a tear from his eye. 'Just having a laugh, Elian.'

The woman named Elian motioned for the boys to come over to the table. 'Sorry about that,' she said. 'They're a good bunch, most of the time.'

'Hi,' said Julius, shaking her hand. 'For a moment, I thought we were on the wrong ship.'

'Don't worry about me,' said Faith. 'I can hold me own.'

'I noticed,' she said, grinning. 'Good for you.'

'Hi, I'm Skye,' he said, stepping forward. Maybe it was because of the surprisingly deep voice that came out of him, but Julius and Faith whirled around as if they were expecting to see someone else entirely. When all they saw standing there was the one and only Mr Skye Miller, they realised that their friend had no doubt just developed another one of his crushes. This was further backed up by the way he was suavely cocking his left eyebrow.

'Hello, handsome,' said Elian, with a smile, evidently playing along. 'Call me back in a few years' time, will you?'

'I'm already counting the days,' he replied in the same low drawl.

Elian laughed. 'Grab some food and join us,' she said.

The boys headed for the food counter, where a selection of reasonably appetising platters had been laid out.

'Skye,' said Julius, 'what happened to you when you were young?'

'She is *so* hot,' cooed Skye, ignoring him.

'Forget it, man,' said Faith to Julius. 'He's possessed by his own hormones. When they take over like this, you just gotta wait till it's over.'

Julius shook his head, and patted Skye on his shoulder as he scooped a helping of mashed potatoes onto his plate. 'I won't tell Morales, I promise.'

After grabbing a tray of food each, they returned to the table and sat down opposite Elian and Kelly, who properly introduced himself. 'Welcome aboard, Mizkis. No hard feelings, I hope.'

'I'm sorry to hear about Morgana,' said Elian, brushing a lock of her long, chestnut hair behind her ear.

Julius looked up in surprise. 'Do you know her?'

'I met her last summer, in the Canis Major. I was one of the instructors at the apprentice flying camp. I've never seen talent like that in someone so young before.'

'Yeah, she's the best,' Julius said.

'We'll get them all back,' said Kelly, quietly. 'You'll see.'

Julius stared for a few seconds at the man as he slowly ate his food. The scar extended from his left jaw up to his cheekbone. Whatever had caused the injury, it had missed his eye by no more than half an inch. Surprisingly, it made Julius feel more at ease, knowing that he was clearly in the presence of someone who had seen some proper action before, and so was more likely to know what to do if things turned bad. And, judging by the number of officers onboard, it seemed that a bad scenario was definitely on the menu.

For the next while, their conversation steered away from the mission ahead. It was as if they had made a silent agreement to keep the chat light and give themselves a chance to relax before the meeting. At 19:50, Cress arrived in the mess hall.

'First Officer on deck!' cried Kelly, standing swiftly to attention.

Julius, Faith and Skye quickly did likewise and bowed to the Tijaran Master.

'At ease,' said Cress, bowing back to them. 'Mizkis, if you are done we should make our way to the ready room.'

The boys immediately moved over to the door and waited for Cress.

'Second Officer Kelly, your presence is also requested.'

'Yes, sir,' he answered, promptly.

Julius waited as Cress and Kelly exited, and then followed them with the others. He was vaguely aware that his heart had begun to beat rapidly, as the thought dawned on him that soon he would be in the same room as all three of Zed's Grand Masters.

The ready room was near the front deck of the ship. As they entered, Julius was relieved to find they were the first ones in – he hadn't been looking forward to having all eyes trained on him when he arrived. A glass-top table occupied the middle of the room, surrounded by several black leather armchairs running down either side of the table, which stretched from a few metres in front of the door to the far wall to their right. Cress walked around the head of the table, where a single chair had been placed, and indicated for the rest of them to join him. Kelly sat down next to Cress, with Faith to his left, followed by Julius and Skye at the end.

Julius looked around him as they waited silently for the others to arrive. The walls were covered in monitors of various sizes and all manner of control panels. There was also a metal plaque on the wall opposite him, which read "Ahura Mazda – Captain John D Kelly".

'*Faith!*' said Julius, calling to his friend with his mind. '*It says on that plaque that Kelly is the Captain of the ship! Didn't Cress call him Second Officer?*'

'*Yes, but the Grand Masters are also onboard, remember,*' answered Faith, pretending to look at his fingernails. '*Kelly may very well be the Captain normally, but the crew on this ship would still answer to the Heads of the schools. So, if they're here too, then they're the highest ranked.*'

'*Do you think maybe Elian is his girlfriend, then?*'

'*Probably, given how much of a liberty she took before, shutting Kelly up like that.*'

'Hey! She didn't shut me up!' said Kelly, out loud. Julius and Faith froze and looked at him, blushing wildly.

'How did you ...' began Julius.

'First off,' said Kelly, looking quite amused, 'give me *some* credit at least. I did study on Zed too, you know. Secondly, you guys aren't exactly subtle.'

'He's right,' said Master Cress, trying to look serious. 'I heard you from here. You may want to use a Scrambler next time. It'll give you some privacy.'

Julius and Faith turned a shade of magenta and sunk deeper into their chairs.

'I take it I missed something there, right?' asked Skye, leaning in towards Julius.

231

'Later,' whispered Julius, making a shooing gesture with his hand.

When the clock struck eight, the door of the ready room swished open and Freja entered. Kelly promptly stood up and called, 'Captain on deck!'

Everyone, including Cress this time, stood and bowed. Freja dipped his head and then waited by the entrance for his guests to step inside.

'Grand Master Sield – Edwina Milson,' announced Kelly, and then bowed.

Everyone else in the room followed suit as a stout, distinguished woman walked in. She responded in the same fashion, and then stood by her seat, just across from Julius.

'Grand Master Tuala – Roland Kloister,' continued Kelly, as a broad-shouldered man of average height entered the room.

Once again, there was an exchange of bows and Kloister stepped over to the seat beside Milson. Freja moved away from the entrance, to the chair at Kloister's left hand. There was now only one seat left empty – the one at the head of the table. After a brief pause, Kelly made a final introduction: 'Curio Maximus – Aldobrando Roversi.'

As he said this, a holographic image appeared in the empty seat, that of a tall, grey-haired man. Julius, who was feeling distinctly awestruck, seeing as he was now in the presence of the head of the Curia, bowed low.

'At ease,' said Freja and invited them all to sit.

Julius was filled with wonder as it hit home just how remarkable a line-up was assembled there at the table. Kloister, a sturdy, middle aged Austrian, was wearing the dark red uniform of his school. His fair, cropped hair and bright blue eyes gave a pleasant youthfulness to his face, which compensated for his stern gaze.

232

Julius had been told that Edwina Milson was from South Africa, and that she was the only Grand Master ever to continue playing in the Hologram Palace after being elected as Head of a school, which of course made her rather popular among her students. She was also dressed in full uniform, sporting Sield's official colour, a lively olive-green shade.

Although being in the same room as the heads of Tuala and Sield for the first time was a genuine treat, the real highlight for Julius was the presence of Roversi. The Curio Maximus rarely visited Satras, and only then for certain formal occasions. From his studies, Julius was well aware of how important the Curia was, being the political heart of Zed and a major link between Earth and the rest of the galaxy. He remembered reading about how the Curia had been formed with the express purpose of developing Earth's defences and overseeing the running of Zed and the colonies. This was in direct response to the defection of the Arneshians and the deaths of Marcus Tijara and Clodagh Arnesh back in 2628. Over time, its remit had changed, as responsibility for Earth's military protection had been handed over to the three Grand Masters, leaving the Curia in charge of diplomatic affairs and the exploration of the galaxy through its Colonial Affairs division.

'Thank you all for coming,' said Freja. 'I am reminded at times like this how grateful I am for Zed and the work we do. As you know, we are gathered here tonight to discuss a most pressing matter: the Oracle of Life. Each one of us sitting here in this council knows some part, but not the entirety, of this complex story. Therefore, for the benefit of us all, we shall begin by laying it out in full. Mr McCoy, would you tell us about your discovery, please?'

Julius took a deep breath and tried to fight back the embarrassment of having to speak in front of such an important audience. He began to recount their first chance encounter with Clodagh Arnesh, and spoke of how they had successfully managed to work their way through each clue, until that last fateful night in Gassendi. Admitting to breaking curfew, barging into private property and lying to superiors in front of these people, was probably the hardest thing that Julius had ever been asked to do; knowing Freja though, it could have been his idea of a *moral* punishment. He was mindful not to leave anything out, even admitting about how they hadn't recognised that the Oracle was actually Clodagh Arnesh. However, when it came to Red Cap and his part in all of it, Julius hesitated and looked over at Freja. The Grand Master nodded his head understandingly in reply.

'The hologram responsible for the Gassendi kidnappings,' said Julius, 'is the same one that organised the attack on Tijara last April. I call him Red Cap, but I have no idea who he really is.'

'Yes,' said Milson. 'Freja told us about him. He must be quite an important piece of Salgoria's puzzle to have spared him after the attack failed.'

'Carlos,' said Roversi, 'I take it you invited this young man here tonight on account of him being a White Child, am I right? But what of the other two?'

'You're partly right, Aldobrando,' answered Freja. 'Clodagh Arnesh herself made the other half of the decision for us. You see, the last message indicated that those who had been there at the beginning must be there to deliver her gift at the end. These three Mizkis, along with Miss Ruthier and Red Cap, were there at the start.'

The Curio Maximus seemed content enough with Freja's explanation, and Julius wasn't about to add anything else on that front. Besides, he was feeling quite distracted by how casually he had been referred to as a White Child. It was noticeable too how no one had flinched when they heard that. Obviously his secret was more widespread than he had thought. Even this Kelly guy knew, and they had only just met. Why would Freja tell *him* something like that? He was only a spaceship captain, after all.

'Very well,' said Roversi. 'Please continue.'

'We come now to the crucial question,' said Freja. 'What is the true nature of this "precious possession" of hers, and why exactly did Clodagh Arnesh go to the painstaking trouble of hiding it in such an involved way. Kloister, if you will.'

Grand Master Kloister straightened up in his chair. 'Thank you, Freja; I'll be brief. The three Grand Masters have long been entrusted with Marcus Tijara's legacy: his original scripts, notes, files, the lot. The majority of these items are in the public domain, accessible to Mizkis, officers and even the general public. Of these, there are a few which remain highly classified, known of only by the Grand Masters. One such secret, I will reveal now to the rest of this council.

'Everyone around this table knows that Marcus Tijara and Clodagh Arnesh built Zed together in 2620. We know all about their mind-skills and their unsurpassed talent for using them to their very fullest. We also know that, at some point between the foundation of Zed and the banishment of the Arneshians five years later, Tijara and Arnesh became lovers.'

Julius's mouth fell open. Of all the endless possibilities for what was about to be revealed to them, he had certainly not seen *that one* coming. Even Kelly looked a little flustered.

'However, gentlemen,' continued Kloister, 'this is *not* the secret. The fact that you didn't know about their relationship is merely a symptom of the passing years. It seems that, 200 years later, their love affair doesn't make headlines anymore. Next time you're in Satras, though, look around at the various tell-tale signs of their affection. You see, Clodagh built Satras as a place in which to express her love for Tijara, from the emerald lake to the ice cream parlour – ice cream was Marcus's favourite treat after all. There's even a statue by the lake, which was commissioned for their first anniversary and made in Gassendi, another of Clodagh's favourite places.'

'"To M. Forever yours, C.",' said Skye, almost in a trance.

'Correct, Mr Miller,' said Milson, 'I'm glad *somebody* noticed that.'

'I must have seen that inscription a hundred times ... but I never knew,' he replied

'Well, now you do,' she said. 'And it may be worth your while to refresh the memories of the younger Mizkis when you return to school. You too, Captain Kelly. History should not be forgotten, no matter how shocking the truth of it.'

Skye shifted in his chair, and Julius saw a greyish wisp floating above his head. It was obvious to him that his friend wasn't particularly enthused by this idea. He thought back to Skye's angry reaction, in Gassendi, when Julius had dared to mention *anything* good about Clodagh. So he very much doubted that Skye would be in any great hurry to spread this story back in Satras.

'What I am about to tell you,' continued Kloister, 'is something that is known only to the Grand Masters, and which the rest of you are obliged to not share with *anyone* outside this council. Not your fellow Mizkis, boys; nor your crew members, Captain Kelly; not even your staff at Colonial Affairs, Curio Maximus.'

'But of course,' replied Roversi.

'Understood, sir,' answered Kelly.

Julius, Faith and Skye simply bowed their heads in acceptance of this obligation.

'This information was discovered among Tijara's private papers, written by his own hand and confirmed by a series of medical records that accompanied those papers. It appears that, in the year 2624, Clodagh Arnesh fell pregnant.'

Julius stared in disbelief at the Grand Master, his brain working double shifts as it registered this latest news on top of the previous revelation, which had been shocking enough.

'Marcus was absolutely delighted,' said Kloister, 'and he expressed these feelings in his diary. He even decided to propose to her. However, it was around this time that Clodagh decided to steer her course away from peace, and to strive instead for dominion over Earth.'

'We don't believe this idea came to her suddenly either,' added Milson. 'Rather that it had been growing in her for some time. Already, she had gathered a big following, something that Marcus had been largely oblivious of, it seems, or at least the true nature of that following. Love *is* blind, as they say. And it worked both ways – perhaps the joy of Clodagh's union with Marcus made her mistakenly believe that he wouldn't refuse to join her.'

'But refuse he did,' said Kloister. 'And it seems he tried hard to persuade her to let go of her evil thoughts and instead think about their life together as a family. Clodagh was having none of it though. It would cost Marcus everything he held dear, but still he threatened to banish her from Zed if she didn't change her mind.'

Julius thought suddenly of Morgana, and pictured how she surely would have been crying by this point of the story, had she been there with them.

'It was then that Clodagh decided to leave. Marcus's rejection of her was too much to bear. The hatred she nurtured for his mind-skills drove her mad and she did the unthinkable: the medical records show that the two-month-old foetus inside her was removed from her womb and frozen in a secure, secret location on Zed.'

'Say what?' blurted out Faith.

'He meant to say "*sir*", sir,' added Skye quickly.

'Of course, sir,' said Faith, blushing wildly.

'It's quite understandable, Mr Shanigan,' said Milson. 'The gentlemen around this table seem to share those sentiments too.'

Indeed, as Julius looked around him, shock was written large on the faces of those in the room who were finding all this out for the first time.

'As you know,' resumed Kloister, 'in January 2625, Clodagh was banned from Zed, the Earth and all of their colonies. She took her favourite ship, the Angra Mainyu, while her followers were given enough vessels to take them all far away, and enough resources to terraform a new planet. Eventually, she did find a new home in the Taurus constellation, and called it Arnesh. Three years later, Clodagh and Marcus were both dead ... but that is another tale.'

'After she first left,' said Freja, picking the story up, 'Marcus discovered a note, left behind by Clodagh. In it, she begged him to reconsider and join her. If he wanted to do so, he could find her and their child through the Oracle of Life. We had never understood that part, up until recent events.'

'The messages we heard were for *him*!' said Julius, as realisation dawned in his mind. 'The first time we met her, she said, "I knew you would come back to me" and the second time, at the lovers' statue, she said we were at their favourite spot. She was talking to Marcus Tijara!'

'Yes, Mr McCoy,' said Freja. 'She believed that, in the end, he would come back to her.'

'Sir,' asked Skye, 'how did Salgoria know about the Oracle?'

'We're not sure,' said Freja, 'but the most likely answer would be from Clodagh herself. Maybe, when Marcus continued to ignore her pleas, she decided to leave some kind of record of it for her own Arneshian successors. This is all guesswork of course, but it seems the most logical explanation.'

'But what can Salgoria possibly do with Clodagh's foetus, anyway?' asked Skye.

'She can build the army she's always wanted,' answered Julius. 'She won't need me or any other White Child.'

'If she's capable of reviving the foetus,' explained Milson, 'Salgoria would have the perfect being in her hands – the child of the two most powerful practitioners of the White and Grey Arts. The DNA would be astounding, you can imagine. She could clone it as many times as she needs.'

'Wait a minute; what do they want the girls for, then?' asked Faith.

Freja looked at the other Grand Masters, then back at the Mizkis. 'She needs a mother, a female carrier: my guess is they've taken a few so they can select the most suitable one.'

A deep silence descended upon the room. It took Julius a few moments to fully realise the dreadful meaning of Freja's words. Then, an idea started to form in his mind, like a growing ray of light. 'That really *does* mean the girls are still OK, right?' he said excitedly. 'They can't harm *any* of the girls until the Oracle's ... I mean, Clodagh's gift is delivered, and by then we'll be there to stop them!'

'I believe you are correct,' said Freja. 'It's what we're counting on, anyway.'

'And now for our plan,' said Kloister, clearing his throat and turning to the Curio Maximus. 'We have managed to track down the precise co-ordinates of Angra Mainyu. Between our present warp-speed and a further hyperjump, which we'll use for the last leg to catch them by surprise, we believe we *will* reach it in time. Clodagh's precise birthday is at 20:37 tomorrow night so, all going according to plan, we will board the ship ten minutes before then. We have no way of knowing what we'll find waiting for us onboard, but the three Mizkis should be with us. I wish we could avoid taking them altogether, but Freja is right: they may be needed to trigger the final Oracle message.'

'What do you intend to do with the foetus and the ship?' asked Roversi.

'Destroy them both,' replied Freja.

'The Grand Masters of Zed don't need the Curia's approval in these matters of course,' said Roversi. 'But, for what it's worth, you have our support. You are free to act in the best interests of Earth and Zed.'

Freja, Kloister and Milson bowed their heads courteously to the Curio Maximus.

'Cress will return to Tijara,' said Freja, 'and inform Master Lim and Master Carrero of our plans.' Then he turned to the boys. 'Mizkis, you are dismissed and at liberty until tomorrow evening. At 19:00 hours, you will meet Lieutenant Elian Flywheel in the mess hall. She will equip you for the mission. This council is now adjourned.'

Julius, Faith and Skye stood up, bowed to the others and quietly filed out of the room. None of them were quite able to believe what they had just heard. They wandered over to the mess hall, grabbed three cups of hot barley and returned to their cabin. There they sat for the next couple of hours discussing everything they had just heard, trying to somehow digest these revelations and, most of all, to fathom the consequences of what the Arneshians were planning to do with the kidnapped girls.

Julius could feel rage growing in him. How could he have led Morgana into this awful situation? He should have protected her better, but instead he had failed and she was now facing the incredible prospect of becoming the surrogate mother of Tijara's own son. The thought of it was so hard to comprehend that he was unable to dwell on it that night for too long. It was easy to tell that Faith and Skye felt the same – every time the conversation turned to Salgoria's plan, little grey wisps sprung up around their heads and hung there for a few seconds before dissipating again into thin air. Eventually, they grew tired of talking and lay back in their beds, each one lost in their own thoughts. Julius could feel a headache coming on, so he closed his eyes and slowly drifted off into a restless sleep.

*

The following evening, Julius sat anxiously waiting in the ready room. It was ten minutes until mission time. Faith and Skye were sitting at the opposite end of the table, in the seats that Cress and Kelly had been using the day before, looking every bit as nervous as he felt. They had all been equipped with special protective gear: a type of uniform that none of them had ever seen before on Zed. Elian had given them each a small button-like gadget, called an

Exoskin, to fix onto their jumpers, over their hearts. When they pressed it, their bodies were instantly wrapped in what felt and looked like energy fields, but which quickly transformed into solid armour. The device also had a setting to extend this armour over the head, like a helmet. Its neutral colour was a dark shade of silver but, if it was pressed a second time, it created a chameleon effect and blended perfectly with the surrounding environment: this cloaking device mechanism could render a subject practically invisible. It was incredibly light in weight, to the point where Julius couldn't tell whether it was activated or not, unless he looked at it. They were all wearing their Gauntlets, which under different circumstances might have been quite enthralling, being entrusted with them like that outside the classroom for the first time. Not that that seemed to register much with Faith, he was so ecstatic about the new gadget Elian had given them. He kept pressing away on it, marvelling at its various functions, especially the chameleon setting. It was quite amusing to Julius, every time Faith activated it, seeing his friend blink in and out of visibility.

After watching Faith for a few minutes, Julius got up and stood in front of the plaque on the wall. He passed his fingers lightly over the ship's name and smiled. He liked it here. The crew seemed like a well-knit, close unit, and he thought that if one day he was ever given command of a ship, he would want it to be like this one. Maybe he would have Faith adjust a few bits and pieces on it, but the essentials were already there.

'What do you think of the name – Ahura Mazda?' said Kelly, entering the ready room.

Faith and Skye instantly stood and bowed to the Captain. Julius turned, bowed, and watched as Kelly approached him.

'It's a strange one, sir. What does it mean?' he replied.

'It's taken from ancient Iran – it represents the principles of goodness and truth. Do you want to know the name of its opposite, the principle of darkness?'

Julius nodded, his curiosity fully piqued.

'Angra Mainyu.'

Julius gasped in surprise. 'Salgoria's ship!'

'Yes,' continued Kelly. 'They were designed as mirror images of each other. Both ships were built at the same time, in a place that today we call The Halls of Ahriman.'

'Are the Halls really as bad as they say, Captain Kelly?' asked Faith.

'I'm afraid I can't discuss that. Still, the two ships are identical. One was built for Clodagh and the other for Marcus. She took hers with her when she was banished, and Zed kept the Ahura Mazda.'

'It must be an honour to pilot this ship then, if it belonged to Tijara,' said Julius.

'Oh, it is. I fought hard to become its commander.' As he said this, Kelly unconsciously rubbed the scar on his face. Julius took note of it but, although he was really curious to ask about it, he decided it was best left for some other time.

'I want to command a ship like this one day,' said Julius.

Kelly didn't answer, but observed him silently, as if he was sizing him up. Julius was just beginning to feel a little awkward, when finally the Captain turned to the door and beckoned for the three of them to follow him.

He guided them along a passageway which led onto a landing by the boarding hatch. A large window was set into the hatch, so they could see out into the space outside. The landing was brimming with officers. The Grand Masters were all there, standing off to the right, flanked by several stern faced officers. Julius noticed that everyone there had the Exoskins fixed to their uniforms.

'We're ready for FTL whenever you are,' said Elian, over the intercom.

'Very good, Helmsman. Wait for my order,' said Freja loudly, and then turned to face the boys. 'When we board Angra Mainyu, you three will go with Captain Kelly and his team. Under no circumstances do I want you out of his sight, unless he gives you a direct order. Understood?'

'Yes, sir,' they answered in unison.

'The Grand Masters and I will be with Lieutenant Parker and his team,' continued Freja. 'There will be four more teams on standby, led by Lieutenants Sanders, Molloy, Trond and Berger.' Five men, who had been standing off to the side of them, stepped forward and bowed to the Grand Master. 'May our mission succeed, for the sake of our people!' said Freja solemnly.

'So let it be!' the officers answered, as one.

Kelly led the boys to the left hand side of the room and said, 'Hold on to the banister, Mizkis!'

'FTL engaged,' called Elian over the intercom, 'in five, four, three, two, one. Skip!'

Julius felt as if he just stepped out of his body, exactly like before, when Morgana had fired up the Stork's hyperjump during their fateful flight to Kratos. The sensation didn't last long thankfully and, as he drew a deep breath to steady his stomach, the shape of Angra Mainyu loomed into view through the hatch window. The Ahura Mazda drifted towards it, carefully manoeuvring the airlock so it lined up with that of the Arneshian ship. A couple of minutes later, Julius heard a click and a green light flashed on above the hatch.

'Kelly's team, go!' ordered Freja.

'Mizkis, gear up!' shouted Kelly, pressing the device on his jumper, and then releasing the airlock door.

The boys activated their armour and flicked the safety off on their Gauntlets. At once, Julius, Faith and Skye were surrounded by twelve muscular officers, who formed a ring around them, shielding them completely.

'Skirts!' called Julius, turning to his friends and holding his left hand out to them.

First Faith, and then Skye, clamped their left hands over his. Julius saw scarlet wisps of excitement enveloping their bodies. The hunt had begun.

ANGRA MAINYU

When the airlock opened, Julius was completely taken aback. He knew that the two ships were identical, but to actually step into a darker version of the Ahura Mazda was particularly eerie. Even without the bright lights, Julius could see that the observation deck on the Angra Mainyu was a carbon copy of the Ahura's, and he was willing to bet that the internal layouts similarly mirrored each other. He suddenly wished that someone had told him about this design quirk earlier than Kelly had, because he would have spent some time checking out the blueprints for the Ahura if he had known. Now, however, they would have to rely on the officers around them to navigate.

'This way,' said Kelly, leading them through the hatch and down a corridor to the left.

Julius, Faith and Skye lifted their Gauntlets in front of them, and adopted combat stances, with their right wrists perched on their left arms for support, like Professor Chan had taught them. Faith's skirt hummed gently as he hovered by their side.

Julius heard light footsteps from the airlock behind them. He turned his head and saw Freja and his team heading right. Tiny beads of sweat were starting to form on his forehead and he wiped them off with the back of his arm. The silence in the ship only added to the tension he could feel creeping up on him like a ghostly presence, making the hairs on his arms stand up straight. It was discomforting, the absence of sound in a ship of this size – surely it wasn't natural. He tried to still his mind and tune his senses into everything around him, hoping for some small noise or sign that could lead them towards Morgana and the other girls.

Kelly stopped at the end of the wall on his right side, crouched down and peeked around the corner. When he was sure it was safe, he led them on, around the angle of the wall and up a flight of stairs that jagged back in the direction they had come from. As they reached the floor above, they saw Freja's team emerging from the top of a set of stairs to their left.

The boys watched on as Kelly and Parker nodded to each other and then indicated for each of their teams to split into two smaller units, with quick, precise gestures of their hands. They were now gathered outside an archway which was shrouded in dim shadow. They filed in and moved to the left and right of the chamber beyond – Julius, Faith and Skye with the group on the left – while the sub-teams moved swiftly ahead to secure the farthest sides of the area.

Julius kept looking around him for clues to Morgana's whereabouts but, in the poor light, he couldn't really see much. He could just about make out some kind of pedestal in the centre of the room. It was positioned in the middle of a raised, square platform that had four curved control-desks at each of its corners. Behind this area, Julius could see Freja, Kloister and Milson also staring intently at it.

'*Listen carefully, all of you.*' Freja's voice popped suddenly into

Julius's head, startling him a little. He had never heard the Grand Master communicating in this way before, and he was amazed by how clear and strong it sounded. *'This is it: the core of the ship. The package will be here in about four minutes,'* he continued. Julius instinctively picked up on how Freja had used the word "package", obviously to avoid revealing the nature of its contents to the other officers.

'The Mizkis are present in the room, so Red Cap should be able to activate the last Oracle and deliver the item. We will let him do just that.'

'Sir?' There was a murmur of surprise from several of the officers. Clearly Julius wasn't the only one thinking that might not be such a good idea. Even Kelly was looking a little puzzled.

'In order to fully eliminate the threat of the package, it must be activated and its contents exposed. As soon as Red Cap does that, Kelly's team will take care of him.'

'Yes, sir,' said Julius, along with the other officers. He still wasn't entirely convinced that the best course of action was to actually allow the delivery to go ahead, but he was fully aware that he had also just been authorised to go after Red Cap once that was done.

'No one moves until I give the order – no matter what happens – understood?'

There was a chorus of "*yes, sir!*", which gave a strange echo effect in Julius's head. He was quickly discovering how disconcerting mind-talking could be among large groups like this.

Everyone fell silent again, an air of anticipation hanging over the room. They didn't have to wait too long as, a few minutes later, a door at the top of the chamber opened and Red Cap entered. He walked casually to the centre of the room and onto the platform, and then stopped.

'I wouldn't move if I were you,' he said in an unconcerned voice, to no one in particular, although it was clear that he was aware of his audience, despite their camouflage.

'There goes the element of surprise,' whispered Skye.

Red Cap began his preparations on the central pedestal. At either side of the chamber, no one moved – Julius knew that, unless Freja gave the order, it would stay that way.

'So,' called Red Cap, 'did you bring the White Child, or should we just call this thing off now?'

He was met only by silence. Red Cap sniggered. It was obvious that he already knew the answer to his question and was just taunting them. Not only that, but he had just revealed that there was a "White Child" in the room – word of that would quickly spread among the officers afterwards. Julius was aware that this was a deliberate ploy. Red Cap's arrogance infuriated him and he struggled to contain the anger that was bubbling up inside him like a raging volcano. He thought of everything they had been subjected to by the Arneshians: the girls who had been kidnapped to use like meaningless vessels and discarded as Salgoria saw fit; he thought of the Ruthiers and the other parents – the desperation and worry they must be feeling – and it burned through him. The time had come to settle this score once and for all.

He was so consumed by the thought of vengeance that he was oblivious to how the adrenaline had begun to pump through his veins: waves of energy were rising up in him, causing tiny sparks at the tips of his fingers, creating the illusion that energy was actually dripping from his hands. He didn't even notice how the officers around him were edging away from him. Even Faith and Skye, who had witnessed Julius's abilities at first hand, were unable to stay close

249

to him. It was as if they were being pushed aside by a growing orb of energy around their friend. But Julius remained unaware of this; his mind bent solely on Red Cap. As he watched, every sinew tensed, like a wolf waiting to pounce on its prey, the Arneshian holo spoke again.

'Come now, White Child – enough of the games. Step forward. We both know nothing happens if you don't.'

Julius tried to calm himself and waited for Freja to give him some kind of order, but there was nothing. Maybe the Grand Master was waiting for him to make a move. He decided the only way forward was to see this one out, and he *was* itching to get at Red Cap. He stood up and began to walk forward.

'*Only* you!' said Red Cap menacingly. 'Or your friends don't see another school year.' With that, he held up a small silver controller in his left hand and pointed up to the ceiling. It had been shrouded in darkness before but now bright light illuminated it.

Julius looked up and gasped. High in the air, four pods could be seen gently bobbing below the domed ceiling. He strained his eyes and saw that inside them were the four kidnapped Mizkis: Ife, Sharon, Siena and Morgana, whose dark hair was floating ethereally around her face, as if her pod was filled with some kind of liquid. Red Cap pointed his right hand upwards and shot a small blast of energy towards them – it struck just below them and rippled in the air, revealing for a minute an underlying field of energy.

'If you hurt them-' shouted Julius. To his left, Faith and Skye sprang forward and then stopped dead as Julius shot a mind-message at them: '*Don't! That won't help.*' He wondered why none of the officers had moved yet.

'As long as you're a good boy, and your soldier friends stay where they are, I won't do anything to them. Think fast – time is short, little one,' Red Cap finished mockingly.

A sense of utter desperation filled Julius. This wasn't how it was supposed to go. And what was Freja doing? There was still not even a hint of an order from him. He looked up at the girls again and walked towards him – there really was no other choice. Red Cap smiled and waved Julius closer. He inched forward hesitantly onto the platform; being so near to the Arneshian was a torture in itself. His muscles trembled from the effort of controlling himself.

A few seconds later, a small hole appeared in the pedestal. A ray of turquoise light, like the one that had appeared in the cave before the first Oracle appeared, emanated out of it, scanned Julius from head to toe and blinked out again. There was a loud beep and the last Oracle sprang into dazzling life.

'You fill my heart with joy, my love,' she said, spreading her arms out.

Julius studied Clodagh's face: so beautiful and yet forever tainted now that he knew what she had done, and the suffering that her obsession had caused for so many. In that brief instance, however, her expression was a picture of tenderness and anticipation, a woman longing for a lost love to return to her.

'*She really believed he would come back,*' thought Julius to himself. There was no empathy in that knowledge though – in the grand scheme of things, he couldn't bring himself to feel sorry for her.

'Give it to me,' she said, extending her hands, 'and I shall create it for us.'

Red Cap reached into his chest and pulled out the container, then gently placed it on her outstretched palms. Clodagh's hands closed around it and drew it in towards her belly, where it vanished inside her holographic body.

251

'*Now!*' he heard Freja's voice in his mind. He swung his head from left to right and saw the officers who had been waiting on either side burst forward towards them.

'No, no,' said Red Cap calmly, extending his left hand outwards and flicking a red button on the silver controller. A blue, electric force-field sprung up around the edges of the raised area, blocking them all out and trapping Julius inside with Red Cap. As this happened, a loud buzzing sound filled the room, and an army of Arneshian holograms materialised at the back of the chamber. Julius pointed his Gauntlet at Red Cap but the holo knocked him back with a thrust of energy from his right hand. 'This time we win,' he said, raising the controller up above his head.

'I don't think so!' Freja's voice rang out, clear and commanding, from Julius's right. The outline of a man's shape could just be made out against the inside of the control-desk in that corner.

'*He was hiding there all along,*' thought Julius incredulously,

The Grand Master's camouflage melted away and, quick as lightning, he made a grabbing gesture with his left hand. The controller flew out of Red Cap's hand and into Freja's. Without missing a beat, he fired an energy burst, which the Arneshian just managed to deflect, but the force of it knocked him back against the desk behind him. An instant later, Freja clicked the button on the controller and the force-field disappeared. 'The Oracle!' he shouted and immediately two white rays of energy, coming from the other Grand Masters, enveloped Clodagh, forming a cocoon around her and dragging her slowly toward the right sideline.

The Zed officers were now engaged in a full-on battle with the Arneshian holograms. The room was ablaze with the light of the energy-bursts from their Gauntlets. Julius had been so stunned by how quickly everything had happened, never mind the shock of seeing Freja appear seemingly from out of thin air, that he had been completely caught off guard. Now, clarity returned to his mind and he searched with his eyes for his old enemy. Red Cap had recovered and was on his feet again. He briefly made as if he was going to attack Freja, but hesitated. Instead he swung around, leapt up on the controller desk and hurdled over the heads of a group of soldiers behind it. He landed effortlessly beyond them and sprinted for a door in the far corner of the right wall. A red mist descended over Julius and he dashed after him.

'McCoy! Wait for us!' he heard Kelly shout from his left, but there was no stopping him now.

'Let's go! Let's go!' cried Skye, motioning for Kelly to follow as he took off after Julius.

'Get your blinking shield up, Julius!' shouted Faith, switching his own one on and zooming over to his friend's side to protect him from any stray fire. Julius managed to activate his just in time to block a shot from Red Cap as he sprinted through the door after him.

Kelly and his team advanced after them. A handful of the men crouched down in a row, their shields held out in front of them like a protective wall, and fired at a clump of holos that were trying to stop them. The rest targeted a group that was attempting to follow. Their shots, despite them being on the move, hit their marks and several of the holograms disappeared in an instant.

Julius, Faith and Skye, meanwhile, had just turned a corner in the passageway beyond the doorway. They suddenly found themselves in a large room that was brimming with more of the Arneshian soldiers.

'Aim for the boxes above their heads!' yelled Julius, keeping his eyes fixed on Red Cap. He moved over to Skye, their shields side by side to shelter them from the volley of energy-bursts that the hologram army was firing at them. Kelly's men had fought their way out of the chamber and were now streaming into the room, their defences up to form a barricade, and were advancing steadily forward.

'Wait, where's Faith?' said Skye, and then stopped, his eyes growing wide as he spotted him.

While the Arneshians had been distracted by Julius, Skye and Kelly's team, Faith had taken full advantage of the situation and stealthily snuck over to the centre of the room. There he stopped, hovering just above the ground, and shouted, 'Duck!'

Everyone hit the ground, and the holograms whirled around, suddenly aware of this new threat. It was too late though, as Faith launched himself into a spin, his Gauntlet held out in front of him, firing off a volley of energy while he twirled on the spot, spreading devastation among the holos. 'Behold, the rotating fury!' he cried.

'He's absolutely bonkers!' said Kelly, booming with laughter. 'I like it!'

The holograms were swept away by the carousel of energy crashing into them, their small red controller-boxes clattering to the floor as they blinked out of existence. It was only when there was a small handful of them left that they decided to retreat through the side exit. Kelly and his men leapt to their feet and ran after them.

'Mizkis, follow us!' he shouted, as he led his team out, not stopping to check that they were behind him. So he didn't notice that Julius, Faith and Skye had no intention of following.

Julius stepped into the middle of the room, hot rage coursing through him. 'Show yourself!' he yelled.

'I'm right here, White Child,' said Red Cap, stepping out of the shadows. 'You children have been a nuisance for far too long. How about you all just die now?'

Before any of them had a chance to react, he flung his hands outwards in a pushing motion, and the boys flew across the room. Like an arrow, Faith careened out the door and crashed into a group of Zed officers in the passageway beyond it. Skye smashed into the back wall and was knocked out cold.

Julius landed in a heap on the floor several metres from where he had been standing, his upper teeth biting down as he hit the floor, splitting his lower lip open. He dragged himself up, wiping the blood from his mouth with the back of his hand.

'Is that it?' he shouted. 'You Arneshians are nothing but cowards. Look at you, sending a bunch of bully holos to do your dirty work. You're nothing, you hear me? You don't even exist!'

'Such anger,' said Red Cap, shaking his head in disappointment. He lifted his right hand and Julius was scooped up high into the air, where he hung suspended, wriggling and twisting desperately to try to free himself.

While this was happening, Faith had recovered and rushed back into the room. He hurried over to where Skye was lying and knelt in front of him so they were both protected by his shield. From there, he fired several shots at Red Cap. The holo easily blocked them with his empty hand, however, and deflected them back at Faith, who had to duck behind his shield to avoid being killed by his own energy-bursts.

'Wha ... what hit me?' groaned Skye, regaining consciousness.

'If you're done napping, we could use your help,' said Faith, not turning to look at him.

Skye shook his head, suddenly remembering where he was. He flicked his shield on as he scrambled to his feet, and started to shoot at Red Cap. Unfazed, Red Cap continued to block them with his left hand. As he did this, he began to rotate his right hand in increasingly rapid arcs. Invisible cords of energy wrapped around Julius's upper body and bright dots filled his vision as the breath was squeezed out of him. '*I have to stop him,*' he thought desperately, but there was nothing he could do – he couldn't lift his Gauntlet because his arms were trapped behind his back.

Just as he was beginning to black out he saw, as if through a haze, Kelly and two men rush into the room and charge. It was enough to briefly distract Red Cap and Julius felt the grip around his chest loosen. He strained with all his might and managed to pull his right arm free. With his Gauntlet drawn up in front of him, he took aim and shouted with his mind, for all in the room to hear, '*Shoot his box! The controller box!*'

Red Cap couldn't hear this, but he must have felt something because his head turned toward Julius, a confused expression on his face. Julius stared coldly at him. 'Party's over. Time you were leaving!'

'No-' Red Cap began, but he was cut short as six beams of energy flashed through him, knocking the remote device off his head. His eyes widened in disbelief, and then he was gone.

Julius fell to the floor and quickly got to his feet again. 'Come on – let's finish this,' he said, walking over to the red box lying on the floor.

Captain Kelly, Faith and Skye moved over to his side, surrounding the device. They readied their Gauntlets and pointed them at it.

'On three,' said Julius, breathing heavily. 'One ... two ... th-'

256

Suddenly the red box whisked past them, off to the right, as if pulled by a magnetic force.

'What the-' said Kelly, as they turned on their heels to follow it.

Standing by the door, covered in dust and scratches, Grand Master Kloister was holding the box in his left hand. 'Come with me,' he ordered. 'I'll show you how we're going to do this. And we need a few extra hands over there.'

They looked quickly at each other and then set off after Kloister, who led them along the passageway, back to the central chamber.

'Wow,' said Faith, as they entered the room. 'You guys really didn't like the furniture, did you?'

They stood there, admiring the devastation that had been rained down on the place. The floor was littered with red boxes, some torn in half, some still smoking. Large chunks had been blown out of the control-desks on the platform and the pedestal had been completely destroyed. The Clodagh hologram was nowhere to be seen. Julius looked around and saw Freja and Milson huddled together in quiet discussion. The Grand Masters had their backs to them, making it impossible to hear what they were saying. Julius, like everyone else, waited in anticipation for them to finish, his eyes darting from them to Morgana and back. A minute later, Milson stood up and silently left the chamber.

'Gentlemen,' said Kloister, turning to the teams. 'What say we get our girls down and see how they're doing?'

They all gathered around him. Freja joined them and pushed a blue button on the silver controller he had yanked away from Red Cap. The field of energy below the girls fizzled out, but the pods remained where they were.

'All together now,' said Freja. 'Hold them steady.'

257

They fixed onto the pods with their minds and dragged them gently downwards. As they touched the ground, the pods exploded with small popping sounds, leaving the girls lying on the floor, covered in a goo-like substance. Morgana opened her eyes and let out a couple of wet coughs. She tried to get to her feet, but then thought better of it and instead knelt there, blinking at the mess around her. A second later she was enfolded by two arms.

'Wai ... wha ...' she mumbled weakly.

'Welcome back,' said Julius, squeezing her tight and grinning with delight.

Morgana hugged him, then pushed him gently away and looked at her dripping clothes, before gazing around blankly at the room. When she saw Siena, kneeling off to her left, shivering like a bedraggled cat, she finally remembered. Looking Julius in the eyes, she said, 'You guys came for us.'

'Actually,' said Faith, hovering over to them, with Skye just behind, 'we were tempted to leave you with the Arneshians. But then I figured, if I let the best pilot on Zed go, then who's going to fly me ships?'

'Come here you,' said Morgana, shaking her head and holding her arms out to them. 'Both of you.' They hurried over and she hugged them tight, while tears streamed down her face.

Julius sat with his legs stretched out, his trousers drenched from the liquid that had oozed out of the pods, but he didn't care. He was far too tired, and happy, to worry about a soggy bottom.

'We're not quite finished yet,' said Freja, gently. 'Let's get back to our ship.'

Kelly lifted Morgana off the floor in an easy gesture and carried her off. Three other officers gathered the remaining girls in their arms

258

and followed him. Skye walked beside the man who was carrying Ife, holding her hand in his.

'Grand Master Freja,' said Julius, as they were leaving the chamber.

Freja stopped and turned to him, with a look of contentment which Julius had never seen before, on his face.

'Which one is Red Cap's box, sir?'

'That one there, by the broken pedestal,' he answered. 'Kloister thought it was an appropriate resting place.'

Julius looked back at it. He longed to shoot it himself, there and then, just to be sure. But Kloister had already decided its fate, and it was not for Julius to ignore a Grand Master's wish.

'It's over, McCoy. You did it, and you can finally put *him* out of your mind. Let's go now. I can't wait to blow this vessel to smithereens.'

'I couldn't agree more,' said Julius. 'You know, sir, you were pretty impressive back there, if you don't mind me saying.'

Freja smiled at him. 'I've still got a few tricks up my sleeve, McCoy.'

They walked down to the lower level and, by the time they reached the exit, Julius had just one nagging question that was begging to be answered. 'Sir?'

'Yes, McCoy?'

'Do you think Captain Kelly would let me join him for part of the Summer Camp?' Freja turned to look at him and, as always, seemed to pierce right through him with his gaze.

'Sorry, sir,' said Julius, turning red. 'It was a silly idea. Captain Kelly probably doesn't-'

'I'll see what I can do,' answered Freja, cutting him off.

*

Once they were back on the Ahura Mazda, the Mizkis were told to go to the observation deck. The resident doctor, upon hearing of their success, had hurried up to meet them, and said that he needed to check the girls immediately to make sure they were definitely all right. However, Freja insisted that they be allowed to watch the destruction of the Angra Mainyu – it was, in his opinion, the best possible medicine. Given that they were all now back on their feet, walking unassisted, and seemed to be suffering no obvious after-effects, the doctor relented and agreed to wait a few minutes.

Morgana stood between Julius and Faith, a blanket wrapped around her shoulders. Skye was standing with Ife, while Sharon and Siena sat by the window.

Julius watched the ship slowly moving away from them. When the explosion came, the Ahura Mazda didn't even twitch. A bright, silent wave washed over the hull of their vessel, so intense that Julius had to shield his eyes for a moment. Knowing that Red Cap would forever be buried with it did seem quite fitting now that he thought about it.

Clodagh's spaceship, and everything in it, was destroyed in that blast; its debris destined to travel through space for all eternity.

LEGACY

For the second time in a year, Julius was about to disembark in the Zed docks with dread in his heart. The first time he had been afraid to face Kaori, right after Morgana had been kidnapped. Today, he would be facing her entire family and, although the rescue mission had been successful, there would be a lot of apologising to do.

The Grand Masters had sent word of the successful rescue mission to the girls' immediate families, along with special permission for them to fly in and stay with their daughters in Satras for a few days. Julius thought that was a particularly good idea, especially since the girls were bound to be subjected to a barrage of questions from the Mizkis once they returned to school. Julius had been in that position the year before, so he had a great deal of sympathy for them. It had been a tiring experience. Moreover, before leaving the Ahura Mazda, each of the four girls had to swear, under oath, that the presence of McCoy, Shanigan and Miller would be kept secret. Ife, Sharon and Siena had seemed a little surprised by that, but none of them had objected.

When the doors opened, the three Grand Masters filed out in their pristine uniforms and headed straight for the waiting parents. Through a porthole on the deck, Julius could see numerous handshakes being exchanged, along with heartfelt thanks for bringing back their daughters. Then, it was the turn of the girls to emerge from the ship. As soon as they appeared, all composure left their parents and they were swept up in a whirlpool of joyful tears and crushing embraces. Julius, Faith and Skye waited for a while in the shadows and, when they were sure that no one was paying attention, they hurriedly disembarked. They had just managed to make it to the nearest exit, when a man called out, 'Julius!'

He stopped and turned – it was Morgana's dad. Mr Ruthier jogged towards him and Julius held his breath. Then he noticed a telltale white wisp floating above Mr Ruthier's head and a wave of relief washed over him. A feeling of guilt still lingered but, as he opened his mouth to apologise, he was left speechless by the intensity of the hug that met him. Julius squeezed back gratefully and, for a few seconds, they stood there like that.

Mr Ruthier stepped back and Julius saw that Morgana and the rest of her family were standing there; the same bright, wispy light was surrounding Fujiko and her daughters. As one, they bowed to him, a sign of respect passed on from centuries long gone.

'Thank you, son,' said Mr Ruthier. 'I knew you would bring her back.'

'I ... I'm sorry. I shouldn't have let this happen in the first place,' said Julius. 'I promised I would take care of them, but instead I let you all down.'

'Don't say that, lad,' replied Mr Ruthier kindly. 'We've been shown the footage of Morgana's kidnapping. Grand Master Freja also sent me a message to tell me what went on inside Angra Mainyu. You've done everything in your power to protect her, and then rescue her. I couldn't have asked for more, and most certainly I could not have done what you did. If I *really* wanted to blame someone, I could point to Zed's lack of security. But, since the day my daughters were selected to join the schools, I knew their safety was no longer in my hands, as hard as that may be to accept. They belong to Zed now, and so do you.'

Julius bowed his head gratefully. Deep down, he knew that Mr Ruthier was right, but to actually hear him saying it made a big difference. They shook hands and Julius watched as he led his family away. He waved to Morgana and sent her a quick mind-message: '*I'll see you in a few days.*' She waved back and nodded.

Julius grabbed his bag and turned back towards the exit, where Faith and Skye were waiting for him.

'So,' said Julius, patting Faith on the shoulder. 'Care to explain where you learned to do that "rotating fury" stunt?'

'Yeah,' said Skye, 'and I'd like to know exactly what was behind that "rabbit in the headlights" glance you threw at Siena back on the shuttle.'

'I'd almost forgotten about that – I wanna know too,' said Julius, laughing and elbowing Faith in the ribs.

'She was going to hug me!' exclaimed Faith defensively, and darted into the Intra-Rail station.

'Come back, *Fury*!' called Julius, who was grinning wildly. 'We wanna know more!'

It was a long train journey back to Tijara for poor old Faith, who was ribbed mercilessly all the way by his two friends.

*

It was nearing midday on that day – Monday, the 16th of May – as the train arrived at their destination. While Julius, Faith and Skye were heading over to their dorms to unpack and freshen up, the rest of the 2MJs were just finishing their Shield lesson with Professor Morales. The boys knew their classmates would want to know why they had skipped class that morning, so they had agreed to simply say that Freja had given them permission to go to the docks with the girls' families and welcome them back. After all, they had been there when Morgana and Siena had been kidnapped.

The story worked, and not one of the Mizkis raised any objections over lunch when they heard this explanation. Julius guessed they were all just too happy that the girls were safe, even though the students would have to wait until they returned to school that Wednesday to hear all about their ordeal. In fact, the excitement was so much that Barth decided to organise a little welcome back party in Tijara's garden for them. The idea turned out to be a great success, with all the teachers in attendance, as were the older students. Even Cress and Freja stopped by for a few minutes. Felice Buongustaio prepared a mouth-watering buffet, which was spread out on a long picnic table in the middle of the garden, and was serving slices of cake to the hungry crowd. The trees had been decorated with colourful fairy lights, compliments of the many students who had volunteered to chip in.

Julius was sitting on a chair under a tree, one foot propped against another seat. Hands in pockets, he watched with delight as the night unfolded. He still found himself feeling a little shy in among such large crowds, so he was quite content to sit there on the outskirts – he wouldn't have missed it for the world.

Not too far from him, Professor Chan was congratulating Faith on his "rotating fury" move, saying that he had showed remarkable

skill adapting a kata to complement the advantages his skirt offered. He even added that he would be teaching that very move to any other student who was accepted into Zed and had to be fitted with a similar skirt. Faith was so pleased with this that he couldn't find anything to say, except to fumble a small thank you.

A few feet to Julius's right, Skye was quietly, but dramatically, explaining to Professor Morales how dangerous the fight on Angra Mainyu had been, and how he had managed to save several soldiers with his Shield manoeuvres. Julius grinned and shook his head.

Further away, Morgana and Siena were at the centre of an ever changing group of people, who flocked around them to hear all about their ordeal. Julius felt sorry for them, but he figured, after that, they'd surely be left in peace again. Eventually, the throng of people thinned out, and Siena walked over to Julius.

'Hey,' she said.

'Hey, Siena,' replied Julius, lifting his feet off the chair and offering her the seat.

'No thanks,' she replied. 'We kept missing each other on the way back home – that ship's huge. Anyway, I've already thanked Faith and Skye, but I wanted to thank you too.'

'That's fine,' said Julius. 'We just did whatever we could.'

She nodded her head and turned to leave but, as she did, Julius said, 'You know, there was one thing I was wondering though.'

She stopped. 'What's that?'

'That night, back in Gassendi, what were you doing in the room? I thought you had gone to bed.'

'I did,' she replied. 'I had a bad dream and then, when I woke up and didn't see Morgana, I went to find her. I guess that's what I get for being curious.'

Julius nodded and Siena wandered off to rejoin Morgana. The rest of the evening went smoothly and, when midnight came, the Mizkis returned to their dorms, tired but happy.

*

There were only twelve days left to the end of the year, and the students had to choose their Summer Camp destinations once again. On the last Saturday of May, the Skirts were sitting under the oak tree, munching on toasted sunflower seeds.

'You lucky sod!' said Faith, throwing a seed at Julius.

As it turned out, Freja had managed to convince Captain Kelly to take Julius with him, and not just for a week or two, but for the entire summer.

'Yeah,' answered Julius, beaming. 'I have no idea how he managed that, but I'm not going to complain about it.'

'I think the real revelation is Skye,' said Morgana. 'Mr Smooth-talk here is going to spend his summer in the Curia!'

'What?' said Faith and Julius in unison.

'Let's just say that I've decided to try something different this year. Hone my talking skills, if you like. And I've heard that girls like a powerful man.'

'I knew there had to be a reason for it,' said Julius, rolling his eyes. 'Seriously, though, you want to be a politician?'

'I'm thinking about it. Maybe a diplomat. Who knows?'

'Well, mate,' said Faith, 'if there's one person who could sell stars to the universe, that person is you. And it *would* be handy to have a friend in Colonial Affairs.'

'So you approve?'

'Of course,' said Morgana. 'And you don't need our approval. We'll support you no matter what.'

'Well said, Morgana,' added Julius. 'Besides, the Skirts already have one fighter.' As he said that, he pretended to shine his fingernails on his jumper, in mock smugness.

'All right then,' said Skye. 'And you guys?'

'Faith and I will stick with last year's plan,' explained Morgana. 'I'll go with him to Pete's, and then head off to meet Elian at the apprentice flying camp.'

'I like Elian,' said Skye, with a long sigh. 'I would *so* go out with her.'

'Who *wouldn't* you go out with?' asked Julius.

'Err ... your ugly face?'

The words were barely out of his mouth before Julius had pounced and wrestled with him, crying, "Revenge!". Faith promptly hovered over them and plonked himself down on their legs, trapping them both and leaving Morgana laughing her head off under the tree.

*

When the last day of term finally arrived, Julius stood on the Zed dock, pushing his rucksack towards the shuttle door with his foot, while sending a message to Faith on his PIP. Suddenly, his bag lifted off the floor and levitated over his head. Julius, who was distracted, didn't realise what had happened and continued to push away at an invisible object for a few steps. When he realised that his foot was finding only fresh air, he stopped and looked down.

'Hey!' he said, searching for his bag.

'You could always wear it on your shoulders, you know?'

Julius turned in the direction of the voice and saw Bernard Docherty standing there, looking rather pleased with himself. The older boy looked up and Julius followed the direction of his gaze: the bag was hovering a few feet above his head. He stretched out his arms and the rucksack fell into them.

'Is that you leaving then?' Julius asked him.

'Yep. It's over.'

'What next?'

'I'm going home to California for the summer. Then back here to start my new job in the Curia.'

'Politics, huh? I can see that.'

'Can you?' asked Bernard, half-smiling at him.

'Sure. You have charisma. Haven't you noticed how people listen to you?'

'You're doing all right for yourself too, you know. Though, you do need to work on your leadership skills a bit more. You're still too shy for a captain.'

'A captain?'

'And a brilliant one you'd make, if I've read you right.'

Julius wasn't sure what to say, but he was quietly pleased with what Bernard had said.

'Anyway, I need to give you something,' said Docherty, pulling out a little box. 'Take it – it's yours.'

Julius took the box, opened it and emptied its contents into the palm of his left hand. It was a black metal ring, with the word "*Solo*" engraved on its inner side.

'Only one person at a time can wear that ring,' explained Bernard. 'If someone overtakes you while you're still in school, you must hand it over to them.'

'What if no one makes it before I leave?'

'Then you hand it back to Master Cress. Marcus himself made it for the Solo champions. It's Zed legacy.'

Julius nodded and slipped the ring onto the middle finger of his right hand. The band, which was loose at first, tightened gently until it fitted him. 'This is just!' he said, admiring it.

'Cool, huh? And everyone knows what it means. It'll earn you respect,' said Bernard.

'Thanks, and good luck.'

'You too, McCoy,' said Bernard. 'I'll see you around.'

Julius stood on the platform, watching him board the shuttle to Earth. It was a shame that he had never managed to challenge him in the Hologram Palace; it could have been fun.

'*The shuttle for Pit-Stop Pete's is departing from dock bay 5. Passengers must make their way to the gate for immediate boarding,*' called a voice over the loudspeaker.

Julius tightened his fist, making the black ring on his finger shine under the artificial light of the Zed shield. It was going to be a great summer. He shouldered his rucksack and headed for the shuttle.

EPILOGUE

Edwina Milson removed the feeding bottle from the heater and let a few drops of milk fall onto the back of her hand. The temperature seemed fine, as far as she could tell. The last time she had fed a baby – her niece – she had still been living in South Africa with her sister. She walked over to the crib and looked at the child wrapped in the sand coloured blanket. The tiny infant was staring up at her with its big blue eyes, its tiny fists pressed against its mouth. The sight of this caused a deep sense of broodiness in Edwina, and she briefly felt a sting of regret in her heart, for letting her career take over her life at the expense of raising a family of her own.

'It is as it was meant to be,' she said. There was a light knock at the door. 'Come in,' she called, but not too loudly – she didn't want to scare the baby, after all.

Freja and Kloister entered the room and walked quietly to her side.

'So,' said Kloister, 'what is it?'

'A girl,' answered Milson. 'Disappointed, Roland?'

'You know me better than that,' he said gently, leaning over the crib and touching one of the tiny fists with his finger. A little smile appeared at the edges of his mouth. 'She's growing faster than I thought.'

'I don't think we've seen just *how* fast she can grow yet,' she said; then to Freja, 'Have we done the right thing, Carlos?'

'We have given her a chance to live,' answered Freja. 'No more, no less. And we'll do our best to ensure she takes after her father's side of the family.'

'Speaking of Tijara,' said Roland, 'I think our holo friend should be kept in *your* school. Here you go.'

Freja opened his hand and Kloister handed him a small, singed red box.

'This is one Pandora's Box I never want to see opened again,' said Kloister.

'Let's hope not, Roland. But you just never know – it may prove useful one day.'

The baby stirred a little and Edwina held a finger up to her lips to shush them. They leaned over the crib again, marvelling in silence at this innocent child who had caused so much fuss.

For the moment, at least, everything was as it was meant to be.

Also available by FT Barbini:

Tijaran Tales: White Child - Book I

You can follow us on Facebook and Twitter.
For more information check out the official website:
www.ftbarbini.com